Birthright
The Immortal Forest

By: J. A. Reed

DEDICATED TO:

Brandey, who inspired me to pick up writing. To Matthews, who helped, and continues to help me realize my dream. To Burt, who was the perfect sounding board for me to bounce ideas off without judgment or negativity. To my family, who I miss every day I'm away from home. And to all of my other friends, stationed both with and away from me, who are too many to name.

TABLE OF CONTENTS:

PROLOGUE:

Lightning. The flash crossed the sky, illuminating the large village of Tuckkar far below. Scattered mud huts ran through the village in uneven rows. Electric blue light could be seen trickling through most of the small bared windows. Another lightning bolt struck the tallest tower of a large castle overlooking the village, followed immediately by roaring thunder.

A large burly villager by the name of Tinus loomed in his small hut, in his small living room, staring through his small window at the storm outside. Tinus stood six and a half feet tall, his head brushing even the highest points of his roof. The glowing blue light that filled the hut revealed thin scars that crisscrossed most of his body, which looked and felt as if it were made of solid stone. He hated being home. He hated the mundane nature of a domestic life. He would much rather be back in his shop. He missed the heat of the forge on his skin, the weight of his hammer in his hand, and the vibrations that recoiled through his body with every strike of his mighty tool as it folded molten metal into various masterpieces of war.

Tinus was one of the town blacksmiths, the other being his brother, Kilik. Even though they shared a mutual career, Tinus preferred to work alone, another thing he had in common with his brother. They each owned their own shop in different corners of the village. The younger, Kilik, covered the smaller southern corner while Tinus, as the older and stronger of the two, controlled the north. Tinus had accomplished much in his life. He had a beautiful wife, a loyal servant, and the finest weapons in all of Tuckkar, but no matter how successful he was, he was still just a blacksmith. And a blacksmith can only live the life of a blacksmith, which meant a little hut, with little rooms, and little windows.

Light footsteps could be heard approaching from the other room. "Sir, it's…" squeaked Silva, his young servant woman. Her tiny, shaky voice barely reached his ears.

"It's time. Yes, I expected as much," Tinus cut her off. He turned away from the window and swiftly approached the servant woman. She quivered as he towered over her. "I'll bring the carriage around. Make sure she's ready when I pull up."

Silva scurried away and into the bedroom. As Tinus heaved his thick coat over his enormous frame, he glanced into the bedroom. On the large, straw-stuffed bed was Tinus's wife, Murel. Murel had her hands on her swelled belly and winced through one of her first labor pains. Silva rushed nervously to her side and offered out a hand. Murel took it gladly and squeezed until the contraction had passed, and her servant's fingers were purple.

Tinus shook his head, clearing out any pesky feelings he may have been having. He gripped the cold steel of the door handle and nearly yanked the brittle door off its hinges. As he walked through the blanket of rain between his carriage and himself, thoughts of worry engulfed his mind. *What if we don't make it in time? It's an old carriage, what if it won't start? What if…* *No!* Tinus was a strong man, fearless. He had been face-to-face with death thousands of times and never turned his back, so why was he thinking like this now?

He pulled up in front of the hut in a metal carriage. The black metal was worn and beaten as if it were very old. The exotic curvatures and accents of the carriage exerted the same blue glow as the light emitted from the huts along the street.

"Hurry milady," Silva pleaded urgently, "before the next one comes." She helped Murel through the threshold and supported most of her weight as they made their way through the downpour and into the back seat. As soon as Murel and Silva were inside Tinus revved the engine and sped down the dark brick road and out of Tuckkar.

Silva dabbed Murel's forehead with a damp rag as she endured another painful contraction. The carriage was far outside the village now, deep in the forest. The thickness of the trees prevented the rainstorm above from reaching the forest floor, keeping the dirt road from turning to mud. The road, which was progressively becoming more and more nonexistent, was scattered with tree branches, vines, and rocks. The treacherous path began causing the carriage to bounce, bob, and weave over and around obstacles.

"Please sir! You must hurry. They are getting too close together, she's almost there." Tinus's heart raced with Silva's words. Tinus had a significant amount of his attention on the road in front of him, but every extra ounce of brain power he had was focused on repressing his fear. He was still trying to figure out why he was afraid; it still didn't make sense to him. The things he had seen, the things he had done, and never even a glimmer of fear. He tried once more to banish it from his mind.

"We'll be fine. We'll make it," Tinus replied as he glanced in the rearview mirror for a short moment. Murel, between her deep breaths, smiled and blew a kiss to the reflection of her beloved husband. Tinus looked back to the road with a jolt as soon as he realized his eyes had been off the road for far too long. He paid for his mistake as the carriage rolled over a fallen tree trunk. They gained a few feet of air for a longer moment than any of them would've liked. Tinus prepared for landing, and fought to keep the carriage from swerving into a tree or rolling outright.

Murel recovered from the bump. "He's quite right my dear, you have nothing to fear. We'll make it, everyone makes it."

Murel shouted out another cry of pain. Silva looked back and forth between Tinus and Murel unsurely. As she wiped the beads of sweat off Murel's forehead once more, she muttered quietly, "Not everyone."

Suddenly, like a war hammer to the chest, it hit him. Love. He hadn't been fearing for his own safety, his own life, but for the safety of Murel, for her life. Tinus had never enjoyed his home life; he always saw it as weakness. Having a weak wife, a weak servant, and no danger or challenge, he only ever felt obligated to be there as long as he had to and get out. Things were different now. Now he realized he couldn't imagine life without Murel. He wanted a family, and he would die to protect them.

Tinus's eyes widened as he saw a clearing in the distance. The road ended at its edge, and the carriage exploded out through the last of the overgrown foliage and into the open clearing. The downpour resumed even more heavily than it was when they had left Tuckkar. The carriage slid to a halt through the muddy grass of the two hundred yard diameter, perfectly circular, field. They came to rest several yards away from a ring of giant stone pillars. Eleven identical pillars were spaced evenly, like that of a clock face with the twelfth position missing. The missing pillar distinguished the direction of the road which led back to Tuckkar. Tinus exited the driver seat and paused to stare at the magnitude of the pillars. Each one was seven feet in diameter, and at least one hundred feet high. They each contained a single deep groove that spiraled its way up to the top, which ended in a sharp point.

"Tinus!" Murel's cry for her husband snapped him out of his daze and he turned to open the rear door. Silva helped Murel out and across the grass. Tinus followed behind the two women to the center of the clearing. In the exact center of the clearing, in the exact center of the ring of pillars, stood a single block of stone, the Altar of Pilgrimage. Unlike the pillars, the Altar was smooth as glass; it didn't have a single groove, chip, or blemish of any kind. The stone looked almost polished. It stood three feet high, four feet wide, and seven feet long. Silva assisted Murel onto the Altar and prepared her for birth. Tinus turned away and walked out of the center ring and peered off into the darkness of the forest, completely indifferent to the heavy rain beating down on him.

The forest was home to many creatures, creatures Tinus knew all too well about. Most stayed away from the Altar. Those that did venture close never entered the clearing; however, there was one species, the most dangerous the forest had to offer, that didn't abide by any rules in the wild. As Tinus stood there he had a strong feeling that one of these forest dwellers had its eye on him right at that moment. He could hear leaves rustle as it moved from branch to branch, and he could see branches bend slightly under its weight as it moved closer. *Getting a better view perhaps? Just watching, or is it waiting?*

Tinus could see it moving from tree to tree. Like a shadow in a shadow it was barely perceivable, but Tinus's sight was well trained for such a thing. As it made its way around the tree line, Tinus leaned closer. He squinted his eyes, trying to peer through the darkness. The movement finally stopped; it stopped in the tree directly in front of him. About nine feet off the ground, a face slowly bled out from the shadows and into the dim light. First, the nose: small, dry, and pale. Next, the eyes: round and a shade of deep blue. Finally, the whole face came into view. There was no snout, no fur, and no bearing teeth or fangs. Actually, there were no teeth whatsoever, it wasn't even a *creature* at all. It was a child, a human child, no more than a few months old.

"Tinus!" Silva's voice thundered across the empty space to break the silence. Tinus turned back to face the Altar. He didn't know she could speak that loudly. "It's coming!"

Tinus spun back around to the tree line only to find the infant gone, and the fading sound of branches bending as it retreated back into the forest. Murel's screams filled the clearing and Tinus rushed back to her side paying no more mind to anything outside of those pillars. "Don't worry my sweet, I am here."

Murel gave one last big push, followed by a much needed sigh of relief. Tinus looked with as much hope as worry in his eyes down the Altar to see his servant starting to wrap his child in a dirty brown cloth. There was a long silence, and a noticeable absence of the distinctive ring of a newborn's cry, or the coughing of a first breath. The only sound in the air was the *splat-splat* of raindrops on stone and mud. Tinus looked back at his wife. She tiredly gazed back at him, weak from giving birth. "I... I don't hear any crying. Does that mean...?"

Silva approached her with the little bundle. "Yes, it's a healthy baby boy." Tinus smiled one of the first smiles of his life and kissed Murel joyfully.

Silva handed the boy over to his mother. Her face lit up the moment her beautiful green eyes met his matching pair that blinked back up at her. Murel brought up her other hand and brushed his cheek lovingly. The boy fought to pull one of his thick arms out from under the wrapping and shoved her hand away. Tinus laughed, pleased. "Yes! Yes! That's my boy, he's a strong one." Tinus took his son and held him up and out in front of him. The blanket fell like a leaf off of the boy and floated to the muddy ground beside the Altar. The child remained steadfast, not a single sign of discomfort on his little, emotionless face. Not from the rain that pelted down on him, not from the cold wind against his unprotected skin, not even the loud crack of thunder that shook their eardrums to the brink dismayed him.

"Help me up," Murel gestured for Silva, "help me to the carriage."

Tinus didn't budge, he stayed behind as he gave his

son a thorough look over. The boy looked perfectly healthy, no visual defects. The only notable thing about this child was his hand. Located in his left hand, imbedded in the center of the boy's palm was a glowing blue orb. Tinus gripped his son's left arm and held the hand open to get a good look at it. Blue sparkling light rose out of his palm and twisted around in a helix shape. After a short moment, an image appeared in the middle of the light. The image of a hammer and anvil floated and rotated an inch above the skin. Tinus released the hand and the image retreated back into the magical round stone, and then it faded back, leaving only a dark purple glow.

Tinus set his son back down on the Altar where the boy stood fully upright with the mirrored stone cold stare of his father. Tinus knelt down to his son's eye level. "Stay strong my son. Fulfill your Birthright and return to us." Tinus turned and walked back to the carriage. The boy turned the other way and jumped off the Altar. Tinus slid into the driver's seat of the carriage. The boy ran into the forest. Neither of them looked back.

CHAPTER 1: THE KING'S CABINET

"And on this day, the last day of his seventeenth year, Gylum shall smile upon him with His internal light. For the boy's strength of flesh and will of spirit, he shall cease to be a boy, but a man. Welcomed back into his home, the man receives three gifts from Gylum: the life and blood of Birthright, the appointment of a name, and the honor of a wife."

- The Xyrith: 155:15-17

The hulking figure of the young King Rynok busted through the large red and gold double doors of his chambers. He strode through his magnificent castle halls with his elegant robes flowing behind him, much unlike his thick course dark brown hair that, while it reached as far down as his shoulder blades, clung to his body under its own weight. Rynok loved this part of the morning. Every day right after he awoke he would walk his castle grounds, and walk the entirety of the forest wall. There was so much to being king. There were meetings, decisions, rulings and way too much politics for his liking; but these mornings, these mornings were just for him.

Rynok walked out into the open air of the front courtyard. The slight moisture that clung to his skin told him last night's storm had just recently ended. The smell of fresh rain hung in his nostrils, a pleasant smell that was fairly uncommon to him. As he crossed the damp mud, his mind began to drift away from his relaxed morning and into his later work schedule. *Is that meeting with the cabinet today or tomorrow? It is today, damn it.* Rynok hated meeting with his cabinet. Every week it was the same old bickering between councilmen: these people needed more funding, those people were getting too much funding, taxes were too high, or taxes weren't high enough. No one was ever happy, and it all fell down on the king. All he ever wanted was to do right by his people; to give them everything they needed, even if it wasn't always what they thought they wanted.

Rynok reached the base of the forest wall, awaiting him was Nimm, one of his many servants, and Rynok's personal favorite. Nimm had been with Rynok ever since he returned from Pilgrimage; yet, the Nimm that stood before him now was the shadow of his former self. His age and inactivity had really caught up to him. Rynok used him as a constant reminder to never allow himself to ever become that weak. Nimm's eye caught Rynok approaching and he stood up straighter. "Good morning, sir. You're a bit early today, aren't you?"

"Unfortunately, yes. Busy day ahead, must make today's walk a swift one." Rynok stopped face-to-face with Nimm and gave him the traditional Tuckkar greeting. They each held out their right forearms across their chests and trusted them into one another with great force. Just like everything in their culture, this greeting was meant to favor the strong. Nimm was at an obvious disadvantage. Rynok saw the telltale signs of pain in Nimm's face, but he hid it very well. Rynok was impressed, while his physical strength had faded, his mental willpower was still very much intact.

After about an hour, Rynok and Nimm were nearing the last corner of the forest wall. They walked side by side but Rynok's steps were much harder now, his jaw was clenched, there was a burning rage on the verge of erupting, for in that time he had been bothered by four of his townspeople with gripes and complaints. *So much for alone time.* Despite the disappointment in his morning thus far, he continued on.

Every twenty feet or so stood a wall guard fully armored in shiny black armor reminiscent of coral with white accents of a web-like network. Equally spaced, some had giant seven foot long bows around their torsos. The thickness of them suggested they could only be drawn by men of incredible strength, making them devastatingly powerful. Massive quivers slung over the other shoulders contained hundreds of beautifully crafted arrows. The feathered ends protruding out blended together into a single ball of razor blades. Between each of these archers stood guards with nine foot long halberds piercing into the dark sky, thick round shields with heavy swords that probably should have required two hands, but seemed to be wielded effortlessly in one, or three hundred pound war hammers hoisted over a single shoulder.

Another man approached from the opposite direction. He seemed to be inspecting the guards, flanked by two wearing a very different type of armor. The man in the middle Rynok knew to be the head of his royal guard, Moryn, who wore very light armor, nothing but a chest plate and light pads on his arms and legs. His escorts both had full head-to-toe blood red plating that ended in sharp points at every joint. At first glance, it would appear they were unarmed, but nothing could be further from the truth. On each forearm were two hidden retractable blades that could slice through at least two feet of solid stone. Rynok had seen this demonstrated years ago before his own eyes, he was glad these men were on his side.

Moryn did a double take when he saw Rynok, and extended his arms in pleasant surprise. "My king, quite early this morning, are you not?" Moryn reached Rynok and they bashed forearms. Each one impressed with the others strength, they laughed and hugged joyfully, but violently.

"Ah, yes, yes. As you may know, it is becoming increasingly difficult for me to find solitary peace. I am afraid today especially is no exception." Rynok turned Moryn around and swung his arm around his shoulder as they resumed walking. "I should hope you are not having too many issues up here that you will be bringing to the table this evening."

Moryn laughed. "Oh my king, I know how much you dread the cabinet meetings, but please, you have nothing to fear from me. These are some of the finest men I've ever had the pleasure of training." Moryn stopped walking. Rynok noticed his eyes were darting back and forth between two wall guards side by side, one was noticeably stronger than the other. "Actually, I can't take the credit for them. I don't know what's happening out there, but the Pilgrimage has been returning me stronger and stronger men this past year."

Rynok grabbed Moryn by the shoulders and turned him to face him. "It is not the forest that has changed my friend, it is our sons. We are passing our own strength unto them, someday when you have a son you will know this." Moryn nodded in understanding. They continued along the wall. "Speaking of, is your wife…"

"Not yet, we are still trying."

"These things take time, nothing to fear. Just look at how long it took us." Rynok wished he had chosen his words more carefully the moment they left his lips. Moryn was 30, just over eight years older than he was. While it was true that many wives can take as long as a decade to conceive, Rynok felt like he came off more gloating than comforting.

"Yes, of course." The look on Moryn's face confirmed Rynok's fears, but thankfully, it disappeared as quickly as it had emerged. "That reminds me, I have not seen Ivary in months, how is she?"

"I have made sure the carriage is fully powered and ready to go at a moment's notice. He's due any day now."

"Ah, confidence, a noble trait; However, unfounded confidence I have seen be the downfall of many."

Rynok's demeanor changed. *What does he mean 'unfounded confidence'?* Rynok knew his child would be a son. It wasn't a hopeful wish like most men have for a strong son over a weak daughter. Rynok had a distinct advantage over his villagers: in all recorded history, the first born child of the king was a boy. No one knew the reason behind this for sure, but it was as widely accepted as the Birthright itself.

Just as Rynok's mouth began to open to vocalize his anger at such a blatantly disrespectful comment, a thin twenty year-old boy flew up from the side of the wall and landed between the king and his guards. "My Lord, I bring word from Prince Athan." The boy stood upright at a miniscule six feet even. His torso was almost as thick around as Rynok's wrist, his arms and legs were even more slender. Rynok recognized him at once, there were few of his kind in Tuckkar. Eddan was a runner. Unlike most of the men of Tuckkar that relied on brute strength to survive, runners were built for speed, quickness, and agility. In his opinion, they were cowards, always running away from a fight rather than facing it head on as a man should.

"Yes, what does my dear little brother want now?"

"He's called for the cabinet meeting to begin at once. He says there is a matter that requires immediate attention."

Rynok turned his back to Eddan and Moryn. He walked to the lip of the wall that overlooked into the forest. That was it, the final straw for him. Rynok's rage burned in every molecule in his body. He placed his hands on the ledge just to stop them from shaking. His blood boiled in his veins, it could no longer be contained, but he had to. He was in front of his soldiers, his friends, his people. Somehow, he had to find a way to deal with his overwhelming stress. He was their king; he couldn't just grab the little pipsqueak runner and use him like a club to beat his brother to death, no matter how much he wanted to right now. Instead Rynok just tightened his grip on the cold hard stone of the wall. He squeezed with his tough calloused fingers till they began to bleed, and then only squeezed harder. He closed his eyes and tried to channel all his anger, all his stress, everything that was bottled up inside through his fingers and into the bricks. After a minute of this, Rynok finally felt bearable. He laxed his grip and looked down at where his hands had been a moment before. The wall now had a series of compacted divots, one for each of his fingers.

-O-

The grand doors of the dining hall parted before King Rynok. He strode through them towards the polished, hundred foot long dining table that cut through the room. Rynok had used the time it took for him to arrive to gain his composure despite the extreme anger that bubbled just below his skin. He knew this was not the time and definitely not the place to show any signs of weakness. It was a good thing he took the time to do this before entering the room as opposed to after, because the moment he crossed the threshold the eyes of his entire cabinet turned on him.

Along the far side, near the king's empty chair that waited patiently for him at the head, were three of the five councilmen, Burmin, Jossif, and Brantt. All three of them were young, younger even than Rynok. On the one hand, that meant they were still strong from their Pilgrimages, they hadn't had enough time to go soft. However, their youth was not an appealing quality for a councilman. None of them showed very much prowess in the diplomatic affairs, so their opinions held very little weight in these types of meetings. Moryn walked past Rynok and took the next open seat beside Burmin. On the other side of the table sat the remaining two eldest councilmen, Ardo and Rukor, his royal treasurer, Garm, and the last person he wanted to see right now, his brother, Athan.

Rynok took his seat. It was warm and soft, he hated it. The others took their seats after the king out of respect, all of them except for Athan. He took an unnecessarily extended moment to arrange his loose leaf pages and fix his already perfect blonde shoulder length hair before sitting. Even if Rynok had not been furious with Athan up until now, this act of disrespect, intentional or not, had pushed him further towards the brink.

"Well, now that we are all here *early*," Rynok glanced at Athan as the last word slid between gritted teeth, "shall we begin? Athan, since your matter was so urgent, please."

"Actually my Lord, this will require much discussion. I would prefer we resolve any other business before we dive into this one."

Another stabbing pain of hatred shot through his body. *Now he is trying to control the flow of the meeting? My meeting?* Rynok forced his body not to shake with rage, it took every ounce of might he had, but he did. "Very well. Moryn. The boarder sentries, how are they fairing?"

It took only fifteen minutes to go around the table. One of two things was happening: either everything in all of Tuckkar was perfectly fine on that day because these meetings would always last for hours, or everyone at the table was just as interested in Athan's big important situation as Rynok was. When Rynok was convinced he wasn't going to hear another word from the rest of his cabinet, he turned back to Athan. He sat there silently, his eyes said it better than words could. *This better be good.*

Athan shuffled through his notes again. "Several months ago, an unusual trend caught my eye. It was subtle at first, I wasn't even sure it was anything at all, but after some time this trend was getting more and more predominate. I've been spending this last month doing some research, and... Well, take a look for yourselves." He passed his papers around the table. Rynok let out a frustrated sigh as he peeled the top page off of the polished surface. The page might as well have been blank, he would have gained just as much from it. A graph and chart took up the bulk of the page, the blank spaces around and between were blanketed in random and unorganized scribbles of advanced equations. Rynok began leafing through the other half dozen pages, all with different graphs and numbers.

Rynok looked up at his brother, who was smirking

back at him. *Smug bastard. Just five minutes alone with you, then we'll see who is smiling.* Alas, he couldn't do that. Sometimes he wondered if that was the reason Athan enjoyed poking the bear so much. If you needed something broken, beaten, or killed Rynok was your man, but Athan made up for his physical shortcomings with intelligence and political finesse. Rynok needed him more than he liked to admit, and they both knew it.

"What exactly are you trying to get at here, boy?" Garm snarled from the other end of the table. The tone in his voice suggested he actually understood what was in front of him, and he didn't like it one bit.

"Well, as you can see, for the past hundreds of years, as far back as our records show, on average only one out of every five reaches Fulfillment, a steady twenty percent every year."

"Of course," Moryn cut in, "that is the purpose of the Pilgrimage; the weak have no place among us. I have yet to see a problem. We compensate, we always have, enough of our sons return to keep our bloodlines strong."

"Exactly. We compensate for the twenty percent, but look at the last pages." Athan stood up now, he took out the last two pages of his copies and slammed them in the center of the table. Athan was panting now. Whether it was his concern of whatever he was trying to say or frustration in being the only one to care, Rynok wasn't sure, but his anger was beginning to fade into genuine curiosity. "It started ten years ago, a slight increase of one or two percent three years in a row. Then another jump, another four percent here, the past two years have seen a six percent leap each."

Rynok looked around the table, everyone was silent. Athan was looking desperately for someone to speak. Rynok still didn't fully understand what Athan saw, but he tried to ease the tension. "A few percent isn't the end of the world, we just…"

"This year was fifty-one percent," Athan said, cutting him off.

Silence followed his words once more. This time it was Rukor who broke it. "One for every two, it is quite a change yes, but it's still manageable."

"Is it? As Moryn stated earlier, we've been compensating for twenty percent. How many sons have you had?"

Rukor hesitated, taken aback by the question. He glanced across the table where Jossif and Burmin sat, both his boys. He answered softly, "Only three so far."

"And as I recall, your wife is carrying as we speak. Ardo, you've already had four sons, you're eldest Brantt already Fulfilled. And Garm," Athan turned to the treasurer, the rest of the room followed suit, "how many sons have you had?"

Garm stood up defiantly, locking gaze with Athan. "Six. I have had six strong, worthy sons." Despite his age he was still bigger and stronger than Athan was.

"And how many have Fulfilled?"

"Two."

"And how many would have reached eighteen by now?"

"Two."

"Precisely." Athan broke his stare down with Garm to resume getting his point across. Garm sat back in his seat, his eyes still burning and jaw clenched tight. "We are still in the mindset of ten years ago. We have multiple sons to ensure at least one returns, but times have changed. We need to get ahead of this before it becomes a bigger problem. If this trend continues to grow at this rate, in another ten years we won't have the room, the food, or the resources to cope."

That was when it finally hit him, Rynok knew why Athan had called the meeting early. This would not be an easy fix, far from it. When dealing with the Birthright things get complicated; options were limited to one. There was no other choice but to follow its will. "So what then do you suggest? Birth restrictions?"

Athan hesitated, with faint workings behind his eyes. He chose his next words carefully. "Not necessarily, that could be a viable solution, yes, but…" Another hesitation, more gears moving tactfully in that big brain of his. "The true problem isn't the increase in Fulfillments itself, as I said, we won't have the resources to sustain them."

"Just spit it out, boy!" Rukor shouted impatiently.

"Then, ten years from now, we need to have more

resources."

That was it. That's what he was dancing around. It was absurd. "And how is that possible? Our walls are in place where they are, where they have always been. Where would we put new homes? Where would we get these things?" Rynok feared where this was going.

"Then we build somewhere else."

"Oh really? We just build somewhere else? And who may I ask are going to risk their lives for this impossible task? Clearing out that much forest…" Rynok's voice rose, "we don't even have people for that kind of work!"

"Well…" Athan started.

He wouldn't dare. It would be impossibly stupid of him to even think it. The room froze as everyone prepared for Athan's next words.

"We could reassign some people."

The cabinet members unified in their shock. Rynok exploded out of his seat, his fists slamming into the table with tremendous might. Spider-web cracks rippled out from the impact points. "You cannot be serious!"

"I am!" Athan's voice raised, he was standing up for himself for once. "Fulfillments are rising, there are just some jobs that don't need the numbers we're getting."

"So you would deny them their Birthright? A tradition as old as Ghor itself?"

"Times are changing my Lord, whether you like it or not. We need to be prepared to change with it. We have been contained within the borders of Tuckkar for millennia! It's about time we pull our heads out from that stupid book and…" Athan stopped. He slipped up and he knew it. He had been so careful to hide it, but anger clouded his mind and he made a fatal mistake for his cause.

"Stupid book? So that is what this whole thing is about?" Rynok moved around the table and paced behind Athan, "Just because you have lost faith now all of Tuckkar must as well?"

"I know you don't believe as we believe, but…"

"We? When did this become a *we*?" Rynok stopped for a moment, "Any of you wish to help out dear Athan? Who here agrees with him?" The only responses were averted gazes and nervous shuffling.

Athan was on his own. "I'm just trying to say we shouldn't remain stunted. Our civilization hasn't grown in thousands of years and it's because of the Xyrith. It's time we put away ancient superstitions and embrace science."

"Science? You think just because you have figured out how a few little things here and there work that you no longer need a god? The Birthrights, the Fulfillments, the strength given to our newborn sons, can your science explain any of these? Because the Xyrith answers all of these and more."

"Stop it!"

"Stop what?"

"Stop avoiding the true problem. Your faith is duly noted, but it doesn't get us any closer to a solution."

"The solution seems fairly simple. When one in five returned, people had an average of five sons, with one in two returning, people will only be allowed two sons."

Confused looks surrounded the table. Moryn managed to stutter out a few words, "B-but my Lord, you can't…"

Rynok turned on him sharply. "Yes I can! This is my village, I am its king! I can do whatever I wish."

"That won't help," Athan interjected, the focus landing firmly back on him. "There are still eighteen years' worth of Birthrights waiting to be Fulfilled out there. You can't stop those ones."

Rynok made his way to the door. As far as he was concerned, the meeting was over. He stopped just before the door and turned to make one last closing remark. "Things might get a bit crowded for a year or two, but it will balance out soon enough. I am not worried about it." As he left the room behind him, a painful little seed of doubt popped into his gut. His brother knew what he was talking about in situations like this, but admitting that would be the last thing he would do right now.

CHAPTER 2: SCHEMING AND SCREAMING

"Under the unblinking, all-seeing eye of Gylum, strength is of most value above all else. His blessing of all children is absolute, for those too weak to voyage or too fearful of judgment are sentenced to damnation. Upon His Altar, Gylum looks upon not the child, but upon the father. If strength is found in his heart, he is granted the honor of a son. Should weakness be found plaguing his mind, he shall be punished with the burden of a daughter."

- The Xyrith: 34:1-5

The king moved through the room. He was in his personal armory now, a fairly large room considering it was only for one man. Massive powerful weapons lined the walls; no two alike. Rynok had no need for small fast weapons, they wouldn't have done him much good anyway. He was all about raw, crushing, unstoppable power. The smallest item in the room was a knife that could be considered a broadsword in other hands.

The meeting had only ended a few short hours ago, but it still plagued his thoughts. He began pacing the room looking for anything to distract his mind. He passed by his war hammer. He ran his finger along the decorative pattern that curled up and down the sides of its giant head. Every few inches, he felt the chips and cracks from use. It was intended for display, but on more than one occasion Rynok liked to take it hunting. It reminded him of the club he used on his Pilgrimage. Things were so much easier in the forest, not like they are now.

He moved on from the hammer. It had helped ease his mind for a moment, but his trail of thought still found a way to lead him back to the place he was trying desperately to avoid. A few paces later, he stopped at his crescent axe. Rynok approached the blade and inspected it closely. It was dull. Not that it would alter the weapon's effectiveness at all; that axe would go through whatever Rynok swung it at even if he used the broad end.

He lifted it off its rack and carried it across the room to his sharpening wheel. Maintenance of his gear was his favorite pastime, right up there with his morning walks. As his foot reached the pedal, his body connected with the wheel. The faster he pumped, the louder the spin of the wheel, the quieter his thoughts became in his own head. As he pressed the dull axe blade against the moving stone, his mind was finally free. Nothing existed in that moment but a single entity, body, stone, and steel all one. Rynok moved the crescent shape along the wheel with elegant precision, up and down, and back again. He flipped it over, and glided the blade from top to bottom once again. He ran his calloused fingertip along the edge, feeling every minute variance in thickness. He went back and corrected the areas that needed it until the entire edge was uniform.

Rynok, satisfied with his work, dusted off the metal flakes and stone dust and stood to return the weapon to its rightful home. As soon as he turned, he was taken aback by his wife, Ivary, leaning against a rack of swords watching him with loving bright blue eyes.

"I love watching you work," she said softly.

Rynok moved past her to put the axe back up. As he did so, the slight breeze he created was enough to cause her long, flowing golden hair to flutter around her shoulder. Part of him was ashamed that someone, anyone, could have got that close to him without realizing. *It's Ivary though. She is small, quiet, and I had been intentionally blocking everything out.* He was satisfied with that excuse. He almost turned to greet her, when a thought popped in his head. He stopped and stared at the ground. "You would not be so loving of my real work."

"The meeting didn't go well, then?" concern in her voice.

"Not particularly," the words came with a sigh. Rynok always felt safe letting his guard down with Ivary.

She moved closer, "Whatever it is, I know you'll figure it out. You are the strongest king this village has ever known."

He knew it was true, everyone did. The halls of his castle contained portraits of every king dating back a hundred generations, they all pale in comparison to him. "That is what I fear. Strength is good for many things, but for a king?" Rynok held his hands out in front of him. "These hands can crush stone, bend steel, but that means nil for governing a kingdom."

"You are more than this," Ivary gently placed her

slender hands on his. "You are resourceful, creative, and incredibly stubborn, in a good way of course." Rynok laughed. Ivary reached up to grab his head and pull his forehead to hers.

"I am at my end. I do not know how much longer I can go on like this."

Ivary took one of Rynok's hands and brought it down to her belly. Despite being nine months pregnant, her belly only bulged out slightly. "Any moment our child will be born, and will carry your strength with him. Years from now when he returns to us, he will need his father."

Rynok moved away and looked into his beautiful wife's eyes. She had done it. She had eased his mind in a way only she could. Now when he reflected back on the meeting, his worry was transformed to confidence. He gave her a long, passionate kiss before leading her to the door. Rynok heard a slight *pop* and stopped when Ivary tugged on his arm. She looked to the ground, his eyes followed. A small pool of water now rested beneath her feet. He noticed the gleaming of light off what appeared to be a trickle of water streaming down her leg. They both looked up to each other at once. "Is it…?"

"It's time."

-O-

Moryn rushed towards the elegant double doors of the throne room. He stopped for a fraction of a moment to order his twin guards to stay behind. They obeyed without hesitation. Moryn plowed through the doors into the grand, but empty room. Besides Moryn, only three other things resided in the room. The thick velvet carpet that ran down the center, the goliath-sized throne at its end, and Garm, standing where the two met. Garm turned to face Moryn. *Wait, no, he isn't facing me. What is he doing?* He was getting ready to sit in the throne, the king's throne. Garm closed his eyes, placed his hands on the cushions of the arm rests, and bent his knees slowly as he sat back into the powerful seat. An expression of sheer joy overcame his weathered face.

"Garm! What are you thinking?" Moryn shouted as he double and triple checked that the room was indeed void of onlookers.

Garm opened his eyes, but continued to look extremely relaxed. "Don't worry, I'm well aware that this mantle shall never be mine." He closed his eyes again and sank even further into the throne. "Doesn't mean it doesn't feel good though."

"Stop your daydreaming." Moryn reached the base of the raised platform which held the throne above the rest of the room. He finally eased up a bit. "I take it you've heard then?"

Garm stood up and eased himself down onto Moryn's level, "Of course."

"Yes, but it's ahead of schedule."

"That's why I always keep an ear to the ground. Things rarely abide the plans of men."

"But we aren't ready, we still have a week's worth of preparations, we don't even…"

"Then," Garm cut him off, "you should be off making those preparations. Labor can take several hours." Garm motioned for the two of them to leave for the door. They walked slowly down the long carpet. "Besides, once the king returns, there will be much celebration. The festivities should provide adequate cover for us."

"Only if he has a son," Moryn murmured. He partially didn't want Garm to hear it, all he had was a wild theory.

Garm laughed. "My boy, you're not that old yet. You know the history, no king…"

"Yes, no king has ever had a firstborn daughter but as you should have guessed, Rynok is no ordinary king."

Garm stopped walking. "I know what you're getting at, but it changes nothing."

"It could, you don't know. He is the first king in recorded history to be born outside of the royal bloodline." Moryn knew this to be true, and even though no one would ever bring it up, they all knew too.

"Bloodlines matter not. Rynok Fulfilled the Birthright of Royalty; therefore he *is* Royalty, end of discussion." Garm resumed walking, leaving Moryn to catch up. "Even if that was a factor, he is without question, the strongest king Tuckkar has ever had. He will produce a son."

"Actually, that's my second point." Moryn grabbed Garm by the shoulder and forced him to stop and face him.

"You must have seen what I have seen. He is slipping, he is beginning to buckle under his responsibilities."

"Of course I've seen it, why else would we be here right now? You think I want to do this? Rynok is like a son to me, as I'm sure he is to you." Garm looked away, cursing under his breath. He was right though, Moryn had watched over the previous king for eight years before Rynok returned. He helped him learn how to lead, and was always there for him after he succeeded. Garm looked back at Moryn with a renewed resolve. "But it's what's best for Tuckkar. That is why we do it."

Moryn nodded in agreement, "And you're sure Athan is ready to lead?"

"Any doubts I may have had yesterday are gone now. The way he stood up for himself today, the conviction in his words, and this new information on Fulfillments. Rynok is too stubborn in his outdated ways. We will need Athan's adaptability."

"Then I shall hurry, I want to get as much ready before they return as possible." Moryn placed his hand on the door to leave. Before he did, he noticed Garm with a strange thought all over his face. "What now?"

"Oh, it's nothing," Garm shook his head, but he said it anyway, "It's just now you have me thinking. If you're right, and the king has a firstborn female, then all this planning and subterfuge will have been for naught. It would show the whole village he was weak, and unfit to lead. We would be completely justified in killing him."

-O-

Rynok felt the carriage slam to a halt. They were there. They had arrived at the Altar of Pilgrimage. He didn't wait for his driver to so much as open the door, he was already out and helping Ivary through a contraction. His driver, Nimm, finally stepped out of the front and hurried to Ivary's side. He took over and carried her the rest of the way, up onto the Altar.

Rynok followed slowly behind, he looked around in awe at the magnificence before him. He had almost forgotten what it looked like. After all, that was twenty-two years ago, and he only stayed for a short moment before venturing into the forest. His memories from those first days were elusive and foggy, but being here they flooded back vividly. The Altar and its pillars, his mother and father, and the bright blue glow of the Birthright they had stuck him with. Rynok tried to pour the rekindled memories out, back into the deepest darkest region of his brain once more. It was enough that he was plagued by constant reminders that the life he lived was not the one he was destined for. He didn't need the faces of his blood-born parents nagging at him as well.

A scream from the lips of the woman he loved snapped him back to the present. With the day of his own birth successfully banished from his thoughts, he charged to be at his wife's side. He grabbed her hand and let her squeeze through her own pain. Rynok cracked a smile. Small as she may be, she had one hell of a grip.

Rynok grabbed a cloth and started to dab the beads of sweat that were pooling on Ivary's pearly white brow. A single loose strand of hair got caught on the rag as he worked. He used his free hand to pull it away. Rynok loved her hair. Despite the fact that Tuckkar was far from the cleanest place in the universe, he had never seen so much as a speck of dirt or a tangled knot in all four years of marriage. It was a rare trait; in all his life he had only met three others to have it. Her father and his mentor, and her two brothers: the older one that lived in the castle with them and the younger one that Rynok had murdered. He hoped it passed on to his son.

"I can see the head!" Nimm shouted from the far end of the Altar, "Keep pushing milady! You're almost done!"

Rynok started to move further down the Altar to witness the miracle with his own eyes, but Ivary tightened her grip. "No, please. I need you here."

He exchanged glances with Nimm. Nimm nodded confidently. Rynok trusted him, if he said he could handle it, then he could, so he stayed. "Yes dear, anything you wish."

Rynok kissed his queen's forehead, but had to pull away abruptly when she yelled out in pain once again. "This is it! Just one last push!" Nimm shouted overflowing with excitement. Ivary took several quick breaths, and gritted her teeth in anticipation for her final exertion. Her final cry of pain quickly turned into a sign of relief. She fell back, exhausted and covered in a thin blanket of moisture.

Rynok turned to greet his son, but stopped dead in his tracks. The most terrifying noise he could ever have imagined pierced his eardrums. His eyes and pupils widened as his heartbeat tripled, it practically rattled against his breastplate. The look of pure shock and horror on Nimm's face confirmed what Rynok knew couldn't be. The shrill sound was originating from within the bundle of blankets Nimm held at arm's length. The sound was a crying baby.

CHAPTER 3: A WALK THROUGH THE WOODS

"In the Ghor of old, the Immortal Forest existed as a place of fear and certain death. As Gylum looked upon His people, He wept for them. As His tears fell to Ghor, His people stretched out their hands to catch them. Pooling in their palms, the liquid turned to stone, and thus the Birthright was born. Feeling His sorrow, the men vowed to end it. They ventured into the Forest to shed their weakness. The women ignored His plea, and thus were denied His gifts."

- The Xyrith: 15:37-43

Ivary pushed herself up with her elbows. She was still so weak from labor, everything ached. Her abdomen was the worst of it. The drastic change of losing six pounds from the core of her body took quite a toll. The crying continued, and her maternal instincts kicked in. *My baby needs her mother.* She painfully sat upright enough that she could take her weight off her hands and elbows. "Bring her to me. Let me see her," she pleaded with outstretched arms. In the corner of her eye she saw Rynok cringe at each utterance of the word, "her".

Nimm stood in shock, his gaze bouncing between Ivary, Rynok, and the small ball of cloth in his hands. He eventually rested on Ivary. "Y-yes, of course ma'am." He placed the bundle gently in her arms, he then preceded to back away slowly and cautiously. The look in his eyes and overall demeanor suggested he just handed over live explosives. Ivary parted through the outermost layer, and beneath it was the most beautiful thing she had ever seen: her daughter's tiny, dirty little face.

"Rynok, my love. Come. Look," she was speaking to him, but her eyes were locked in place. The newborn opened her eyes and Ivary cried. The girl flailed her arms and her mother laughed. The infant squeaked the beginnings of a cry, but the calming, gentle voice she had always known for the previous nine months soothed her. Ivary had lost track of time in those little blue eyes; it could have been a few seconds, it could have been half the night. When she looked up, Rynok was halfway to the carriage pacing a very small line in the ground. He was muttering incomprehensibly, his hands danced randomly around him, one minute they were interlocked in his hair, the next they were in fists pounding against his thighs.

Ivary brought her head around to the other side of the clearing. Nimm stood a dozen feet away, his expression unchanged. "Come! I need your help," she called to him. Nimm moved closer, still slow, still stone faced. She grabbed him with her free hand and shook him till his attention was firmly on her. "Something's wrong with Rynok. I need you to help me up." Nimm nodded silently and placed his arms around his queen. It wasn't a good idea, she knew that before she had even asked, but she knew she needed to get to her husband even more. Nimm finally seemed to be in control of himself again. Even with him back at his peak, his help just caused her more pain. Every time her weight shifted, every time her body twisted or bent, fiery hot lightning shot throughout her nerves.

Nimm gave up and eased her back into a comfortable position. She was frustrated. Even though strength wasn't even close to as necessary for women, the simple fact that she couldn't even stand or walk a few feet when someone needed her killed her inside. Nimm must have seen this on her face, because he started heading towards Rynok. She never was very good at hiding her emotions. "I'll bring him to you," he said over his shoulder.

Not a moment after Nimm finished, Rynok turned to them with a shout, "That's it!" Nimm stopped walking, Rynok was coming to them now. His steps were slow, heavy, and uneven. She could tell something was different about him. When he was only two strides away from the Altar, there was a fire in his eyes. "Give her to me!"

Ivary had seen this side of the king before, but never directed to her like that. She hesitated a millisecond too long, and their child was now in his hands. Realizing her mistake, she clawed out after her daughter. "No! Stop!" She was too late, he had already stepped out of reach with the child screaming in his tight grip. The pain was too great, she couldn't move herself back. She fell off the Altar and slammed into the cold hard dirt. She tried to scream, the agony was overwhelming, but no sound left her lips.

Rynok hadn't even looked back when she fell. He left her to crawl painfully after him. Every inch she gained on him was excruciating. "I am not going to return to my kingdom with this weak puny child!" he shouted. Rynok already towered over her, but from there on the ground he seemed as large as the stone pillars surrounding him. When he lifted his massive arms up above his head, it looked like the tiny baby was a mile above her. It seemed hopeless.

She had to do something. She looked to Nimm, but he resorted to his useless state once again. It was all on her, she had to say something. "And what will you tell your people?" Rynok's face turned first. His arms came down easily and he turned the rest of the way. She had bought some time, for whatever that was worth. "Will you lie to them? Tell them you have a son? A son that will never return?"

He smiled, not a smile she ever wished to see again. "No, that will only delay the problem. Instead of looking weak today, I will look weak in the future."

Fear stabbed into her heart. He was way too calm with his answer. "T-then, what are you going to do?"

"I have enemies, but they would never attack me directly. No, I am much too strong for that. They would target those close to me. My wife. My unborn son." He bent over and dropped the child onto the ground beside him. Her cries told Ivary she was still alive. The fall had seemed low enough, but she couldn't know for sure.

Rynok stalked towards his wife, that look in his eyes again. That look he only had in the heat of battle. She already knew what was going on. For whatever reason, denial, hope, delaying, she cried out, "What are you doing?" He remained silent. If anything, he intensified from her words.

Nimm stepped in from the side. She didn't know what had caused him to snap back into the right state of mind, but it wasn't a moment too late. He now stood between the homicidal king and the helpless queen. He blocked the king from her view. "My Lord, think about this! There must be…" The sounds of metal on metal, and then metal on meat, were so close together they blended into a single noise. A dark red point protruded out of his back. Nimm fell to the side, the hilt of Rynok's sword stuck firmly in his gut. Rynok's hand still wrapped around it, he pulled it from his friend with a strong tug. Nimm remained on his knees, fighting to stay conscious.

"They would have paid my trusted friend and driver. I never saw it coming." Rynok dropped his own sword and unsheathed Nimm's from the scabbard on his waist. He examined the curved blade. Satisfied, he kicked Nimm just enough to aid him on his way to the ground. Rynok resumed his advance. "Unfortunately I was too late to save my dear wife." He twirled the scimitar in his hand. He was getting a feel for the weapon. "And my unborn son died in the womb."

Ivary backed up along the ground, trying to put distance between them. She was in unbearable pain everywhere, but the back of her head hitting something hard drew her attention. It was the Altar; she was out of room to run, but she couldn't give up. She used the side of the Altar to push herself further. *If I could only reach the other side, no, he'll get me no matter what.*

It was over now, he was right on top of her. He raised the steel, his whole body moved with each heavy breath. "Why? Why did you not just give me my son?"

Ivary covered her face, she was ready. Ready to feel the sharp metal pierce her body, but the moment that should have come didn't. She opened her eyes to find Nimm with one bloody hand clutched to his giant wound and the other arm wrapped around the king's throat. "Run! Save the child!" he spit out along with streaks of blood, "I can't hold him much longer! Go!"

Ivary didn't even wait for him to finish his sentence. She scrambled to her feet. The pain of being on her own two feet was worse than anything before that point, but her blood was pure adrenaline now. She only slowed enough to scoop up her daughter, and then picked back up to a full sprint. Tears were pouring off her face in the wind. The carriage was behind her, on the other side of Rynok. It was the only hope to get back to Tuckkar, but she would never get past him in the clearing. Her only other choice was a certain death sentence, to head into the forest.

Just after the first branches passed over her head, Rynok's thunderous voice rang in her ears. "You have nowhere to go! You will not last five minutes in that forest!" he sounded uncontested. That could mean only one thing; Nimm was dead.

Ivary held her baby tight to her chest. She ran around

trees and over roots; every rustle in the distance caused her to jump. She had never been in the forest, no women ever had. She never took the time to even learn what was out there. She searched her memories, anything that could help. She knew that every creature that called the Immortal Forest home was extremely deadly, and she was completely unarmed. But even if she had a weapon, she wouldn't know how to use it.

Rynok's footsteps were growing louder. Ivary stopped to take a moment and check behind her. Through thick foliage, she could make out his unmistakable figure. *Oh Gylum! He's so close. I don't know what to do.* He appeared to be wrestling a giant snake. It must've been a Knixx Viper; she had only heard of them before. Before she knew it he threw its lifeless body aside. He killed it so fast one would hardly call it a fight at all. She only had a few seconds before he would come smashing through the vines between them, she had to act fast. Near her feet there were thick roots arching out of a massive tree and into the ground, the space made a pocket just large enough to hide the child.

Ivary bent down and slid her into the space. She knew that she should leave immediately to lure Rynok away before he spotted them, but her maternal instinct wouldn't let her. She had to say something, anything, just in case this was indeed the end. "I love you my little Princess. I'm so sorry." She kissed her fingers and pressed them softly against the girl's cheek. She was sleeping peacefully; if she started crying this would have all been for nothing. Ivary turned and ran. As much as every fiber in her body wanted to look back, she refrained. She couldn't afford giving her position away to Rynok.

She made it almost a hundred feet, but it was too quiet. She couldn't hear any twigs snapping or branches bending. Nothing but fearful silence rang in her ears. She knew she couldn't afford to stop running, but curiosity got the better of her. Keeping the same pace, she turned her head over her shoulder. She scanned the area behind her; there were nothing but trees, leaves, and vines. Ivary slammed into something stiff and unmoving. She ricocheted off hard, landing several feet away in a heap. *What was that? A tree? It hadn't felt like bark.* She never should have looked back, but Rynok wasn't following her anymore. Maybe, just maybe, she stood a chance now. She clutched her head. Her vision was blurry, but returning fast. Her obstacle began to take shape. It wasn't a tree, it wasn't some wild beast either, it was much worse. It was Rynok. Somehow he got ahead of her and there was no hope now. She was going to die that night.

Once again, Ivary prepared herself for his blade, but once again, death never came. He wasn't even looking at her, his eyes were darting through the darkness. She tried to see what he saw, but it was too dark. She tried to listen for what he heard, but the calm silence gave no indication. He turned suddenly away from where she sat; this was her moment. She had no idea what was going on, but she knew she had to take advantage of it. She scurried to her feet and started off, away from her husband's back.

Terror nearly stopped her heart. Yellow emotionless eyes peered at her through the darkness. Trying to stop, she tripped over her own feet and landed painfully on her chest. As the bright eyes moved out of the shadows, the ugly, twisted snout of a Zed Wolf came into view behind them. Jet black fur grew in patches around the scarred lines on its face. Four thick grey horns protruded from the base of its skull and curved around its head, encompassing it in stone-like armor. The wolf stalked closer, yellow and black teeth rotted the air between them, and massive paws crushed the dirt from severe weight. Ivary got back to her feet and turned to her right. She made it two steps when another Zed Wolf landed directly in front of her. A whimper escaped her lips. The silence was broken by the sound of snarling. It was coming from everywhere, not just the two she had seen; there were more hiding and waiting under the veil of darkness.

She backed away slowly, she had nowhere to go. When she moved further away from one, she was moving closer to another. The Zed Wolf in front of her pounced. She wasn't scared of death anymore. She had almost died a dozen times in the past few minutes. Ivary was getting tired of the waiting more than anything now, but she would have to wait a little bit longer. Rynok had appeared out of nowhere in a blur of motion. He knelt underneath the wolf with it skewered on his sword. He spun around and kicked it free of his blade towards the second wolf. It bucked the body of its brother off to the side with its horns and charged Rynok. He shot out both his own sword and Nimm's, catching the beast in the mouth with one and the heart with the other. Before he could get either sword free, a third exploded out of the foliage and caught him by the arm. He released the hilt of his weapon and took the creature by the throat. He pried it off his forearm single-handedly. It shook and writhed in his grip. With a single flex of his wrist, the spinal column snapped loudly in two. The wolf stopped kicking; its lifeless carcass sagging from Rynok's hand. He dropped it beside him when he turned to her.

"Y-you saved my life. Thank…" she started, but the tip of Nimm's sword cut off her sentence, luckily not her head. Not yet at least.

"Do not thank me." There was a defiant look in his eyes and no emotion in his words. "Where is the child?"

"You mean your child? Your daughter! It's your duty as her father to protect her, not kill her!"

"It's my duty as king to have a son! Now I will not ask again!" He pressed the metal edge into her neck. A small drop of blood ran down onto her dress.

"Somewhere you'll never find her."

He pulled the blade away. "We are deep in the Immortal Forest. Nothing is safe out here, where could you have possibly hidden her?"

She stared into his cold dead eyes. Rustling sounds came crawling over her shoulder and into her ear. She looked in that direction and saw one of the dead Zed Wolves on the ground near a tree's base; the same type of tree that made up her daughter's hiding spot. The roots of this tree broke free of the ground and wrapped around the bloody mass like thin boney fingers. The skeleton of the wolf was cracking and breaking inside the wooden cocoon. The roots shot back into the ground beneath the tree's trunk, taking the body with it. Rynok must have seen the look of horror growing on her face, because he bursted into a wretched laughter.

"Oh my, you put her under a tree? You did!"

No! I need to get back to her! Ivary got to her feet and ran back, but Rynok grabbed her waist. "No!" she screamed. Tears fell down her cheeks. She fought against his grip, but it was no use. She stopped fighting and sobbed in his arms.

"Honestly, are you surprised? What did you think was going to happen?"

"I don't know," she said through her tears. She fell to her knees. Her eyes were dry now; she had no more tears left to give. "Just get it over with." She placed her hands on his. She made him raise Nimm's weapon. He never said a word. He didn't say 'I'm sorry' or 'I love you.' Nothing.

He made it quick and clean. She felt no pain, only cold numbness. She fell forward, but he caught her. He lifted her over his shoulder as the last bit of life drained from her and carried her back into the clearing. Now her eyes were just as cold and empty as his; she was gone.

-O-

He watched as a beautiful young woman with gorgeous gold hair placed a bundle of cloth under the roots of a Grim Wood. He stood on one of the lower branches of the adjacent tree. *What is she doing? Why would she put something there? And what is it anyway?*

"I love you my little Princess. I'm so sorry," she said softly to the bundle she had just, probably unknowingly, put in grave danger. She turned and ran away.

He was in shock. *Is that...? Is that a child? 'Princess' she said. She called it her little Princess. Is that a girl? What is going on?* There wasn't time for questions. The roots began shifting. Normally, Grim Woods would only eat dead animals and clean up the scraps left behind after battle. They were scavengers, but how could it resist a weak, helpless little meal presented on a silver platter?

He jumped from his perch. It was only eight feet off the ground, but standing at barely over two feet tall himself it was quite the leap. Halfway down, he slung the foot-long blade from his back out in front of him. It was a crude weapon; the sharp metallic feather of a Dao Wing, with a leather strap making a safe place to grab. With one movement he sliced through half of the long brittle roots and landed hard in a kneeling position. The other branches fled back into the dirt. They were smart enough to know this meal wasn't worth losing anymore limbs.

He surveyed the area; it was safe, for now. In the forest, the term *safe* was used very loosely. He had to know what was going on. None of this made sense. *Why was there a woman in the forest? Why did she bring her daughter in the forest? She must have been running from something, but from what?*

He turned to run after the woman. He made it halfway up a tree when he stopped. *The girl!* He looked back. Only half her face and a lock of hair were visible through the soiled wrapping. Her eyes were closed and her breathing shallow. Her hair was the same beautiful gold as her mother's. *I can't just leave her, but I can't take her either. How am I supposed to look after a baby?* He placed a hand on a viper skull that hung around his neck. Painful memories bubbled up inside him. *I can barely look after myself.*

He jumped back down and walked to her side. He picked her up, but his small stature made it awkward to hold her. He pursued after the woman with gold hair slowly; he had to stay on the forest floor and try not to wake the sleeping newborn. He could hear sounds of battle. It was the snarl of a Zed Wolf. *No, make that three wolves.* One by one by one he heard the death of each in quick succession. *There's no way that she could kill three Zed Wolves, there must be someone else with her.* What was still unclear though was if she been running to him or away from him.

He was close now. He could smell the blood in the air, hear a man's voice, and a woman's fearful breathing. "No!" the woman shouted. He clasped his hand around the baby girl's ear and pulled her tight to his chest. She hadn't woken, *good.* He was afraid to move closer. He didn't wish to be seen, but he had to see. He had to know what was going on. He peered around a tree and made sure to stick to the shadows.

The woman was on her knees and a man stood behind her. He was massive, the largest he had ever seen. *He's much older than eighteen, so why is he out here?* Instead of finding answers, there were just more questions piling up.

"Just get it over with," she said softly, void of meaning. The man lifted the smaller of his two swords and held it to her.

What is he doing? What is she doing? I have to help… It was too late. Blood pooled out of the woman, the man hoisted her onto his shoulder, and he left. *He just killed her. He just murdered her in cold blood.* The forest had rules. Murder was allowed, but only between boys on their Pilgrimages, for Birthrights or survival. This was neither.

He followed the man to a clearing. The boy recognized it; it was the Altar of Pilgrimage. It was strange, just over a year since he was born there and he still hadn't ventured out very far. He watched as the man placed the woman's body into his carriage and walk away from it. It was only then that he realized there was another body in the clearing; an older man in a bloody pool near the Altar. The man wiped off the hilt of the sword he used on the woman, and placed it in the man's hand. He then left him there, and returned to his vehicle. He drove away, down the road back to Tuckkar.

The crack of thunder was followed swiftly by the wakeful crying of the baby. A downpour slowly grew around them. The young warrior was in shock. He didn't grasp the full nature of what he just witnessed, but he understood the gist of it. There was one final thing he had to know. He rifled through the blanket and searched for the girl's left hand. She was kicking and flailing, but he got it. He pulled it out in front of him, and his jaw dropped when he saw the swirling blue image of a crown. *Royalty!* 'Princess' wasn't just a loving nickname, she actually was the Princess. He looked at his own Birthright. The pickaxe of a Miner stared back at him. If he wanted to, he could take it from her. He could cut it from her flesh and swap it out with his own. In seventeen years when he reaches eighteen, he could be king.

The thought stuck in his mind for a time; the shrieking of the child being a constant reminder of how bleak the alternative would be. *If I take it, and let her die... No, there's no honor in that. But if I let her live, she can't take care of herself.* The forest was a dangerous place for anyone to live, but for a one year old to raise and protect a newborn girl, it would be impossible. He looked down his chest at the viper skull, and remembered the promise he made that day. He thought of Gylum's teachings, and the words of the Xyrith imprinted in his genetic knowledge. He knew there was only one choice for him. He would take her as his own and he would be her guardian, her protector. She was his Princess and he was her Paladin.

CHAPTER 4: CHANGE OF PLANS

"All things are as they should be. Gylum gives a man pain to make him tough and obstacles to make him cunning. A setback in the eyes of the ignorant is truly the unseen hand guiding His child towards destiny. Fear not, for the fortunate are destined for nothing, the mediocre for little, and those with the greatest plights, they are the chosen few meant for greatness."

- The Xyrith: 67: 23-27

Moryn stood in the throne room with Garm and ten of his finest most trusted guards. If anyone else had asked, they were waiting the king's return to celebrate the birth of a prince, but that was just half the truth. They were the first step in a carefully planned out plot to overthrow him. Moryn had been spending hours trying to rush the last few pieces into place. It hadn't been easy and he cut it a little close, but now everything was set. By this time the following day Athan would be sitting on the throne for the first time, and Rynok would be safely tucked away in the catacombs.

Moments before, Moryn was grateful for Rynok's tardiness; it gave him the time he needed. However, now he was worried. His feet were getting antsy, he began to pace up and down along the twin rows of guards standing still at attention. "Where is he? He's been gone too long."

Garm remained calm and collected, "Patience old friend, everything is in place, and it will still be in place no matter how much longer we must wait."

"No, no, no. Something's gone wrong, I can feel it. We must send a search party." Moryn snapped his fingers, and the first guard in each row came to him.

Garm placed a hand on Moryn's shoulder and whispered into his ear, "Easy now, you aren't thinking clearly. We can't afford to show our hand, not yet. Our moment will come, I assure you."

He was right. They had put too much effort into their plan. If he jeopardized it now they wouldn't have another shot. He raised his hand again and his men fell back into formation. "Yes, yes you're right, quite right. My apologies."

Garm grabbed Moryn by the back of the neck and

brought their foreheads together. It was a sign of trust; Moryn appreciated it. He felt calm now, everything was going to be…

The main doors exploded open. Moryn and Garm pulled away from each other and looked with confusion towards the front of the room. Rynok was limping across the velvet carpet, deep red blood falling onto it as he went. There was a body in his arms, it was thin and small. The face was covered with a blood soaked rag but Moryn knew who it was; nobody else had blonde hair that bright. It was Ivary.

"Oh my. W-what has happened?" Garm stuttered.

"Where is my brother? Where is Athan?" the king demanded. Moryn looked at Garm, both looked equally confounded. Moryn started to answer, but was cut off before his lips could open. "Tell me now!"

"Um, he's in the study. Why? What happened?" Garm said. He looked to Moryn for help.

"Please my Lord, how did this happen?"

"Moryn, send your men to the study! Arrest him at once. Athan has plotted against me!"

This can't be right. How did he find out? Athan didn't even know this plan existed, very few did. He would have to sort this out later, he had no choice but to do as the king said for now. "You heard your king! To the study, now!" His men began to march down the room.

Rynok turned and shouted after the guards, "He is to be bound and gagged immediately!" He turned back and looked down at the cold body in his arms. "I will not have him turning anymore of my men against me," he whispered. He brushed between Moryn and Garm without another word. They turned to follow him into the hallway.

"I still don't understand my Lord, what happened out there?" Moryn pleaded. His reluctance to answer had him worried. How much of the plot against him did he know? Did he know of their involvement too? Was he leading them into a trap, where he would get his revenge?

The king finally spoke, "It was Nimm. Somehow Athan corrupted him, convinced him to turn on me, to turn on my family." The sounds of marching armor rumbled overhead. *That wasn't part of our plan. Could Athan have really been trying to overthrow his brother himself? That didn't sound like Athan.*

Garm cut in. "Nimm? But he would never."

"Forget Nimm, Athan would never take action against you. He's your brother. It must have been someone else."

Rynok stopped in the doorway to the conservatory, a large open room with a rounded ceiling of glass. He had been through so much in such a short amount of time; it was clear by the look on his face. "It was him, I questioned Nimm myself before I killed him. Trust me when I say, his final words were no lies."

Moryn followed after Rynok into the vast room. The conservatory was one of the most beautiful rooms in the castle. It was a shame the current mood completely contrasted. The whole far side of the room up across the ceiling was mostly comprised of rain soaked glass, separated with a spider web of stone. Within the room, many of the less dangerous plant life grew in massive pots, suspended above the ground. Outside, the view overlooked the village of Tuckkar; the dim flickering of blue light emitted from the small huts looked like little stars. The periodic flashes of lightning illuminated the forest stretching out from the village's boarders in all directions, to the horizon and beyond.

Rynok had reached a stone table in the center of the room. He cleared the table with one swipe of his giant forearm before laying his late wife down upon its surface.

"And, what of your son? Did he…? Is he out there?" Garm asked cautiously.

The king slammed both hands on the table, his head drooped low. He stayed that way for a full minute. "No, he is not. He was still in the womb when it happened. No matter how strong, there is no surviving that."

Garm placed a hand on Rynok's shoulder. He shot a glance at Moryn. The look showed zero trace of disappointment in their plan going up in smoke. He was mourning for his friend. Whatever was to happen regarding Tuckkar's leadership would have to wait. Right there, in that moment, Rynok was more important. "I shall send for the undertaker then."

Rynok removed Garm's hand from his shoulder. He stood up straight, as straight and tall as was physically possible for him. He turned his back to the body. All emotion, all sadness, all weakness was removed from his face now. "No. I'll prepare the body…" A flash of pain overcame him, but he recovered just as quickly as it came, "The bodies, for the catacombs myself."

"But my Lord, that's not necessary. You don't need to put yourself through…" Moryn pleaded.

"But I do, I need…" another hesitation, and another momentary look of emotion, "closure."

"Very well, then. I shall send for the supplies you need," Garm said as he started for the door.

"If you could, yes. But I need a moment first."

Garm left the room. Moryn stopped at the door, knob in hand. He watched for a moment as Rynok removed the rag covering Ivary's cold white face, straightened out her body, and placed her hands on top of one another over her chest. Rynok's body blocked the view of her blood and mud stained lower portion. All Moryn could see was his peaceful, sleeping, precious queen. She wasn't sleeping though, and that terrible truth was stuck in his mind. He closed the door slowly. Once it clicked shut he would never see Ivary ever again.

-O-

The Paladin entered his small tucked away dwelling with the infant Princess in a makeshift sling. She was sleeping again, finally. It had been three days since he rescued her, three terrible days for him. He had tried to head straight for his home, but fifteen minutes out she woke up screaming. For fear of giving away the position of his hideout he had to retreat. If that wasn't bad enough, her cries were like a dinner bell for anything within earshot.

He had always survived by running and hiding, because he knew he wasn't strong enough to stand and fight everything that crossed his past like many on Pilgrimage do. Although, after experiencing those three days, all of that would have to change. Hiding wasn't always an option, not with that siren going off constantly. Running wasn't always an option, for the precious few moments she was quiet or sleeping, moving her would just upset her again. He had to relearn how to survive, assess every situation with a new mindset and new priorities.

Running and hiding still had their place, but more often than not he would have to stand and fight.

Now, seventy-two grueling hours later he was home. Just seeing this place again caused feelings to well up inside of him. This had always been his safe haven. He would only venture out in search of food and to collect more water, but that was before. Princess was silent for now, but for how long?

Paladin's father had a daughter before he was born, so the genetic knowledge passed down to him contained a wealth of information on raising a girl. He knew that she would remain in this helpless state for years. His sister was six years old when he was conceived, and even at that age a female child is barely capable of doing things on its own. It would take many more years before she could be taught to protect herself.

Luckily, feeding Princess wasn't as big a problem as it could have been. Paladin was still very adept at getting food edible for a baby; he had only just started getting his teeth in. It had been a little difficult to get while on the move, but now he had access to his stores again. She was probably very hungry by this point. When he had come across her he was looking to refill his new diet, one that required teeth. He never got that chance, so he still didn't have anything for himself, but the food he had outgrown hadn't rotted yet so he packed it up.

Paladin used this moment of peace to prepare for the new life he was about to lead. He checked his rudimentary armor for cracks or weak spots. His armor mainly consisted of bark off the Niku tree, surprisingly durable, albeit a little scratchy. Curved plates of the bark made good arm bracers, shin protection, and vest pieces, but he was still small and there was plenty of room for growth. He sharpened his knife. The strap of Zed Wolf leather had worn down too much and he was fresh out; hunting Zed Wolves had never been high on his to-do list. Quickly, he applied a new strap of Knixx skin to it. It wasn't as strong as the leather, but it was much easier to come across. Lastly, he packed away some of his medical herbs. Carrying Princess meant he would have to travel as lightly as possible, so he only took a few Integro roots. These roots were the jack-of-all-trades when it came to herbal medicine. Ground up, the powder could be put in open wounds to accelerate healing and prevent infection. Boil them in water to brew a tea that helps with fever, poisons and even an upset stomach. He would have to leave behind all the others, they were usually easy enough to find.

He was done. Everything he could prep, everything he could pack, everything he could think of he had done. He wished he had known before he started that she was going to be sleeping for that long. He hadn't had more than an hour of sleep a day since all this began. Adrenaline kept him awake when they were in danger, and fear kept him awake when they weren't. He knew she would wake up any minute; she had already been down for so long. He couldn't get rest now, but being back in his dwelling, his home, where he felt safe made it impossible to resist the calling from that bed. His bed, the one he slept in every night for the majority of his life. *Maybe I can just rest my eyes for a bit, just until she wakes up.* He crawled lazily onto the soft, plump pad. *I'll get up as soon as she does. No way could I sleep through her crying.* He eased her close to him, right next to his ear, just to be safe. *This will be good, I'm no good to either of us if I'm this tired.*

Something hit Paladin in the back of the head. It was strange, he was expecting the roar of a baby's cry to wake him, not sudden pain. There was something else strange, he could hear her sobbing but it was so very quiet. *No, not quiet. It's far away?* It couldn't be, she was right next to his head when he fell asleep.

He opened his eyes. He wasn't in his bed, *how is this possible?* Looking around, he wasn't even in his dwelling anymore. That pain hadn't been something hitting his head, it was his head hitting the ground. He had been thrown from his resting place. *But how? By what?* He searched for wherever his home was located, and he found it. The only problem was, he found it everywhere. The walls, ceiling, furniture, everything was scattered in crumpled heaps all around him. He hadn't been the only thing tossed.

The sobbing Princess wasn't quiet anymore. She was letting out a full blown screech. It came from the far side of a Niku tree. The tree was thick; it took him a moment to round the side of it. When he did, he stopped dead in his tracks.

He knew something had to have destroyed his home, but not a Djinn. Standing ten feet tall on its bipedal cloven legs, the creature flung another of his walls aside like a ball of trash. It dug back into his former home with its massive clawed hands. Each of its five claws were thin, curved, and blacker than the darkness around it. It got hold of a bushel of Integro roots and raised it to its long lizard-like snout. Its nostrils flared as it investigated. Satisfied, it opened its wide mouth revealing foot long curved fangs running from corner to corner, on top and bottom. After eating the herbs, it returned its focus to the dwelling and to the cries still coming from within. Its back was fully towards Paladin now, his field of vision blocked completely by the outstretched bat-like wings jetting from the beast's armor plated body.

The good news was it hadn't reached her yet, she was still alive. The bad news, Paladin had never even been close to taking down a full grown Djinn before. If circumstances were different, he would run without question. There was no hiding from these things, they could get through anything put in front of them. There was no fighting them either, at least not for another ten years or so. Time was running short. Every moment he didn't act, the beast was one claw swipe closer to finding his target.

He wasn't sure what his plan was yet, but first things first, he had to arm himself. He scanned the wreckage for his knife. No luck. He checked the terrain for any place to get an advantageous position for a fight, anyplace to set a trap or anything at all. There was a pattern of Dao Wing feathers stuck in the trees around the area. They hadn't been there before, he was sure of it. It must have happened recently. Dao Wings never launched their feathers for no reason, so there had to be a reason. *Either one heard the crying Princess before the Djinn showed up, or one of them attacked the beast.* If the former, there wasn't much for him to do without something to protect his hand, they were useless as a weapon. If the latter, then he might be in luck. He studied the pattern, he pictured the fight in his mind. *It definitely fought with the beast, good. Claw marks start there.* He followed the signs of battle around quickly. *The pattern ends there. The Djinn must have killed it. If so, it would have fallen right... Yes!* On the ground a few feet away was the mangled remnants of a Dao Wing.

Paladin made a beeline for it. The nearest Grim

Wood was already reaching out its tentacle-like branches. He reached it but was too late. The branches already had a firm hold of the bird. He wasn't going to give up that easy though. With no weapon to speak of, he pulled at the twigs. Every time one snapped, two more took its place. He glanced back at the Djinn. It wasn't digging anymore. The terrible thought that it already found her crossed his mind, but the ringing of her weeping reminded him she was still alive.

A pack of Zed Wolves were circling the Djinn. *Great, because a Djinn wasn't enough, let's throw in some wolves.* The lead wolf attacked the beast and then the other's joined in, but it began cutting them down. *Never mind, this might just buy me the time I need. But even so, I need to hurry.* Paladin abandoned the bulk of the wooden cocoon for the tendrils that attached it to the tree. With each strike, a dozen or more crumbled to his feet. The Grim Wood finally retreated, the prize was his.

He pried through the branches until he found the birds head. That's what he needed, that was his only chance for defeating the beast behind him. While the feathers of a Dao Wing made useful knives and small blades, the creature's beak made them look like brittle sticks by comparison. Thin and razor sharp, the beak was just shy of three feet long. This bird must have been an adolescent, because they could easily reach five. He wasn't complaining though, it would be difficult enough for him to wield as it was. Realizing that too much time had already passed, he tore the head from the rest of the bird and stuck his hand inside. His fingers found a comfortable enough grip and then he took off to protect his Princess.

Rushing in was a huge mistake. He was supposed to get the drop on the beast from behind as it dug through his former home, but it was just barely finished with the pack of Zed Wolves and still on high alert for threats. The beast roared an ear shattering war cry. Hot stinking wind pushed him back. Even at a full sprint he was losing ground. It charged him, but he stayed his course. He still had no idea what he was doing or how he would take this thing down, but it was away from Princess, so that was progress. He waited until the very last second. The beast's claw came for his head, but he slid into the dirt. It was faster than he had accounted for. It still missed him, but his short hair just got a lot shorter. As he slid beneath the beast, he jabbed his blade into the creature's abdomen. Once again his timing was only slightly off. He hit just above his mark, where the impenetrable armor scales blend into the fur covering its legs. The sword glanced off the armor plating and he didn't have time for a second strike.

That tactic wouldn't work again. Djinn were extremely smart. The longer anything fought one, the more it learned about how its enemy fought, so his best bet was to finish it quickly. A tall order for a one year old. If attacking from below wasn't an option anymore, he would try from above.

He scaled the nearest Niku tree. Niku trees had fewer branches, and are much harder for someone his size to climb than a Grim Wood, but they were also very defensive so he hoped his hunch played out. The Djinn didn't let up, he swung for Paladin at every turn. Each time it missed, it hit the trunk or branch of the tree he had just moved from. Just when he started to think his plan wasn't working, one of the larger branches fell down from above and cracked the beast on the head. The beast was hardly phased, but that momentary break was all he needed to get high enough to be out of its reach.

He took a quick moment to collect himself, but it was cut short. He must have been slipping, because he had completely forgotten: Djinn can fly. It was level with him again after just a few powerful beats of its massive wings. His new sword was useless at this range; he had to get in close and get it back on the ground. Parrying its claws with his sword, he lept from the Niku to a nearby Grim. Running along the branch, he reached his free hand down and pulled one of the Dao feathers out of the wood. The sharp edge broke the skin without any protection, but he was running out of options. He flung it at the beast, aiming for its left wing. A direct hit. It passed clean through the thin film of skin leaving an open slit. He repeated this six more times in immediate succession, all aiming for the same wing. With only one missing its target, the beast screamed with pain, and dropped like a stone. It was unable to keep aloft on only one good wing.

This was it. This was his shot. The Djinn landed on its chest, and Paladin dove from his perch thirty feet above. He had to get the timing right this time. After this, there would be no more opportunities. Even if he survived the fall he didn't have any moves left. If this worked though, he would proudly be able to walk away from a Djinn corpse. He spread out his arms and legs, slowing his descent just enough; just until the right moment. The beast rolled onto its back trying to stand. *There!* He pulled his limbs in, stuck his blade out in front of him and plunged it deep into the beast's abdomen and landed his feet on either side. Any higher, he would have glanced off again. Any lower, it would have been a superficial flesh wound. As he jumped off the beast's stomach he twisted his sword around and right up into the major organs.

It fell backwards like a chopped down tree. The ground quaked when it hit. Dark red blood, thick as oil, oozed from the wound like a waterfall onto the dirt. Paladin breathed heavy, staring at the magnitude of his fallen foe. He had been so focused on the battle, it wasn't until this moment that the surrounding world came back to him. He ran to the rubble of his dwelling; the sound from beneath the destruction was a quiet sob now. He dug and dug. It took him ten full minutes to pull enough out to get a visual on her. She had been safer than he thought. None of the fallen debris had landed within a foot of her. She hadn't been a single claw swipe away from death as he feared. She was wrapped up, in the far, completely untouched, corner. The Djinn had destroyed so much of the dwellings other sections, it created a sort of barrier between itself and Princess.

When he reached her, he fed her, cleaned up the mess she made in the blanket, and she fell right to sleep. He desperately wanted to sleep again too, but he knew he couldn't risk that again. Besides, the Djinn would be forfeit to scavengers if he didn't jump on it now. He collected a few fangs, one of its claws, and pried up enough of the scales to make a new set of armor. He cut out the skin from the good wing to make a new sling for Princess, and skinned the lower half for its warm fur. He returned to the peacefully sleeping girl, loaded her up along with the rest of his supplies, and took off. Where he was going, he didn't know; however, wherever he went and whatever he faced, he now had a justified confidence that he could handle whatever the forest threw at them.

-O-

Moryn watched as Athan was dragged through the halls of the castle; his hands bound behind his back in chains, his mouth gagged with a thick roll of cloth tied firmly in place. He still didn't understand why. Athan would never betray Rynok, let alone like that. That was the main reason they had kept him firmly out of the loop; he never would have agreed to their plot to overthrow Rynok. And to use Nimm? Nimm was one of Rynok's most trusted servants. He would never have crossed his king. And killing Ivary? Athan loved her, she was his sister. He would have died before ordering her death.

Something was terribly off, and he wasn't the only one who thought so. "How did this happen?" Garm hissed, he didn't want to be overheard.

"I don't know. I've sent a team to the Altar. They will report their findings directly to me once they return."

"But what about the plan?"

"Are you serious? The plan is finished; no child, no Athan. There is no plan without either."

Garm threw his hands over his eyes, "Of course, I know, I know. It's just..." He slowly lowered his hands down his face. "What does that mean for Tuckkar?"

"We can work through this. We just need to think it through." Moryn had no idea what to do. Their first plan was hard enough, and look where they were now. "If we can't put a new king in power, then we're just going to have to make the most of the one we have now."

"And how do you propose we do that? If it were that easy, we would have done that from the start. We both know Rynok well enough, he can't handle what's coming."

Garm was right. They had considered this completely and thoroughly before they settled on removing him from the throne their way. He was completely stubborn and could never be made to change his mind once it was set. He had always been that way, the only person who could really reach him had been Ivary and now she was gone. "Wait. That could be it."

"What? What could be it?"

"Ivary's gone; without her he just might be willing to listen to someone else."

"That's a pretty big *if*. His most trusted friend betrayed him. His brother betrayed him. He could just as easily become completely closed off to those of us he once trusted."

"I hope for your sake you're wrong."

"For all of Ghor's sake, I do too."

CHAPTER 5: A DECADE OF DESPAIR

"Within the Immortal Forest, there is only Gylum's law; His law is absolute. Knowledge of His law is passed down from the father to the son through blood. For eighteen years, boys are expected to learn from His teachings, to carry them into the next life. Upon Fulfillment a man is no longer held to these laws, but to the laws of man. The laws of man are their freedom, but at the end of their days, they must be prepared to justify them before Gylum."

–   The Xyrith: 136: 49-53

Moryn walked down the hall of the castle, right past the open door to the conservatory. His hair, more gray than black now, had developed a large bald patch on the top of his head. His face drooped and sagged with the wear and tear of a stressful life. The years had not been kind to him. As he passed the open door, that momentary glance inside flooded back memories of that dreadful night ten years prior. He wished he could remember her from before; he wished to think of her happy life rather than only the sorrow of her death. He tried, but failed. His happy memories had run dry a long time ago.

Garm stood outside the small side door to the throne room. He looked very anxious, checking his timepiece impatiently. Moryn was moving as fast as he could short of running, the noise of his footsteps alerted Garm to his presence. "There you are! Hurry, the session has already started."

"I'm sorry. It took longer than I expected," he said with heavy breathing. He could feel his age catching up to him.

"Yes, and congratulations are due, but we must get in there right now."

Moryn cracked the door open and took a peek inside before committing to entering. "And this is everyone? The whole village?"

"Every soul save some of your wall guards."

"And the atmosphere so far? How has it been?"

"How do you think it is? They're running out of food and room. They're pissed off. They want answers, more importantly, they want a solution."

Moryn turned back to Garm, away from the door. He

leaned in close and quietly asked, "And when they realize their king has neither?"

"That's why we must get in there. We must ease their minds before we have a full-fledged revolt on our hands."

Under these circumstances, that really was the best they could hope for. There would be time that night for the cabinet to discuss what was about to be said by the villagers, so long as the villagers didn't kill them all first. "Very well. After you?"

Garm barged into Moryn as he passed. It hurt a bit, *not bad for a man entering his fifties*. They entered the room in the back, near the throne. The expansive room was filled to the brim with dirty and raggedy peasants. Only a wall of armored guards separated the volatile crowd from the king and his cabinet members. The sound of a thousand quiet murmurs in an enclosed space amplified to a thunderous roar.

The king raised one of his hands barely above the height of his own head. The moment he did, the room fell deftly silent. Moryn could finally hear himself think. *That's a good sign. They still have a decent amount of respect for him. That might just be enough.*

"Easy now my people. We all knew this day might come. We have been preparing for years," his words carried through the room. Like most things about Rynok, his speaking voice was very powerful.

Quiet whispering started up again among the masses. One voice distinguished itself, "You told us this wouldn't happen when you forced your birth restrictions on us!" Supportive shouting rung out.

"But it will work. This is just a momentary crossover before the effect of the restrictions bears its fruit." Rynok's voice was calm. His belief in what he was saying was apparent.

"How long are we supposed to wait? Another eight years? We already have two or three, sometimes even four families to one home!" shouted a different voice from the sea of bodies.

"And we're running out of food! How do you expect us to produce strong sons when we ourselves are wasting away?"

This went on for over an hour. The people voiced

their complaints, and Rynok just gave them empty promises and dodged the true problems. For a man who had always hated politics, he wasn't bad at it. Unfortunately, it didn't help. The villagers were smart enough to know that he was just beating around the bush. The longer the session went, the closer they were to erupting into anarchy. When Moryn could almost see the people's patience breaking, he got Garm and put an end to the discussion. There were mixed feelings in the crowd, some were happy just to have the uselessness end, others more upset that nothing had been resolved. Regardless of their individual attitudes, they filed out and back to their homes.

Rynok stepped down from his throne as soon as the front doors closed behind the last villager. "Very well then, I shall see you all in a few hours for the meeting. I'll be in my quarters."

Moryn stopped him from leaving by grabbing his shoulder firmly. "With all due respect sir, I think we need to address this issue now."

Rynok turned, his eyes leered into his soul; an all too familiar look in these later years. Garm stepped in and backed Moryn, "I agree my Lord. This can't wait, not this time."

Rynok glared at Garm now, then he circled the room. Moryn could see it, the whole cabinet was in silent agreement. The king stood alone, and he caved, "So it is. Lead the way." Harshness filled his words. They left the throne room immediately.

They reached the dining hall a few minutes later. They took their usual seats, Athan's old chair, right next to Rynok, remained unfilled. Rukor sat two seats further than anyone else. He was the oldest of them, and he just didn't care anymore. He was there because he had to be, didn't mean he had to enjoy it or put any effort.

"Alright, who would like to start?" Rynok asked his men.

Moryn looked at his fellow cabinet members. They all wanted to speak, but fear of reprisal held their tongues. If they wouldn't address the issue, then he would. "We can't just sit by and wait for this problem to solve itself. We need a new plan. An immediate plan."

They all sat there, quietly, waiting for the king's response. Rynok sat for a moment with his hands folded under his chin. He gave the slightest of nods, and in that moment, everyone suddenly felt very boisterous as they too expressed their support for Moryn. The other four councilmen had lost their backbones these past years. Now they were just a group of worthless yes men. This continued for some time; Moryn and Garm would present clever and original ideas, but then Rynok would reject them, either completely or just slightly. Suddenly the others who had loved the idea realized maybe it wasn't that great after all.

Moryn had enough. "Then please my Lord. Come up with something, anything, better."

The king sat, thinking hard. Suddenly a dull voice broke out, a voice they hadn't heard in a long time. "Why bother asking him?" It was Rukor, "Unless you want him to smash something, you'd better look somewhere else for answers."

"Excuse me!" the king raged. No one spoke to him like that.

"With our queen dead, there's only one member of the true royal bloodline left. We need a king right now, not this sterile wannabe." His demeanor remained relaxed and nonchalant even as his treasonous words crossed the table.

Rynok stood up with an uncontrollable bloodlust in his eyes. He flipped the heavy table like it was nothing. Everyone scurried away except Rukor, who only shifted his weight now that the table was upside down across the room and not under his chin. Rynok drew his blade halfway when Moryn held him back. "Hold on my Lord! Just let me and my men take care of this!"

"I'll kill the dog myself!" Rynok spit the words.

"Ya, because killing is all you think about. It's all you know. If only killing people could solve all your problems, you'd be set."

Garm joined him in trying to hold the king back, but it would be only a matter of time until he overcame the two of them. Moryn cried through gritted teeth, "Why Rukor? What are you doing this for?"

For the first time in a long time, Rukor showed some

form of emotion. There was conviction in his voice as he sat up straight. "For an entire decade I've sat by in silence and watched our beloved city fall to ruin, but my time is short. Today is my last day, I can feel the sickness coursing through my bones." He stood up, not a hint of fear in his eyes. He was prepared for death. "And I'll be damned if I let my life end without speaking what everyone in this room knows to be true, but fears to say themselves."

Rynok got free of Moryn and Garm and plunged his sword right into Rukor's breastplate, hard and deep. Blood gushed out around the exposed metal. Rukor fell to his knees with his final words, "Long live Athan. True king of Tuckkar." He fell forward landing with a smack into his own blood; gone.

Rynok cleaned his blade off and headed back to his seat as if nothing had happened. Moryn needed a moment to collect himself, to adjust to what Rukor said, what the King had done, everything. He called for his men. It took five of them to flip the table back upright, and then two of them collected the body. "Take him downstairs. Call for the undertaker," Moryn ordered.

"That will not be necessary Moryn," Rynok stated coldly, "chuck him off the wall. Let the forest have him."

"But my Lord. Please don't condemn his long life of service for one momentary lack of judgment."

"His treason cannot go unpunished. That is the punishment I have placed upon him." Rynok looked across the table at Rukor's sons, dread on their faces. "He's lucky I don't condemn his whole bloodline."

Moryn hesitated. He looked for a way to salvage the situation, but when Rynok made up his mind, the only choice was to do as he says. "Guards, you heard your king." The men took the body out the door; not the door to the stairwell, but to the outer wall. Moryn reluctantly took his seat again. "Now, if we can get back to the topic at hand? We still don't…"

"I have a solution," Rynok interrupted. "And I should really thank the late Rukor."

"What do you mean *thank him*?" Jossif squeaked.

"Yes, you all heard him, correct?" Rynok looked around the room looking for an answer. He received none.

"He gave us our solution, 'If only killing people could

solve all your problems.' Don't you see now?"

"My Lord, killing Rukor is one thing, he was treasonous, but you can't kill our own people," Garm pleaded.

"No, of course not. I will not be killing anyone."

"Then I fail to see what you're getting at," Ardo added.

"The Birthright. It serves the purpose of weeding out the weak, but clearly, that is not working as well as it used to. And, as we all know, we can't deny it once it has been Fulfilled. So, if two or more men Fulfill the same Birthright, only the strongest should hold a place in Tuckkar."

"Are you suggesting what I think you're suggesting?" Garm asked, appalled.

"You want our own sons to fight each other for the right to live?" Ardo asked.

"Of course, that already happens every day in the forest."

"But that's different."

"Is it? All it will be is one final test. Gylum demands only strength, this is simply the next step."

"Have you thought of how you will present this to the people? They'll never approve," Moryn said, trying to change his mind with a different approach.

"It will be a new law. I think I will call it 'Rukor's Law,' that way everyone knows who came up with the idea."

He was insane. Worst of all, there was nothing they could do to stop him. "The people are on the brink of revolt as it is. This will push them over that edge for sure."

"We can handle the peasants. We have the finest trained guards thanks to you. And they will be exempt from Rukor's Law of course."

The meeting lasted for another ten minutes, but it was already over. Nothing else that was said mattered. The king dismissed the cabinet but remained behind. Moryn watched him from the door before leaving. He always hoped that things might change for the better, but for ten long years things only got worse from one day to the next. He should have snapped out of his denial a long time ago; he never should have let it reach this point. They had to revise their old plan. They had to remove Rynok. They needed Athan now, more than ever.

-O-

Paladin woke with a start, knife in hand. This was the norm for him; an hour of sleep at a time, waking from the slightest sound or vibration through the trees. He got up and put on his armor. He had grown a lot, he was an inch shy of five feet and composed of solid lean muscle. He checked on Princess who was sound asleep. *Good.* He did a quick perimeter check, made sure all his traps and snares were intact and not triggered before heading back inside. They had been staying there for almost six months now, longer than anywhere else before. It was hard to hold down a dwelling. Princess was only ten; she was young and still made mistakes. He had been able to make it very homey in that time, but he wondered how long it would last.

She would be waking up soon, so he prepared breakfast; a chunk of meat from a Niku tree and some dried Zed Wolf jerky. There wasn't much food variety in the forest. The harsh environment weeded out all but a few species, and most of them were either too difficult to hunt regularly, or too lean to provide enough edible meat to be worth the trouble. However, anyone with a blade strong enough to cut through the armored bark of a Niku could access the hearty meat fairly easily. The only hard part would be trying to avoid getting bashed to death by the thick branches.

The smell of the food must have woken her, because the minute he put the food on the table she took her seat. Her eyes were still tired. She didn't have his burden of needing to be alert at all times, not yet. He finished his meal quickly and quietly, but she was poking around her Niku meat, eating it slowly. "You're supposed to eat it, not play with it." She sneered at him, but listened. She tried to get up, but her jerky was still on the plate. "You're not done yet."

"But I don't like Zed jerky, it's too tough." She sulked back into her seat.

"If you don't eat it now, that's all we're having for dinner." Having his father's memories of raising his older sister really came in handy. His parents had some very useful tricks he could incorporate with her.

She pouted for a minute, but when she realized he

wouldn't budge she cleared her plate. "Happy now?"

"Very, now we can crack open those Dao eggs for dinner."

"Really?" She jumped up and gave Paladin a huge hug. "You're the best!"

His face turned stern. "Quiet, do you want to get driven from here like the last place?" He didn't wait for an answer, he went straight for the exit and checked outside. He didn't hear anything, they should be safe. For now.

"I'm sorry," she said, tearing up.

He went over to her and hugged her again. "It's okay, I know you are." She was just a kid, even though everything he did was for her safety, she didn't understand yet. "I have a surprise for you today, but you have to promise to be good."

"I promise." She wiped her face and tried to match his seriousness.

"Okay, you're coming outside with me today."

Her expression changed to fear. "B-but, we haven't been found. I don't wanna leave this place, please?" As far as she knew, the only time she left whichever dwelling they lived in at the time was because they needed to abandon it and find a new home. Once they did, she wouldn't leave until the next time.

"No, no, we'll be coming back. I have something out there I want you to see." He tried to calm her down. She seemed to accept that they weren't leaving for good, but she still looked scared.

"But, you always said it was too dangerous outside."

"I know I did, and it is. That's why I need to show you."

Her fear was still present, but she trusted him. She had trusted him all her life, and with good reason. She didn't ask any more questions, she just took his hand and followed him out into the forest.

Their dwelling was high in a Grim Wood, away from its more carnivorous roots, where Paladin could keep it in check. He climbed down with ease, only slowing to help Princess, and only when she needed it. They reached the forest floor where there was a clearing about twenty feet by fifteen.

She looked around, confused. "What did you want me

to see?"

Paladin crossed the clearing and picked up a chunk of Niku bark. "This." He tossed it to Princess, but she dropped it when she tried to catch it. She picked it up and looked at it. It was carved into the sword-like shape of a Dao Wing's beak.

"What is this?" she asked.

"It's your training sword. It's about time I teach you to defend yourself."

She was still with shock. She lifted the tip of the wooden blade off the ground for a second before setting it back down hard. "It's too heavy."

"It's weighted that way for a reason. It will build your strength, and the real one will feel lighter and nimble by comparison."

She still didn't get it. "B-but why? Why now?"

"Because in six years, two months, and five days I won't be here to protect you anymore. That's how long I have to prepare you so that you can survive your last year here without me."

He always hated mentioning that. He had taught her a lot about Birthrights, Fulfillments, the Xyrith, and everything else he knew. He knew all the laws and all the rules. He knew that no matter how hard he worked to keep her alive, he couldn't stay with her after he turned eighteen.

She gripped the training sword with both hands and heaved it up in front of her. "Then let's get started." He had never been so proud of her in his life.

Their first training session on that day only lasted half an hour. They would have to start out slow, he knew that, but her heart was in it completely and that's all he could ask for. The physical ability would follow soon enough. Her arms were too worn out from using the sword, so they had lunch on the forest floor.

"Are you sure it's safe enough for us to stay down here?" she asked with a worried look around.

"Safe as it is up there. I've placed enough traps around here to keep almost anything out of our hair."

"Almost anything? Now I *really* feel safe." They laughed together. Paladin didn't laugh very often. He didn't think anyone in the forest ever did, but then again, no one had ever had a female child with them before.

"Well, let's see how well you know your beasts of the forest. What do you remember about Knixx Vipers?" If her physical training was done for the day, he could still test her knowledge. Knowing the enemy was just as important in defeating them.

"Um, they are good climbers. They can hunt on the forest floor but prefer to stay in the trees. They constrict their food to eat it, but their bite can paralyze too."

"Right, good. And how do they hunt?"

She scrunched up her face, "Um, sneaky?"

"No, I mean what do they have that other beasts don't?"

"Oh, they can see heat." She looked pleased with herself.

"That's right. They have heat sensors right next to their eyes. And don't forget what uses they can provide. Good meat, their skin, while not the strongest, is flexible enough for joints." He demonstrated with his own armored elbow. "Zed Wolves?"

"They have four horns that protect their heads from most attacks. They hunt in packs of four to six, they are really smart, and their pelts are waterproof." She answered confidently, "And they only taste good fresh, their jerky sucks." She added that last bit with the same pouty face from breakfast.

Paladin laughed. He had brought some more jerky down as a part of lunch, but spared her having to eat it. "Good, very good. What's next?"

"The Dao Wing I guess." He nodded and she continued. "They hunt alone, they have extremely good vision. Their metal feathers are detachable, and they fire them at their prey as they flap their wings. Other than their metal beak and skull, their skeleton is hollow bone. They have almost no good meat on them, but their eggs are delicious." She licked her lips in anticipation of the dinner he had promised her.

"As long as you remember to filter out the metal bits, otherwise that same delicious meal will tear up your insides." She grabbed her belly and pretended to writhe in pain, and then she laughed loudly. "Alright now, keep it down," he said, but nicely this time, "I think that's enough for today, are you ready to head back up?"

"But Djinn are next. Don't you want to know what I remember about them?"

"You still have a long way to go before that will be an issue." He got up and held out his hand to Princess. Before she got up, a loud snap came from the distance. "That's one of the perimeter alarms. Hurry, we need to get inside."

She rose to her feet quickly and they climbed the tree together. Five feet up, another series of three consecutive cracks. *One of the traps, as long as it wasn't a Djinn, it would have killed it.* But another snapping sound meant it was still coming. They were about twelve feet up when they could first see it through the foliage. Paladin grabbed Princess and pulled her to the far side of the tree and stopped the climb.

"Well, here's your chance," he whispered, "what can you tell me about this guy?"

"What? Now? But it'll hear us," she hissed quietly.

"Will it? Here, look at the side of its head, what do you see?"

She peaked around the corner. The first time she cringed back too quickly, but he made her look again. "I don't see anything, just those gross slimy scales."

"Exactly, no ears."

"So they can't hear anything?" she asked a bit louder.

"Shh. They can still hear, but not the way you and I hear. They sense vibrations through the air and ground. They only pick up on higher frequency sounds." He looked at her face and could tell this was way over her head. "Like a wolf howl, but not its bark, the bark is too deep for it to hear. A Dao Wing's caw, or a Knixx Viper's hiss."

"But their roar is so deep, they can't hear themselves? Or each other?"

"They don't need to. They evolved to hunt these creatures, not each other. They hunt alone. so they don't need to communicate. Unless it's mating season, then they sound very different." They waited patiently for the beast to make his way through and out of their territory. When the outer perimeter alarm on the far side sounded, they resumed their climb. *I'll have to reset those traps and alarms before anything else comes through.*

They reached the entrance to the dwelling and he let her go inside. He made quick work of resetting everything. This was their home now. Even though he knew survival was more important and that they couldn't stay here forever, it felt nice to have a place to call home again. Staying there made her happy, and he would do anything in his power to keep her happy.

CHAPTER 6: DON'T DWELL ON THE PAST

"In one's life there are three types of action: those of the past, present, and future. The actions of the future are known only to Gylum; therefore, no one should try to know them. The actions of the past are known to all, but can never be changed; therefore, no one should wish to. The actions of the present are all that matter, for they are the only ones that can be both known and changed at will."

– The Xyrith: 71: 1-4

Moryn waited impatiently in the conservatory. The memories this place raised within him were painful, almost too much to bear, but it was a fitting place for what he had planned. Garm finally arrived, "Were you followed?"

"I don't know, should I have been checking? No one knows what we're doing here." He peeked back outside the door and looked down the hallway. Not very inconspicuous. "I think we're fine."

"Just hurry up and get over here. You've done enough." Moryn was upset, he didn't want Garm's incompetence to get them both killed. Garm came over, but stopped at the table in the center of the room. It was the very same table the queen's body had been laid upon all those years ago. He looked at it in silence. Moryn placed his hand on his shoulder. "I know."

Garm collected himself. "You know what needs to be done?"

"We need Athan."

"Yes, but it won't be easy. And just having Athan won't be enough. He needs to bring with him a solution to the problem."

"Preferably one that doesn't involve the deaths of half our people." Moryn thought about it, but he had nothing. Hopefully Garm had an idea.

"Before he was imprisoned Athan was working on more than just the statistics he showed us," Garm said, "he didn't get very far, just a theory mostly, but I came across his work."

Moryn was curious, "What was it? What did he find?"

"Well, as you know, he wasn't the most devout

believer in the Xyrith, so he was looking for the true source of the Birthrights."

"And he found it?"

"Not quite. In his notes he mentions that there are references to an ancient Warlock, one that lived in the Ghor of old. He believes this Warlock created the Birthright millennia ago." Garm pulled out a tattered notebook.

"But how does that help us now?"

"Because according to this, the Warlock was immortal and still lives somewhere in the forest."

Moryn was caught off guard. What? *Could it be possible? Could the Xyrith be wrong?* "What does that mean for us though? Athan had a plan to build outside the wall before all this happened. Why not just stick with that plan?"

"Rynok isn't the only zealot we must deal with. Many people believe in Gylum wholeheartedly. If we can undo the magic of the Birthright, we can regain control of all our people."

"But…" Moryn started again. He still didn't understand. He felt like there had to be a better solution, even if he couldn't think of one.

"Enough questions!" Garm shouted. "I know it won't be easy. I've thought this out, it's our only option."

"Fine, I trust your judgment. What's our next step?"

"I'll go speak with Athan tomorrow. I'll need you to help me get into the dungeon without Rynok finding out."

"I'll assign the guards I know I can trust to the dungeon tomorrow, and I'll keep Rynok close to me. How long will you need?"

"The longer, the better. But we must work with care. Just recon for now, we must wait for the right moment to free him."

Moryn agreed, they couldn't afford a mistake, not this time. "Very well. We should keep our contact to a minimum from here on out. I'll send word when I'm prepared on my end."

Garm headed for the door, "Until then. Good luck my friend." Garm left, and Moryn waited a few minutes before he left also. He used that time to think about everything going on, and how it differed from the last time the two of them spoke like that. Last time, he felt bad about what they were going to do because Rynok was like a son to him. This time, there was no love left in him. They were still doing it for the greater good, but this time there was no downside to removing Rynok. This time, he might actually take some joy from doing so.

-O-

Paladin watched as Princess went through her training exercises. She was progressing quickly. She was now able to wield the training sword single handedly, and she had most of the basic strikes and blocks down pretty well. He still didn't believe she could actually defend herself in a real world fight though. She was improving, but she still wasn't even as strong as a newborn male. She hadn't been born with that gift, and he had no idea if she was even capable of getting close; they were in uncharted territory.

Their daily training sessions were up to two hours twice a day now. She was only fifteen minutes into the morning endurance training, and the perimeter was secure enough that he felt safe taking his eyes off her for a while. He hopped up into a nearby Niku and decided to take this free moment to inspect his weapons for damage or dullness. His primary sword, a newer, longer Dao Wing beak was four and a half feet long. He could have found a longer one, but he preferred to use it one handed. Besides, it was thicker and stronger than most he had come across. His knife was a Djinn claw, nearly straight and eleven inches long, with the long bone of its finger making a nicely contoured handle. He began training on duel wielding both blades about two years prior; he nearly had it mastered.

His weapons were in prime condition; he liked how they were low maintenance. He was able to spend more time on other, more important, things. Paladin moved on to his armor. He removed each piece carefully, but quickly, and inspected it meticulously. There was a tear in the Knixx skin of his left knee. That would be a project, it was fairly difficult to fuse the joint pieces in a way that made them wear correctly. He didn't find any other wear or tear. This armor was relatively new since his growth spurt after he turned ten.

There was only one piece left he hadn't removed. It wasn't armor though; it was the oldest possession he owned, something he always kept close to his heart. A series of interlocked Knixx Viper vertebrae connected end to end hung around his neck with a rib bone dangling down every inch or two. He grabbed hold of the pendant and lifted it up to his eye level. It was the white broad headed skull of the same viper. He gazed into its empty eye sockets, and he felt a cold rush like it was staring right back at him, at his very soul.

"Why do you wear that?" Princess asked from behind him. He was startled. He hadn't heard her come up, and it didn't help that he was completely naked.

He quickly covered his sensitive bits. "W-what are you doing up here? Shouldn't you be training?"

"I have been, for two hours. Don't tell me you're making them longer, these two-a-days are already killing me."

She was right. He could feel it, it had been two hours. He had been standing up there with no armor, not paying any attention to the outside world for over an hour and a half. He couldn't believe it. "Um, no. Just head back up, I'll be there in a minute." He started grabbing his armor and putting it back on. It was difficult with her still looking at him.

"You still haven't answered my question." She stood firm.

"What question?"

"That necklace. It's a viper skull. I know that much, but you never take it off. You've had it for as long as I can remember. Why?"

He slowed in his dressing. He wondered what to tell her. *Do I tell her the truth?* He was embarrassed just thinking about it. *Do I lie?* He's never lied to her before; they needed absolute trust to survive the forest together. *I could just deflect and avoid it. No.* He knew her well enough, she was too curious for her own good. She would not let up until she knew. "Ya, I've had it since before you were born."

"What was it then? Your first kill?"

He was finished getting dressed now. "No." He turned and headed for their dwelling.

"Well, what then? You can tell me." She chased after him, but he was much faster than her. By the time she reached the entrance, he had already been inside for five minutes. "I'm not going to stop asking."

"Ya, I know. Have a seat." He gestured to her seat across the table from him. She sat down in silence. She was excited to hear another story, but she contained it fairly well. She had to know that this was something private, and she respected that by containing her joy. "I was six months old, I hadn't acquired much at that point. Some rudimentary clothing, nothing of much protection. A feather with poor wrapping as my only weapon. I was living out of a hollowed out dead Grim Wood."

"But you were only six months old, it's not your fault." She wasn't helping.

"I knew what I needed to survive from the day I was born. There's no excuse for why I wasn't living like this by that point." He stood up and threw his arms out showing off what he had now. "But that's not even the worst part." He sank back down into his seat. His gaze was locked onto the ground. "I was out checking my snares, didn't catch a thing that whole week. I was cold and hungry. I was weak."

"No, I'm sure…" she started, but was cut off.

"I was weak! I came across a Knixx Viper, it was barely older than a baby. I was too slow, I got bit." He paused for a minute. Princess didn't interrupt this time, she was listening on the edge of her seat. "It started wrapping itself around me. It started squeezing." He paused again.

"And then?" She asked in quiet anticipation.

"And then, it stopped squeezing." He brought the skull up in between them. "The viper's body fell off me, and still paralyzed, I saw in the corner of my eye its head roll across the dirt."

"B-but, how? What happened?" She was still stunned and confused from the story.

"An older boy, about six and a half, came out from the shadows beside me; blood dripping off his sword. The boy had saved my life. He checked my Birthright, but wasn't interested. Who would be? the life of a Miner, who would choose that? A few minutes later I could move again, and I left, but not before taking something to remind me."

"Remind you of what?" She asked, worried about what

the answer would be.

"That I was weak, that I am weak. That I don't deserve to still be alive today. That I'm not worthy of Gylum, or anything else."

She sat there with her mouth cracked open, but nothing came out. She didn't know what to say and he expected as much. When she finally spoke, her voice was low, "Is that why you rescued me?"

He hadn't expected her to ask that. Of all the questions she could have asked, he never expected that one. He didn't answer.

"You're not weak. I've seen what you can do. I know you, you are worthy," she pleaded.

He jumped from his seat, angry. "You wouldn't understand! You know nothing of strength! You were born weak and you will always be weak! We can't change who we are!"

"Then why bother training me? Why did you bother saving me at all if that's how you really feel?" She was breathing heavily now. She was waiting for his reply. He could bet it wasn't the one she wanted to hear.

"You're right, why do I bother? You can forget about today's second practice." He grabbed her training sword and tossed it under his cot. "In fact, just forget about all of them."

-O-

Garm walked down the hall, the door to the dungeon right in front of him at the end. He was nervous; it was much more difficult to handle this entire cloak-and-dagger thing in his old age than it had been when he was younger. His heart wasn't as healthy these days, and the constant high rate of beats didn't help.

There was only one guard outside the door today. It was a good sign, there were usually two. *This must be Moryn's man. It better be.* He reached the guard and waited. A moment of panic welled up as the guard stood there in his full body armor, eyes hidden behind steel glaring at him. The guard stepped to the side and pushed the door open with a slow eerie creak. Garm swallowed loudly, and then took the first step over the threshold.

Garm descended a spiral stone staircase about three flights down where it melded into wood. The now wooden stairs creaked under his heavy weight. They ran down another thirty feet to the cold stone floor. Garm knew the castle well enough, it was a defensive measure against prisoners escaping. Should there be a breakout, the guards upstairs could easily set fire to the lower staircase without the flames reaching the main body of the castle. The fire would burn up all the oxygen in the dungeon, and even if someone survived, they would be trapped down there with no means of escape, left to starve. Just one of many things he would have to overcome if he wanted to free Athan.

He reached the bottom safely. He was surprised the wood had lasted this long without falling apart, it was mostly rotten. He walked down the first aisle of cells, lighting torches and looking into each one as he passed. For most of his life, these cells were all empty because people in Tuckkar knew how to work together, not against each other. These days were a different story. With overpopulation and poverty plaguing the village for the first time in its history, crime and violence had emerged. It took passing several dozens of cells to find one that was vacant.

The men inside had different means of coping with their fate. Some rambled quietly to themselves while others screamed and clawed through the bars. Most just sat curled up in one corner or another waiting for their next meal or their last breath, whichever came first. These men had only been down here for a few years, three at the most. If they were in this bad of shape, he couldn't imagine how Athan had handled a whole decade.

Garm turned the last corner, it ended in a dead end. The wall at the end of this last aisle contained the steel door of the very last cell. Athan's cell. Garm came to the bars and looked inside. The torchlight only illuminated half of the cell. Garm reached to pull it off the wall when a deep voice rumbled from inside the dark. "Leave it. Why have you come?"

Garm slid it back into place and stammered before getting out an actual sentence. "I, It's me, Garm."

"That's not what I asked," the voice said. It didn't

sound anything like Athan.

"I've come to speak with Athan. Is this the right cell?"

"Names mean nothing here. And who you wish to talk to is of no importance, that is not the *why*. You have one more chance to answer my question, only one more."

Garm thought carefully on his next words. He wasn't sure why this man, if it even was Athan, was speaking to him like that, but he didn't see any other choice than compliance. If it wasn't Athan, he was about to reveal their whole plot to the wrong person. It could be a trap, but he was willing to take that risk. "I've come to learn more of the ancient Warlock, and free the true king of Tuckkar."

A tense moment passed, part of Garm was waiting for the man to reveal himself as one of Rynok's men and arrest him, but that didn't happen. Instead, the figure that presented itself into the light had clean, long, golden blonde hair grown halfway down the back, and a matching beard. It was definitely Athan. "You sure took your sweet time, didn't you?"

Garm was so relieved, "Oh thank Gylum! My Lord." He knelt before Athan. Athan looked annoyed. Garm forgot he didn't believe in Gylum. "You're okay? You haven't gone mad down here?"

"My fellow prisoners know why they were placed here, they have accepted it, and aren't burdened with questions and theories." He stepped up to the bars. "I don't have that luxury."

"So it was a lie then? You never plotted against your brother?" Garm inquired.

"Of course not. I never would have done such a thing," he hesitated for a second, "well, not back then at least."

"Do you have any clue what really happened?"

"I have only theories and speculation. If I agree to help you with whatever you came here for, you must promise to help me solve what unfolded that night." Athan gripped the bars, passion in his words.

Garm nodded frantically, "Yes, however I can help."

Athan released the bars, "Now, what do you need to know? You mentioned the ancient Warlock."

"Yes, I found some reference to him in your notes." Garm pulled the tattered book out of his inside pocket. He passed it through the bars to Athan.

"You found that, did you? Well I have bad news for you then." He handed it back to Garm. "Everything I found out is already in there. I just barely scratched the surface before I landed in here."

Garm hadn't expected that. He wasn't sure what to expect, but at least something. "What does that mean then? Where do we go from here?"

"You need to finish what I started. The royal library has tombs dating back to the Ghor of old. You need to read through them, you need to find anything that could point to where he might be today."

"Will that really work? Could we really find him after all these years through ancient books?" Garm was having a hard time believing that to be true.

"Not entirely, but it could very well narrow down the search. Someone would have to be out there though. Someone needs to be physically searching in the forest."

"It's just Moryn and myself though. I don't think we would be able to hide a search like that from Rynok."

Athan thought for a moment, "It would have to be me then."

Garm had thought of that as well, but he wasn't sure if it was the smartest idea. "Could you survive in the forest again? It's been so long, and you aren't exactly in the best shape anymore."

"I survived the forest once. I survived this wretched place. I'm stronger than you think." He held his hands and arms out, there was very little between the bones and his skin. "Trust me, I can handle just about anything that forest can throw at me."

"Very well then. It might take some time to arrange your escape. Save your strength, I will return when it's time." Garm turned to leave, but thin pale fingers wrapped around his arm, stopping him.

"What about your end of the deal? I must know what happened that night. I must know what my sister died for."

Garm had almost forgotten about his promise. "What do you need of me?"

"Are her remains in the catacombs? Did he bring her

back with him or does she belong to the forest now?"

"She is at rest. He prepared the body himself."

Athan's eyes darted from side to side. He was processing this new information. It was amazing he could have any theories at all, he wouldn't have known even the smallest detail after how quickly he was arrested. He finally spoke, but it was mostly to himself. "Yes, he wouldn't want too many eyes on the body if he had something to hide, but what was he hiding? Blade marks are hard to distinguish, but no guarantee he even used his own. Probably wasn't that. What else would he hide?" His eyes were darting again, this time a bit longer, and more sporadic. "That's it!" He grabbed Garm and pulled him to the bars. "It's the only thing that makes sense!"

"What! What is it?" Garm was worried. Maybe Athan wasn't as sane as he was led to believe.

"He might have removed the Birthright, but he definitely wouldn't remove the child. Search her belly for the bones of a child. If you don't find such bones, which I suspect you won't, then there still may be hope for us all." Athan released Garm and fled back into the dark corner of his cell. He didn't make another sound, at least not so long as Garm was still in earshot.

Garm made his way back upstairs. He had to inform Moryn of everything he learned. He had to go into the catacombs. He had to begin the search for the ancient Warlock. Most important of all, he had to figure out a way to break Athan out of that dungeon, and he had to do it sooner rather than later.

CHAPTER 7: FORGING METTLE

"Gylum rules over all of Ghor, to include the trees and beasts of the Forest. He presents prey when strength is proven, and predators when He wishes to test it. Know that any challenge presented can be overcome so long as one's heart is true and strong. When a life is taken, do not waste the sacrifice, but use His gift and absorb its essence. Only then can growth be attained."

— The Xyrith: 101: 33-37

Athan sat alone in the darkness of his cell. The torch had burned for three days before it ran out of fuel. That was four days ago. It had become significantly more difficult to hold on to his sanity now that there was a glimmer of hope. Before he had known there was no escape for him. He had the questions to drive him, but now he had more answers than questions. It didn't help pass the time nearly as well. He understood why it might be taking so long, but that didn't stop him from growing impatient.

Athan knew the layout of the dungeons extremely well. He had lived in the castle after all, and so had his father before him. Once an occupied cell door opens, the hallway's traps activate, and the staircase is burned immediately. The castle was ancient; its magic and secrets lost to time. He had always been curious as to how the magic worked and how it knew if the cell was occupied or not. However it did work though, it was far beyond him. He had spent years trying to think of a way to escape, but it was utterly impossible.

Another day passed before Garm returned. He carried with him a small rucksack. "Athan? Can you hear me?" he asked as he lit the torch by his door.

"I was starting to think you weren't going to return." Athan stepped into the light and waited by the bars. "What have you brought for me?"

Garm set the rucksack at the base of the cell door and started unpacking it. "I've been studying the layout of the dungeon; its traps, the staircase, there's no possible way to get you out of here alive."

"That's it? You have to have something! You can't just leave me down here!" he raged. *After all this time, this is what he comes back to me with?*

"I didn't say I couldn't get you out." Garm pulled out a small crystal vial filled with black liquid. "I said I couldn't get you out *alive.*"

"W-what is that?" Athan took a step back. He didn't like where this was going.

"It's a little mixture from the village doctor. One third potent Knixx Viper venom, the rest an extract from the sap of a Grim Wood." Garm pulled out the cork and took a whiff. "It was supposed to be a pain killer. The venom was supposed to single out the pain receptors in the brain."

Athan took half a step closer, he was intrigued now. "Supposed to? What does it actually do?"

"It targets the heart instead. Stops it from beating," he said, his eyes still on the vial.

"How long does it last?"

"A small enough dose, the effect only lasts a few seconds." Garm answered. That was good. Enough time to get him out of the cell before it wore off. "But once a heart stops, it can't just start itself back up," Garm finished his answer. It wasn't such good news after all.

"What good does that do us then?" Athan really hoped this was going somewhere. While he didn't really have better things to do, he still didn't like his time being wasted. Garm pulled a glass jar from the bag at his feet. The jar itself was unremarkable, but what was contained within was quite spectacular. "Is that?"

"Yes." It was lightning in a bottle. The little bolts cracked and bounced around the smooth wall of glass, desperately trying to find ground. "We had to wait for a storm to hit us before I could come back down."

So that was his plan. Bypass the dungeon's defenses completely. As far as it would be concerned, the occupant would die, the body be removed, and the traps would remain dormant. *Quite genius really.* "Once I'm out of the cell, how do I escape the castle?"

"The guard at the door is with us and the halls between here and the nearest section of wall are vacant. I have some supplies here you can use to get yourself started, but once you're out there you'll be on your own." Garm opened the rucksack showing Athan its contents. There was a few days food and water, a bushel of Integro roots, a dozen Djeg leaves, and a long hunting knife. Garm closed the bag and put it aside. "Are you ready to die?"

"Do I really have a choice?"

"Not really. Here." Garm handed Athan the vial. "Only drink half, if you take it all, I won't be able to restart your heart in time to prevent brain damage."

Athan wondered why he didn't just fill the vial halfway, but figured asking was unnecessary. He looked at the vial one last time, the deep black liquid was like sludge except it didn't cling to the walls of crystal. He placed the rim to his lips and tilted it back. It glided down his tongue and throat as if it was hovering less than a hair's width. He pulled the vial away quickly. It had been impossible to judge how much of the contents he actually took. Only a quarter of the potion was left, he had taken too much.

He went to give the vial back to Garm, but stumbled and dropped the bottle. It shattered on the mud covered stone floor. Shards of crystal shot out in every direction, and the last few drops of liquid pooled in round puddles on the ground like oil in water.

He was falling to the ground. He could feel his pulse in his chest, his limbs, in each toe and finger. It was racing, but then it slowed. The slower his heart rate became, the slower the ground was coming up to meet him. Halfway down, time all but stopped. Each beat in his chest felt like minutes apart, when finally, he felt the last beat, and then only blackness.

He didn't know where he was. His eyes were open but could not see. His ears were clear but could not hear. He knew his body was whole, but could not feel it. All of his senses were working, but they were providing no information to him. This continued, for how long he couldn't be sure because he had no frame of reference. Suddenly, he felt something. It was slight, just a tingle in his core, but just as quickly it vanished.

Back in the empty void, all he had were his thoughts. *Is this what death is? How long does it last? Eternity? Just long enough for brain function to dissipate? Or is this just a stop on the way to the afterlife?* He felt the tingle return, only this time it felt stronger. It was accompanied with a faint light. The light didn't look like it was either far away or close up. It was all around him and a single point at the same time. His ears picked up a slight sound, nothing distinguishing about it; more just the difference between nothing and something. He could now smell moisture in the air and taste the inside of his own mouth. It was so little, but he welcomed it like a starving man welcomes a crumb.

It vanished again. *What is this? Could I have been wrong? Is this Gylum's punishment for not believing? The Xyrith speaks of the Underealm, the place for weak souls. Could this be that place?* A surge of sensation came back, but unlike the last two this one was painful. The tingle became a searing rush of fire along every fiber of his being. The light blinded his eyes that wouldn't close. A loud crack filled his ears, his own burning flesh loomed in his nostrils, and the cold of metal stuck to his taste buds.

This time when he fell back into the nothingness, he was relieved. *No! I refuse to believe now. There's a reason for this. There's a reason for everything. I just need to think it through and figure it out.* There wasn't time to think though. He felt his heart beat in his chest again, and he sat up with a giant inhale of precious oxygen.

"Thank Gylum!" Garm shouted. He was kneeling over Athan with an empty glass bottle in one hand and the unscrewed lid in the other. Athan panted as he looked around at his surroundings. The closed iron bars to his cell were in front of him. The hallway through the dungeon to the stairs was behind him. To one side, Garm; to the other, three more empty glass jars and their lids littering the ground. "I only brought four bottles. I don't know what I would've done, if…"

Four bottles? That's what that was. The first three that didn't work, and the final one that did. Athan was glad to have figured out what happened, but infinitely more, he was just glad to be alive again. "I never want to go back there." He got to his feet. His body felt strange, almost like he had got used to not having one. "Let's get out of here."

He placed some of his weight on Garm as they moved through the aisles. He looked down to button his shirt back up when he saw four scorched marks on his chest. Each one burned on the left side of his chest, right above the heart. Once he was dressed the material of his shirt brushed and dragged across the burns, but he was no stranger to that kind of pain.

They made the climb up the stairs together, but stopped just short of the door at the top. Garm unslung the bag and handed it to Athan. "This is where I say goodbye. I can't risk being seen in this area, especially not with you."

"Alright. Did you look into the catacombs yet? What have you found?" Athan asked desperately.

"I'm sorry, not yet, but I promise I will. In your bag I left a map. There is a point just off the road to the Altar. We'll use that as a drop point to communicate." Athan opened the bag and found the rolled up parchment. "Anything I learn from the catacombs and the library, I'll relay through that spot."

Garm held out his forearm to Athan. He slung the bag onto his back and bashed his forearm into Garm's. His arm ached afterwards. This was really the first time he realized exactly how weak his imprisonment had made him. But he wasn't lying before, he knew that he would be able to survive anything out there; it was in his blood.

Garm headed through the door and hurried out of there. Athan waited a moment and then walked out into the hallway. There was a guard by the door. He towered over Athan, and his torso was so thick that three of him could easily fit inside that armored chest piece. The guard did nothing, he stood still when Athan passed by slowly, cautiously. Satisfied that the guard truly was with him and not against, he turned and jogged down the hall.

He reached the wall in only a few minutes, and Garm had been true to his word; the hallways were all abandoned. On the other hand, along the wall there were still guards posted at their stations. If he moved quickly and quietly enough he might be able to make it down the wall before getting spotted, but there was no guarantee.

He waited for a minute to see if the guards might shift position or change their routes, but they never did. They were very well trained. He figured out their movements, and when the next window came he was ready and made his move.

He sprinted for the edge of the wall. He realized he may have overestimated how quickly he could cover that amount of ground. He was only halfway when one of the guards was nearing the turnaround point. Athan gritted his teeth and pushed harder. He was breathing heavily now, way too heavily. He was five giant strides from the edge now. *Almost there! Just a few more seconds!* But it wasn't enough. The guard turned and instantly drew his bow.

"Halt!" the guard shouted. Athan made the last leap off the wall, heading straight for the branches of a tall Niku. The guards arrow whistled as it passed behind his head. He landed in the tree and threw himself to the far side. Two more arrows struck into the bark right where his head and chest had been a second prior. He pulled them out quickly *These might come in handy later.* More arrows flew into and around the tree as a loud Zed horn call rang out an alarm. Athan slid down the tree, branch by branch. The further down he got, the more difficult it was for arrows to reach him until none made it past the foliage.

Athan wasn't sure if his brother would send his troops out on foot. Escaped prisoners weren't something any king had ever needed to worry about before. Athan decided it was better to be safe than sorry and ran into the forest. He went as far and as fast as he could go without losing his bearings. He had to make sure he'd be able to find the drop point from wherever he ended up. He only stopped for a moment when he could see a portion of Gylum and its rings through a clearing in the treetops. It felt great to see the sky again. It was great to be free.

-O-

Two days passed and Paladin still hadn't let Princess resume her training. She didn't try very hard the first day, just enjoying the rest, but by the second day she was well rested and antsy to leave the dwelling again. She tried to leave on the third day, but he wouldn't let her. She spent that day doing what she could in the small space. Pushups here, dips there, crunches by her bed, and whatever else she could squeeze in when he was out checking the perimeter.

On the fourth day, she woke up early and tried to sneak out while he was sleeping. She made it outside and closed the door ever so gently, but when she turned around her triumphant look fell off her face. She was face-to-face with

Paladin. He had been waiting for her and sent her back inside immediately. The only thing they had for breakfast on that day was Zed jerky. She promised never to try that again; she learned her lesson.

Another week passed like that. In everything she tried, he was two steps ahead. Every time she failed, she was punished with bad food and busy work. Finally she had enough. She wanted to learn how to fight. She needed to learn how to defend herself.

When he was out resetting the snare that caught their breakfast, she went over to his bed and grabbed his old backup sword. When he came back she raised it, posed to attack.

"And what do you think you're doing?" he asked, turning his back on her to close the door behind him.

"If you won't train me," she shook as she spoke, "well, then I'll just have to go find someone else who will."

He laughed. "With that thing in your hand? Good luck with that." He circled around, away from the door towards his bed.

"Well, you can't stop me this time." She stepped closer to the door, keeping her shaking sword pointed at him.

He laughed even harder. "Seriously? I could stop you with my eyes closed."

She taunted him with her sword. "Let's see it then, come on." He reached his bed and picked up a piece of cloth. He tied it around his eyes and stood up straight and still. "I said come on."

"No, I'm fine. You take the first swing." He cleared his throat and tucked his hands behind his back.

She wasn't sure what kind of trick he was playing with her this time, and she definitely knew she didn't want to actually hurt him. She just wanted to get back to her training. She decided to go for it. She swung the sword exactly as she had learned. The sword was much lighter than her practice one making the movement much more fluid and effortless.

Paladin kicked the practice sword out from under his bed and caught it. The wood was strong, but not strong enough to block the sharpened metal of her sword so he used it to parry the blade's blunt side downward. She fell with her sword and it stuck into the ground away from his feet. Before she could even try and pull the sword out, he already had the wooden tip pressed against her throat. "Would you like to try that again, or are we done here?"

She released the hilt and left the sword sticking out of the ground. "Ugh! It's not fair!" She stormed over to her bed and crawled up on top of the sheets. "You're right. Why should I bother trying, I'll never be good enough." She started sobbing quietly.

She was trying her hardest. It really wasn't fair, he was born this way. It came as easy to him as breathing, but for her, she worked tirelessly and for what? She felt Paladin sit down beside her. He put his hand on her shoulder comfortingly. She shrugged him off, but he didn't stop.

"Look, I'm sorry," he said calmly. "Do you really want to start training again?"

"No, what's the point?"

"It takes time, even for me. I mean, you've seen me practicing my new duel wielding style. Just because you're not great now doesn't mean you can't get there someday."

She rolled over to face him. "You didn't seem to think so a few weeks ago."

He looked away. He had flipped out the last time they talked about this. She really hoped he wouldn't take it so bad this time. "That's different."

"How? I don't understand. Please, help me understand." She was sitting up now.

"Because I should have been strong enough. I had a weapon, it was just a Knixx. I should have died. That's the way it is; the weak die so the strong can strive."

She grabbed his hands with hers. "But you didn't die. You learned from it, and you're strong now. You're striving now."

He stood up and stormed away. He turned back before heading out the door. "And that's why you'll never understand. I'm on borrowed time. I'm not worthy of Gylum or His gifts. That's why I didn't take your Birthright the day you were born. I'm not worthy of Royalty. I'm not even worthy of this." He held up his own Birthright that shined brightly in the darkly lit room.

She looked down at her own Birthright, the crown

shining in her eyes. "You never told me that." She looked up at him, tears in her eyes. "Is that the only reason you saved me?"

"That's why I didn't take your Birthright. I saved you because…" He paused. Princess got up and walked to him. She raised his chin and looked into his eyes. "Because I saw the way your mother loved you, she wanted you to live. She wanted you safe." She hugged him harder than she had ever hugged him before. Eventually, she let go of him and wiped her tears away. "Now get some rest. You have a big day tomorrow."

She stayed up late from excitement, but she finally dozed off around midnight. The next morning, she woke with a start. She wasn't sure how long she had slept; she didn't have the same ability to tell time like Paladin did. Since it was always night, she had been learning to use the stars. She looked out a tiny window near her bed with a view through the trees. It was morning, pretty late in the morning really. *Either that or it's an hour before I went to sleep.* She still wasn't perfect at this. She decided to go with her first guess, but if that was right, where was he? *Why didn't he wake me? I thought I was going to start training again this morning.*

She went to get dressed when she saw Paladin's armor resting where her clothes should have been. As she got close, she noticed something different about it. She examined it. It was way too small to be his. *It's for me?* She took one of the arm bracers and tried it on. It fit perfectly. She put the rest of the armor on and tried it out. She bent her knees and elbows; the joints were flexible. She checked the plating, it was Djinn scales layered over Niku bark with Zed fur as a comfortable lining just like his.

She looked around for her training sword. It wasn't there. *Maybe he has it with him. He must be waiting for me, I'm probably late already.* She went to the door and left quickly. She made her way down to the clearing hastily, the armor felt like a second skin. She landed at the edge of the tree line. *He's not here. Where is he then?* The only thing down there was his old sword; the one she used against him the night before. It was sticking out of the center of the clearing.

She walked up to it and looked around again. She wasn't sure what was going on. *New armor? A real blade? What is he planning?* She grabbed the sword and pulled it from the soil.

The moment the metal was free, she heard a noise behind her. It definitely wasn't Paladin. It did sound familiar though, like a snake slithering along the forest floor.

She turned to face the sound, her sword at the ready. Sure enough she was now face-to-face with a Knixx Viper. Most of its bulk was hidden behind a nearby tree, but it must have been at least twenty feet long. It lunged at her with its mouth open wide, fangs folded outward straight towards her chest. She dropped to her knees and covered her head with her hands. The viper shot right over her and landed on the other side.

Its thick body landed on her and she shoved it aside. The viper coiled its upper portion around another nearby tree. The body moved past her in a blur, but it was so long, she had an opening. She held the sword above her head and swung it down as hard as she could. Before the sword could find its target, the viper's tail whipped around from behind her and she flew through the air, landing hard. When she regained her bearings, she noticed she lost her sword. She found it, but it was halfway between where she stood and where the viper was wrapped around its tree. It didn't strike right away; it was just watching her. *What's it doing? Waiting for me to make a move?* She wasn't going to wait around to find out.

She took off for the sword at a full sprint. As soon as she moved, it began unwinding itself down the tree. She was going to make it to the sword first, but just barely. She pushed herself harder; she exploded more and more with each step. She dove for the weapon. She grabbed a handful of dirt along with the hilt, but at least she was armed now. She rolled end over end and stopped herself in a kneeling position. The snake was less than a foot from her face now. She reacted without thinking. She raised her left forearm out in front of her to block. She regretted it the moment she did it. She registered that she should have swung her sword and killed it right then and there, but she didn't. She winced behind her arm waiting for the painful fangs to clasp around it. When they did, she realized just how strong her armor really was. She wouldn't make the same mistake twice. She brought her sword up as hard as she could straight through the neck of the creature, right below the base of its head.

The tightness on her arm from the viper's grip loosened. She shook her arm until the head fell off and rolled over to rest next to the body it was once attached to. She couldn't believe it, she did it. She actually did it, she killed a Knixx Viper all on her own.

"Well done," a voice cried out from above. She looked up just in time to see Paladin falling from a high branch. He landed gently right in front of her. "You did well, considering."

She hit him on the arm. "Where were you? I could have died, and you just watched?"

"Yes, I was watching. I promise you were in no real danger." He smiled proudly at her, but she was still upset. The adrenaline was still in her system making her shake like crazy.

"What do you mean? That thing was inside our perimeter. It almost killed me."

"It was here because I trapped it last night. I told you, you were completely safe. I just needed to get a feel for how you would react in a real fight."

Is he insane? She hadn't practiced for two weeks, and she was only a few months into her training before that. The fact that she won at all was dumb luck and a good piece of armor. Surely, he saw that as well. He had been up there and saw all of her mistakes. *What's he going to do? Does he finally realize I'm a lost cause?* That was just what she needed, another reason for him to stop training her. The questions were driving her crazy, she had to know. "So, what did you see? How did I do?"

He circled the dead viper and examined it closely. "Your reflexes are pretty fast, you just need to learn to utilize them better." He turned and walked towards her. "You handle the sword well, just work on never losing your grip. That could be the difference between life and death." He grabbed her left arm and inspected the damage to the armor. "It was a good move, blocking the second attack. Why did you do it though?"

What does he mean? Good move? It was terrible. With any less armor, she would have been dead. "I flinched. I should have swung instead, I know." She turned away in shame.

"No, you made the right call." He pulled her head back up. "You wouldn't have had time to bring the sword around. I saw everything, remember. If you had tried, it would have gotten you right in the chest."

Really? She thought back to it. The viper had been pretty close. She barely had time to block as it was and that arm was much, much closer. He was right, but she hadn't known that. "It was just a lucky mistake. I didn't know…"

"There is no luck in battle. Gylum gives us what we can handle. He guides our movements through reflexes and, as you call it, flinching." He turned and looked around the trees.

"Was that it? Did you see anything else? Am I good enough?" she asked.

"Of course you are. I'll make a warrior out of you yet. But there's just one more thing." He stopped on the thickest Niku in the area. "There. I think we should change up your fighting style. You need a shield."

-O-

Garm heard the Zed horn being blown in the distance. Athan wasn't supposed to have been spotted. If anyone saw his face or had figured out he came from the dungeon, they would be in big trouble. The plan was for his absence to go unnoticed for several days. No one ever checked on the prisoners, and it would take about that long for the people bringing down food to notice something was wrong.

He could hear the footsteps of soldiers approaching down the hall ahead of him. He didn't want to be seen this close to the escape, so he ducked into the nearest door. Garm closed the door behind him and checked to see where he was. He didn't know this side of the castle very well. There were red, pink, and yellow ropes and cloth draped all throughout the room. *Oh no. This is the concubine's room.* Ever since the queen died, Rynok had begun taking concubines to try and heir a son. It often took years for a couple to get pregnant, but he would grow impatient and have them thrown out in under a year.

He hoped she wasn't there. It would be difficult to conceal his reason for barging in like he did.

"My Lord, is that you?" a female voice rang out.

No such luck. "Um, no. My apologies, I must have made a wrong turn."

"Garm? Is that you?" She walked out from behind the large veil blocking the view to the bed.

"Oh, yes milady. So sorry to intrude like this. I'll just be on my way now." He started backing up to the door, bowing respectfully.

"No, no. Please, stay. I don't get many visitors."

So much told him to leave, but the bruises on her cheek and the look in her eyes made him stay. "Of course, my dear. I suppose I could stay a moment." He went over to a nearby ottoman and took a seat. Garm figured it would look bad if he were found sitting on her bed. "Would you like to talk about it?" He gestured to the black and blue lump on her cheekbone.

She turned her face away to hide it. "It's fine. It's nothing, really."

Garm had only seen her a few times. Concubines were never really paraded around, but he knew well enough that this one had been with Rynok almost a year now. Longer than any before but by the looks of it, she wouldn't be around much longer. "If you're worried about ending up like the others, it's not your fault. These things take time, for some reason he doesn't seem to…"

"I know it's not my fault," she said before he could finish. He sat waiting for her to say more, wondering what she meant. He hated to think it, but she was giving off a kind of self-loathing vibe. That answer didn't fit.

"What do you mean? What's the problem then?" He shifted his weight and turned his chest towards her.

"We haven't…" She couldn't find the words. "He hasn't been able to…" He was unsure if she just couldn't find the right word or if she was embarrassed, but he got the idea.

"But how? You've been here for a year. You mean to say the whole time? Not once?" She shook her head and started sobbing. "But why?" He was caught so off guard. *Had this same thing happened with all the ones before her? Is that why he threw them out after such a short amount of time? Why isn't he trying to have a son?*

She grabbed his hands and pulled him close to her. Her eyes were wide and she looked terrified. "He's not right. I do everything I can to help him, but he gives up and starts rambling and talking to himself. He's gone mad, he has."

"What does he say?" Garm had never seen the king do

anything like what she described, but he knew something had been off about him for years.

"Always about *Her*! She's all he'll talk about. 'She ruined my life!' 'Why did she do this to me?' 'All she had to do was give me my son!' He never stops!"

"Wait, what was that last one?" Garm asked, but she was sobbing again. She wasn't listening anymore. *'All she had to do was give him a son'? Why would he say that? He had a son, it died in the womb.* That was what Rynok told them had happened. *He blames her for ruining his life, because she didn't give him a son… That's it!* He figured it out. Ivary gave birth to a daughter that night, and he killed her for it.

Garm looked at the woman and felt bad, but he didn't feel like he could help her very much at this point. He got up and left the room. He felt he didn't need to go to the Catacombs anymore, but he wanted to be certain. He had to wait till the next day because Rynok had monopolized their night with crazy rants as soon as he learned that Athan was the reason for the alarm. He put Moryn in charge of finding Athan, and discovering how he escaped, so Garm felt relatively safe.

Garm made it through the catacombs easily enough; there was no real reason to guard it. He reached the section for the royal family and stopped over Ivary's body. A wave of memories filled his mind. Every happy moment of watching her grow up in the castle with her father, the former king, who also happened to be his greatest friend. All the saddest moments like when she almost died from a bad illness as a child and the night Rynok carried her back from the Altar. It made him angry. Her very own killer held her, prepared her body, and worst of all, he got away with it.

He began to unravel the bandages around the stomach. He went slowly; he didn't want to desecrate her remains. She deserved better than that.

The lower half of her torso was revealed now. Ten years of decay left little more than bone and stench. He breathed as little and as lightly as possible while he checked the abdominal cavity. *Nothing.* There was no trace of a child. If Rynok had told the truth, if he did have a son die while still within the mother, he never would have dishonored the child by removing him. It was official, Garm had no more doubts of what really happened to his beloved queen. He had to tell Moryn of what he learned. He had to relay this to Athan. He reapplied the wrappings and left the catacombs as quickly as he could.

-O-

Paladin hopped down from the tree with a large circular chunk of bark. He made some quick touch ups on the edges making it as round as possible for the time, and fastened straps of Zed leather to the inside. It only took him ten minutes to finish. He would probably add more plating to it later, but for the next test he had in store for her it would suffice.

He handed the shield to Princess and had her try it out. She seemed to adjust to it quickly; she wasn't off balanced or clumsy with it. It was a good thing, because just on the other side of the tree line he had a trapped Zed Wolf, and it was itching for a fight. "Okay, you ready for your next test?"

"What? No, I had a hard enough time with the first one."

"You'll do fine. This one will be a bit tougher, but I'll be right here to guide you the whole time." He was almost to the edge of the clearing. She sighed and gave up fighting him. She didn't really have a choice in the matter, she must have realized it. He turned behind the tree to where he left the wolf, but what he found made his hairs stand on end. "Run!" he shouted at Princess. All that was left of the Zed Wolf was its hind legs and tail. The front half was inside the black oily mouth of a Shade. The creature saw him and bit the wolf in half where it was, then melted into the shadow of the tree nearby.

Paladin turned and ran straight for Princess. *Not a Shade, anything but a Shade.* Shades were hands down the deadliest creatures in the forest, and that was saying something. The Shade, in its non-corporeal form jumped from shadow to shadow, getting as close to them as the shadows could reach.

"What is it? What's wrong?" she asked, worry all over her face.

"A Shade!" he shouted. She froze in fear. He had told her about them before, but she hadn't seen one since she was a baby. They were fairly rare and those that crossed paths with them usually didn't live to tell the tale, so not much was known about them. Luckily, Paladin inadvertently came across a way to repel them several years ago. They hated light.

The Shade took its physical form and glided out into the clearing. Shades didn't have legs; what they did have looked more like a thick tail that they stood vertically on. Its body was an oily black blob that seemed to take whatever shape it wanted at the time. Its wide mouth opened like a hole through its body with the trees on the far side visible through it.

Princess was finally able to speak. "D-djeg leaves. We need Djeg leaves. Please tell me you have some."

He glanced to his right, where his bag was hidden against a tree. "Ya, but they're in my bag." There wasn't much time to formulate a plan, the beast was getting closer every second. He'd have to do it on the fly. "Go for the bag, I'll hold it off." He charged with both blades at the ready.

"Wait! You can't fight that thing!" she shouted after him.

It was too late, he reached it and dove off to the left. He wanted to attract its attention away from the bag. He made a clean hit with his sword as he dove. The gash looked just like the mouth, an empty space with the background showing through. It was a large cut, but the Shade didn't seem affected by it at all. "The faster you move the less time I have to fight this thing!"

That got her moving. She ran towards the tree, but he lost her when she passed on the far side of it. He would just have to hope he trained her enough to know what to do. The beast extended a thick tentacle-like arm out from the side of its body. Paladin spun out of the way and sliced it off with his knife, preceded by a stab to the center of its mass with his primary blade. The piece that had been cut off slithered its way back to the Shade's tail and fused back into it. As for the sword in its gut, he was having a hard time getting it out. Its mouth had moved to close around the blade and was sucking it in.

Two more arms appeared, one on each side and started closing in on him. He had two choices: Let go of the sword and fall back, or risk it all for the win. He always went for the win. He took his knife and stabbed the creature several times all throughout its body before leaving the blade in at what he assumed was the top of its head. He dug his knife deeper and deeper. The two arms had grabbed hold of him and were pulling him into its mouth, but he kept digging and twisting his knife. Finally, in the last moments before he was devoured, the Shade released his sword in an attempt to take the knife instead. In this millisecond that its mouth was moving from one to the other, he ripped both weapons out of its body violently. It had massive pieces missing from its body now, but still didn't seem any weaker.

The Shade didn't resume its attack just yet. It circled around him and passed by the tree line. Its tail stretched out and connected with the shadows and instantly went back to its non-corporeal form. It jumped a few shadows over and reappeared, only this time it was whole again. All the damage he had caused it was healed just like that.

Paladin raised his weapons ready for its second charge, but fiery light poured out from over his shoulder. Princess stepped out in front of him holding a torch and she shook it at the Shade. It let out a banshee roar. Paladin had to cover his ears; he was surprised Princess didn't drop the light to cover her own. It must have been painful, but he was glad she didn't. She jabbed the flames closer and the Shade silenced and retreated into the shadows. It screamed again as it fled, but the sound faded into the distance. It was gone.

She turned and came back towards Paladin. "You're welcome," she joked.

"I totally had that under control." She tried to walk past him, but he stepped in front of her. "Let me see it." She handed the torch to him. He shook his head. "You know what I mean."

She pouted and then held out the hand she was hiding behind her back. A bleeding gash ran along the palm. "It's not that bad, I swear."

He examined the wound. It would leave a scar, but nothing too noticeable. He would have to wait till they got back to treat it properly. "You didn't have to do that. You were supposed to bring it to me."

"In case you hadn't noticed, you were kinda busy." She yanked her hand away from him. "Besides, you weren't even bleeding. So unless you know another way to light Djeg leaves that you haven't told me about, it wouldn't have really mattered." She brushed past him towards the tree. She started to climb and then winced from the pain in her hand.

"The difference being, I can climb with a cut hand." He tore off a shred of cloth from a larger piece inside his bag. "And I don't have training to do." She reluctantly took the cloth and bandaged her hand. He helped her back up to the dwelling and started treating her cut. She probably wouldn't be back to one hundred percent for a week or two, but that didn't mean he would let up on her. The Immortal Forest waited for no one.

CHAPTER 8: YOU SHOULDN'T TAKE WHAT'S NOT YOURS

"Nothing is ever truly taken, all things are gifts given by Gylum. When one of His children attempts to take that which has not been given, His rage will be unleashed upon them. The desperate soul looking to gain will instead find only loss."

–   The Xyrith: 28: 48-51

Moryn was on his way down into the dungeon. He had just finished meeting with Garm where he was told everything: the details of the escape, the conversation with the concubine, and what he found in the catacombs. It had been a lot to take in, that his king whom he had known so well for so long could do something like that. However, it also explained a lot. The Rynok he knew before and the one he knew now were two very different people.

He reached Athan's old cell and opened the door. He was sent down there to gather evidence on how Athan had escaped without triggering the ancient traps. He already knew exactly how because he had helped plan it. Now the question was, how would he cover it up without looking like he's covering it up.

He went to collect the shards from the crystal vial Athan had dropped. There would be traces of the potion they used that could be traced back to Garm. When he found it, there was something wrong. There were only a dozen tiny pieces; definitely not enough to make up a vial even half the size of the one they used. He searched among the pieces and didn't find a single drop of the liquid either.

Something wasn't right. He went back into the hall and looked for the empty jars that once contained the lightning bolts used to restart Athan's heart. They weren't there. *Did Garm collect them before he left? He didn't say that he had.* He didn't specifically say that he had left them either. *He must have left them, he gave his rucksack to Athan. If that's the case, then who has the bottles?* Moryn feared the answer. *Did one of my men come down here first?* Whatever the case, he would have to make it a part of his official findings. That meant Athan definitely didn't escape without outside help. Moryn would have to find a scapegoat.

As Moryn made his way back upstairs, he was trying to think what he could do. He couldn't frame anyone, he wasn't as sadistic as the king, but he couldn't be in charge of the investigation and never find the man responsible. Rynok would have his head if he didn't provide results. When he reached the door at the top, there was a runner waiting for him.

"Sir, the king wishes an audience with you in the dining hall immediately," the young man said.

"Thank you." The runner took off and Moryn headed down the hallway to the dining hall. Time was running short. He would reach his destination in a matter of minutes. He still didn't know what to do. He decided the best course of action would be to report what was, or what should have been, found outside Athan's cell and tell Rynok he needed more time. It would make him angry, but Moryn just couldn't bring himself to point his finger at an innocent man.

He entered the dining hall prepared to give his report, but he wasn't prepared for what he saw. Garm was on his knees beside Rynok, surrounded by three members of the royal guard. Garm's face had been beaten to a pulp and it looked as if one of his shoulders was free from its socket. When Garm saw him enter, he tried to get up and run to him, but the guards put a stop to that. The crackling of his knee breaking echoed around the room's walls.

What is this? Did they lure me here to arrest me too? Did Garm give me up from torture? How did they even know he was involved? Moryn wasn't sure, so he played it safe. "What's going on here? What have you done to Garm?"

"I did a little investigating of my own," the king said as he started walking around Garm. "I found some very peculiar things down in the dungeon. First I found a shattered vial with a strange substance. I asked the doctor in town if he knew what it was. He told me a vial went missing a few days ago, and only a handful of people actually knew what it was." He bent over Garm and grabbed him by the chin. "Garm's name was among them." He let him go and then walked over to Moryn. "But I also found four empty glass jars, the kind that are used to trap lightning. So I started asking around, and Garm's name came up again. A few of the wall guards had seen him collecting lightning during that storm a few nights ago." He finished circling Moryn and headed for the far side of the table. "Of course, it was all circumstantial. I needed proof." He reached down and lifted the badly beaten unarmored body of his guard, the one he posted to the dungeon.

The guard spoke through shattered teeth. "I'm so sorry, sir. I've betrayed you."

What? Did he tell Rynok I was the one who put him up to this? Moryn slid his hand closer to his sword, ready to defend himself.

"That's right. He trusted you to keep those filthy prisoners locked up." Rynok lifted his sword and skewered the young man right through the center of his torso. "He was brave though. He tried to take sole credit. It took hours for him to finally confirm what I already knew." He dropped the body and moved back to Garm. Moryn moved his hand back away from his sword. It sounded like Rynok didn't suspect him at all, he was safe. The king grabbed Garm by the throat and dragged him towards Moryn. "This is the bastard that I sent you to find. He was the one that freed that traitor. I give him to you my friend."

Moryn was confused. "What do you mean, my Lord?"

"I asked you to kill the man that freed my wife's murderer. I will not deprive you that honor."

Moryn looked down at the bloody face of his friend and partner in this scheme. It was too late for Garm now, and if Moryn refused he would look suspicious. He didn't have a choice, but that didn't mean it was any easier to make.

Garm looked up at Moryn with pleading eyes; not pleading for him to spare his life, but for him to take it. "You know what you must do. Do it." As far as Rynok was concerned he was talking about killing him, but Moryn knew what he really meant. Moryn was going to have to take his place and help Athan find the ancient Warlock. Moryn drew his sword and held it high. As he brought it down Garm shouted, "Long live Athan!" The blade pierced through his chest. Garm gargled his final words through blood. "True king of Tuckkar." Moryn ripped his sword free of his friend's body and Garm fell to the floor, a pool of blood growing around him.

Rynok patted Moryn on the shoulder. "Very good my friend. Very good." He headed for the door without giving a second thought to the two bodies behind him. "This calls for a celebration, does it not?"

Moryn wanted nothing more than to kill Rynok right then and there for what he had done, for what he had made him do. But he knew better. He would have to be patient, and know that the more he helped Athan the sooner that day could come. The sooner he could spit on Rynok's dead body.

-O-

He hugged tight to a Grim Wood, checking around the corner carefully. His long oily black hair fell over his eyes, but he quickly brushed it out of the way. He had to be careful; he had made it seventeen years, eleven months, and twenty-three days in the forest so far and he didn't want all of that to mean nothing by making a mistake now. The coast was clear, so he made his way to the next tree. He had a pack slung over his shoulder half full of food. It would be plenty to last him his last week. All he needed now was water. Once he filled up, he would head back to his well hidden dugout shelter and hide out until his Fulfillment.

As he neared the watering hole he had been using for years, he started wishing he had planned better. He only had another day's water and the food he did have would begin to spoil soon. He wasn't sure why he was so worried. He had never been afraid before. He had hunted, trapped, and even used himself as bait when the occasion called for it, but still he was nervous now. It could have been just because he was so close, the final stretch. He really hoped that's what it was, because he had a strange tingling in the back of his neck ever since he left that morning.

He was just on the other side of the pool when he heard something moving in the water. He ducked down and waited, listening. He listened to the pattern to determine what it was. It could have been a Zed Wolf drinking, but there was only one set of sounds and they hunt in packs. It definitely wasn't a Knixx Viper because they swam through the water, not splash around like that. It couldn't be a Djinn either, they were extremely noisy when they found water. The only other option was another boy on Pilgrimage gathering water, just like he was there to do.

If that were so, what would he do? There was no chance the other boy would be older than him, he could be stronger though. One way or another it was a risk, and what would the reward be? A Birthright? He already had a great one. His father was a member of the king's cabinet, a Councilman. It was a great job, especially for someone as smart and manipulative as he was. They lived well, better than anyone short of royalty.

He was content with letting this one go. He would stay hidden until he was sure whoever was on the other side left. He had to admit that he was curious to see who it was though. *I wonder how old he is. What's his Birthright?* He wanted to know, but he forced himself to stay down. At least until he heard a laugh.

He perked his head up. *What was that? That laugh? It was so feminine.* Now his curiosity was beyond quelling. He would just move far enough to get a peek. When he got closer, the first thing he saw was the most beautiful golden color. He had seen that color before but only in Yuma Berries, and he knew to stay away from those. *But it's not a berry, it's hair.* He moved closer and at the other end of the flowing locks of hair was the naked body of a young... *Girl? What is a female doing out here?* He watched her in awe, not because she was naked but because she was a girl.

Am I hallucinating? Did I eat some Yuma Berries and not remember it? No. He knew better than that, but he found it difficult to find another answer. It took him a while to accept that he wasn't going crazy. By that time, she was getting out of her bath and she grabbed a Zed pelt to towel herself off. When she reached for it, he was hit by another breathtaking sight. *Royalty!* Her Birthright was Royalty. It was shining clear through the darkness.

Now he really had to think. He always dreamed about finding a Royalty Birthright, but he never thought it would happen. And he found it on a girl no less. He didn't know how she survived out here and he didn't know why, but he did know that there was no way she could be even close to as strong as him. *Gylum, is this Your doing? Is this my destiny?* He had to assume that it was. What else could it be? She was starting to put her armor on, he had to move now while he could still catch her off guard. He readied his knife, leapt over the small ridge, and landed right in front of her.

The young girl jumped when he landed. She had only her under armor cloth and one leg of her armor fastened. She had been working on the other leg before he interrupted her. He charged and she dove for her weapons. He caught her before she could get there. He was faster than her, that was good. She shrieked, but he grabbed her head and cupped his hand over her mouth. She bit down hard, but he could take it. A droplet of blood oozed down his hand. He let go of her mouth, but just so he could punch her in the gut.

He felt all the air in her lungs leave her body. He took her left wrist and held it up to his eyelevel. When she caught her breath, she wriggled and writhed to break free, but he had her completely pinned. She tried to yell, but his grip around her throat would tighten every time she tried. He just stared into the beautiful blue light of her amazing Birthright. The magical blue light reflected in his dark brown eyes. *It's so beautiful. And it's all mine.*

He had to cut it out of her hand. He kicked her feet out from under her and took her to the ground. She started kicking and hitting him with her free right hand. Her hits were so soft, it almost made him laugh. He placed his knee on her chest and pulled out his Djinn claw knife. He twisted her wrist almost to its breaking point. She cried out in pain. The back of his hand kept her quiet. His attention on the Birthright again, he raised his knife, and cut the skin just above the glowing orb. He dug the knife in and popped the Birthright out.

He caught it before it hit the ground, and held it in his hand. It was his. He had it. He couldn't believe it. He raised it up and it even shined brighter than the one still in his own hand. He would just finish her off real quick and then he could head back to his dugout, and in a week he would be king. She was still under his knee. He put his right hand on her neck again, and with both his new Birthright and knife in his left, he brought the blade high over his head. He was ready to plunge it right through her forehead.

White hot pain shot through his wrist. He gritted his teeth in reaction to the agony. He brought his hand down to see what had happened, but there was nothing coming out of his wrist but a stream of bright red blood. He saw his hand fall to the ground beside him, the knife and Royalty Birthright rolled free of the lifeless fingers. There wasn't time to think, only time to react. An armored leg came swinging at his head with great speed and power, but he raised the armor bracer of his good arm and deflected the strike. He rolled forward and picked up his knife. There was no sign of his attacker; he spun around and around several times.

He was losing a lot of blood and his vision was starting to fade. He noticed that the young girl had vanished also. He heard a voice from the darkness behind him. "Leave now and you can leave with your life."

He couldn't fight like this, he would have to accept. He sheathed his knife and stumbled over to his hand in the dirt. He picked it up, but couldn't find the new Birthright. He searched frantically. "No! Where is it!" he screamed. "Where is it?"

"Leave now!" the voice repeated.

No! I need it. It's mine. No, I won't leave without it. It's not fair. I had it. I had it! He finally had to accept that it was lost, and if he didn't treat his wound soon, he would bleed out. He would die if he stayed any longer. He stumbled away from the watering hole and into the trees.

He searched for Djeg leaves because they would be able to stop the bleeding. It was difficult finding anything with his vision crossed at this point, but soon enough he found some. He tried to wipe as much blood off his one hand as he could, he didn't want the leaf to ignite too early. He plucked one and set it on the ground. He braced himself for the pain to come. Blood dripped from his stump, and the leaf began to burn at each point the blood landed. He shoved the bloody end of what was left of his arm into the leaf. The whole thing burst into flames and the clacking sound of the flames was drowned out by his cries of pain. After a short moment, the bleeding had stopped and the wound was cauterized. Darkness fell over him. He lost consciousness, but at least he was still alive.

-O-

If Moryn was stressed before, it was nothing compared

to how he felt now. Rynok had informed the villagers of Rukor's Law two weeks ago, and it was Moryn and his men's job to enforce it. On that day, just as he had predicted, the people revolted. Moryn had to order his guards to put a stop to it, even though he himself knew that they had every right. He had to continue to play the part of the king's right hand. His guards killed five men and wounded dozens more before the people were finally calmed.

The past two weeks had been a series of tracking down each line of Birthrights, finding all of the sons and hunting down runaways, and then forcing them to fight to the death. If they refused to fight or if they couldn't deliver that final killing blow, both were to be executed on the spot. It wasn't enough for Rynok to only apply Rukor's Law to the newly Fulfilled; he had to apply it to anyone with a Fulfillment ten years or less.

Moryn had to watch as mothers and fathers cried and pleaded for them not to take their loved ones. He had to see the look in the eyes of young men, triumphant from surviving the forest only to turn to despair when they learned of this new law. He had to watch brothers killing brothers. It was making him sick. It made him want to kill Rynok all the more. There was so much blood on Rynok's hands now, he was amazed the king hadn't drowned in it.

Moryn was on his way to deliver a status report on how the fights were progressing. He didn't know if he would be able to do it while holding his tongue, but he didn't have much choice. The stress of having to pretend to still be loyal to that monster was worse than any torture he could imagine.

Moryn reached the throne where Rynok sat. He bowed to show respect, but in actuality, he was just using it as an excuse to avoid looking at the man he hated for a few extra seconds. "My Lord."

"Right on time, good. Please, rise. What news have you?"

Moryn rose and tried as hard as he could not to scowl. "We are hitting heavy resistance. The people are still very much opposed to Rukor's Law." *As they should be.* "But we are averaging five battles a day, not to include those that refuse."

"Fools, why would anyone refuse? A chance of dying versus certain death, how is the choice not obvious?"

"Well, my Lord, most of those that refuse are the ones that have lived with their brothers for years. They've grown to love them." Moryn toyed with an idea, it might get him caught, but in the end he couldn't resist the jab at Rynok. "I mean, it's like asking someone to kill his own wife, they are family, no sane man would." There was a slight look of remorse and fear in Rynok's eyes. That made it all worth it. Now he was having trouble not smirking.

"Not exactly like that." His eyes were cold and stern again. "Where are we on the backlog? How much longer until we only have to worry about new Fulfillments?"

"There are still a few families we need to locate, but we should be caught up by the end of the week."

Rynok smiled and clasped his hands together. "Ah, do you see? We were on the brink of starvation and poverty, and in just three short weeks my new law has solved all of that." He was proud of himself. He was even more sick than he realized, which wasn't easy at this point.

"If that's all my Lord, I have other business to attend to." Moryn started to leave.

"Actually," the king said. Moryn turned and came back. "I wanted to know where you were on locating Athan."

He wasn't sure what to tell him. He hadn't had much spare time to do much of anything to help Athan these past weeks. He had to start going to the library more often, and he had to find a reasonable excuse for Rynok to let him. *Maybe if I tell Rynok about the notebook and the ancient Warlock, I could claim to be doing it to hunt Athan instead of actually helping him.* There was some risk in revealing that information, but it was his best bet. "I have found something, just the other day in fact. This is Athan's old notebook. He was looking for the origin of the Birthright. As you remember, he doesn't believe as we do in Gylum."

"Of course, but what good does that do us?" The king was looking impatient.

"Well, he notes to an ancient Warlock, I think he believes he can find him out there and undo the Birthrights through him."

"So my brother is searching for something that does not exist. I fail to see how this helps us!"

"He read about it in the library, from books that date back to the Ghor of old. If I can read through these, I may be able to find what he found. Then we'll know where he's looking."

Rynok thought about it for a moment. "That sounds fair. Alright, I want you to focus all your efforts on finding out where my brother is headed. Your men should be capable of enforcing the people on their own by now, yes?"

"Yes my Lord. They are more than capable." He couldn't believe that worked. All he would have to do now was try and feed as little real information to Rynok to keep him hopeful, but not enough to look suspicious. It wasn't going to be easy, but at least now he had a shot of helping Athan. Moryn turned and left. He headed straight for the library. There wasn't a minute to waste.

Moryn spent all of his days in that library. He only left for three reasons: to sleep, to eat, and to trade information with Athan at the designated spot. Sometimes not even those; a few times he would wake up with his face in one of those musty old books. He wasn't getting very far because the books varied drastically, but no matter how unlikely it was that there was anything of relevance, he still had to read them all cover to cover. Some were so worn they were almost impossible to read. Others were in ancient languages, so he would save those for last. He hoped that they outdated what he was looking for.

After a month of searching, he only came across three references to the Warlock; two of which were already in Athan's notebook. He was beginning to lose hope, but he wasn't even one percent through the books in the oldest section. *This would be so much easier if Garm were here.* He was all alone now. He lost Garm, and after what had happened to the guard he posted on the dungeon that day he would never risk the lives of his men like that again. If anything happened to him, Athan would be stranded in the forest with no clue where to go or what to do. If anything happened to Athan, which given what he knew about the forest was very likely, everything would be lost.

Moryn set aside his own misery and self-pity, and grabbed the next book. The sooner he could find a lead, the sooner all of this would be over. He had to suck it up for

Garm, for Ivary, and for all of the other lives that Rynok's rule had ruined.

CHAPTER 9: YOU'LL GET THERE SOMEDAY

"Greatness cannot be rushed; although, born with the strength to achieve it and the knowledge to use it, only through patience will it be granted. Be wary of the success that comes with ease, for it will be lost just as easily; just as that which is earned of blood and sweat is far more difficult to lose."

– The Xyrith: 67: 28-30

Athan made his way to the drop point. He had set up camp a few hours walk away; the road to the Altar was the only traffic through the forest and he wanted to make sure he wouldn't be easy to come across. He usually only took trips out there once every few days. Every time he left his hut, he was risking his life. Even though he had been back in the forest for three months now, he was still relatively scrawny. He had put on thirty pounds since the dungeon, but it still wasn't enough.

In that time, he had used the knife Garm gave him to shave off his beard. He always did prefer the clean cut look. He was very grateful for that knife. Tuckkar had some extremely skilled blacksmiths; this blade would be stronger than anything he could find in the forest. The only drawback was that it would eventually dull, but not for a year at least. He still wore the same rags he had been wearing when he escaped. It was difficult to make a suit of armor when he wasn't strong enough to kill anything bigger than a Knixx Viper.

Athan was almost there, just a few more minutes. A few days ago when he last came out, he found a message from Moryn. While most of his messages recently had all been a whole lot of nothing, that one was different. He said he finally made a breakthrough and that he needed to meet in person. He didn't want to get his hopes too high, but it was hard not to.

When he reached the spot, Moryn was already waiting for him. "Athan? Hurry up. Over here."

Athan walked out cautiously. "Right by the road? But if anyone drives past, we'll be seen."

Moryn closed his eyes and listened. To what he didn't know, but the forest was still tonight. "No one's coming. We'll be fine for now."

Athan stepped all the way out. He was confused.

"How can you know that for sure?"

Moryn looked up at a nearby Grim Wood. "The trees. They talk to each other."

Athan was shocked. "I've read about that. That some people sensitive enough can hear the forest. I never knew it was real. I never knew you were one of them."

"Not something people advertise. Bet you never knew Garm had it too."

Athan still found it hard to believe. He blamed himself for Garm's death. If only he hadn't been seen. If he had been more careful with that vial. *I'm the reason he's dead.*

Moryn must have seen how he was feeling because he put his hand on Athan's shoulder. "It wasn't your fault. The only one to blame here is Rynok."

He was right. Garm knew the risks, and he had been willing to take those risks to put an end to Rynok's tyranny. He could dwell on that later; he was there for business. "Please tell me you bring good news."

Moryn unslung a bag from his back. "Yes. I found this old journal." He pulled a half molded notebook from the bag. "It belonged to some member of an ancient order. A lot of it is illegible, but he does make references to the Warlock a few times. Here, read this one."

Athan took the old book. Pieces of it crumbled in his hands as he held it. He read what he could, but a lot was missing.

"I went to check on the Warlock responsible for the Birthright again today. He still remains… …him to. His powers are se… …still present. I have pleaded with what… …le area around Blood Lake, but… …that he will remain there for… …his immortality, b…"

Athan finished reading. The next legible words were on the next page and seemed to be a completely different topic. "But there is so much missing. How can you be sure it means what you think it does?"

Moryn took the journal back and put it back in his bag. "But there's enough. It's not a specific location, but he's somewhere near a Blood Lake. If you find that lake, you'll have a much higher chance of finding him."

"I've never even heard of this *Blood Lake*. How do you expect me to find it?"

"With this." Moryn pulled a long rolled up parchment from his bag. "It's a map of Ghor. It's a bit outdated and missing some areas, but the lake is on it." He handed the map over.

Athan unrolled it and looked at what he had to work with. "Missing 'some areas'?" Over half the map had giant round areas of blank space. There was no legend, no rose, no point of reference of any kind. Blood Lake was one of the few things actually on it. "How am I supposed to find anything with this thing?"

"It's either that or nothing. No one has mapped out the forest in thousands of years. Believe it or not, there were maps even more incomplete than that one."

Athan thought about it for a minute before an idea popped into his head. "Did you bring any of them with you?"

"A few, I was going to destroy them. I don't want Rynok getting his hands on them." Moryn gestured to his carriage.

"Bring them. All of them."

Moryn ran off to retrieve them. If he could use all of the incomplete maps together, he might have more to work with. Moryn returned with five more rolls, five more maps. Athan laid them all out. This wasn't going to be as easy as he thought. They were all very different. He started with the only one that had a rose. Now he had some direction. Next he looked for any landmarks or unique details that he could cross reference with the others. There weren't many, but there was enough. Moryn fetched him some ink and he started copying details from the other maps onto a single one. Only two of them had scales for distance. They were both different, but he used them to create one for his map.

It took several hours, but he finished. Moryn had left halfway through to avoid suspicion from his absence, but Athan had hardly noticed. There were still a few missing spots. Six near perfect circles of varying sizes remained void of any detail. One of them must have been Tuckkar, because it wasn't anywhere else on the map. All he needed to do now was find something, anything, that could tell him where he was, and then he could find Blood Lake from there.

He had a long walk back to his hut. He had plenty of

time to think on his next move. Once he headed out for the lake, he wouldn't be able to keep in contact with Moryn. More importantly, it would not be easy to find his location with the map he had. The map was of the Ghor of old, several thousands of years old; things change over that much time. He would need to start mapping out his local area and continue to expand it until something matched up. It wasn't going to be easy and it could take a long time, but it's what had to happen, he was up for the challenge. If it meant stopping Rynok, he would do anything.

-O-

Paladin stormed through the door into their dwelling. Princess came in behind him pleading. "I'm sorry, okay. Please, can't we just talk about it?"

"No! That was too close. From now on you don't leave the perimeter. You got that?" He was furious, but not at her, at himself. *What were you thinking leaving her like that? If you had got there even a second later… She's not ready to be out there like that, not with this.* He looked down at his hand. He still had it, her Birthright. They left so quickly he didn't want to waste time putting it back until they got home safely. He turned to her. "Come here. Give me your hand."

She came over and unwrapped her hand. He took a look at it and moved the skin out of the way. She winced and looked away. The blood had stopped and he could clearly see the empty cavity through to the inside of the skin on the back of her hand. The white of the bones that curved outward to make room radically contrasted the dark red that coated everything else. "Well, I have good news and bad news. Do you want the bad news first?"

"What? You can put it back, right?" She sounded panicked.

"Well yes, but the bad news is it's going to leave a nasty scar."

"But you can put it back. Is that the good news?"

He tried to keep a straight face but snickered. "The good news is now you'll match." He held out her other hand, the scar from the Shade attack ran in the same pattern as the gash she had just received.

She hit him on the shoulder. "Oh shut up. Just hurry up and do it already."

They laughed a second longer and then he focused on her injured hand again. He carefully placed the small glowing ball back in place. When it was firmly in place, the light it gave off brightened for a moment. Shortly it faded back to its original dim blue. "There you go. Does it hurt?"

"I'm fine, I can take it." She said as she lowered her hand back to her side.

He turned to get some Integro roots from the corner. "I didn't ask if you were fine, I asked if it hurt. You don't have to act tough for me." When he turned back, she did not look happy.

"Who says I'm acting? I'm not as weak as you think I am."

"And you're not as strong as you think you are. That little run in back there proves that." He placed one of the roots into a small stone mortar and began grinding it with a pestle.

"Don't even use that as an example. That boy was bigger than even you." She turned her back to him. She was right though. He was much older; about a week away from his eighteenth birthday. If Paladin hadn't got the drop on him the way he did, he doubted if he would've been able to beat the boy.

He was done grinding the Integro. "Bring it over here."

She came over and gave him her hand, but still didn't look at him. "It's just… I'm trying my best."

Paladin poured the ground root into the cut on her hand. "I know you are, and you'll get there someday, you will." He started wrapping it tightly with a fresh cloth. "But until then, I don't think we should take any unnecessary risks. We'll stick to areas we know well."

He was done with the bandage. She curled and flexed her fingers testing how it held up. It would. "But I've been running that route for a month now. Nothing bad ever happened before."

"A month's not a long time out here."

"Well, where am I supposed to go? Where else can I

run fifteen miles?" She sat down in her chair at the table.

He walked over to his seat. "You won't be needing your runs anymore." He sat down. She looked at him questioningly. "I'm going to change up your training regimen starting tomorrow. We've been going too easy. It's time we move past this kiddy stuff."

She leaned so far forward she was practically standing. "What? You call everything I've been doing 'kiddy stuff'?"

"Yes, I do. You'll see in the morning." He stood up and headed to his bed. "And a long morning it'll be."

"But my hand." She pointed to the bandage.

"Your left hand. Your shield hand. You'll be fine." He sat on his bed now. "After all, you did say you were fine, didn't you?"

She pouted and went to her own bed. "You're so unfair!"

"I know I am."

-O-

It was cold. Five hours of lying unconscious in the middle of the Immortal Forest was anything but a good idea, especially reeking of blood. It was a wonder the boy hadn't already been eaten by something in all of that time. *What? Where am I? Please tell me I was dreaming.* He didn't want to look. A large part of him knew it had really happened. He had sworn to himself that he'd play it safe his final days; unfortunately, what should have been a sure thing ended up being a gamble that cost him everything.

That reminded him. *Where's my hand? Did I bring it with me? Did I drop it at some point? No.* He had it right next to him before he passed out. He looked frantically for it. He was still light headed, and it was going to take quite some time for his body to replenish the blood he lost. He left his pack behind, so he didn't even have any of his food. *Things are just getting worse and worse.*

Not even a moment after the thought crossed his mind that the deafening roar of a Djinn echoed around him. It was unclear what direction it was coming from until the snapping of tree trunks gave it away. It was getting closer; it must have been following the blood trail. The tree directly in front of him fell sideways, the roots breaking free of the soil and up into the air. The large clawed hand that pushed it aside with ease dug into the bark and snapped the thick trunk into splinters. Among the wood chips, a dim blue glow fell to the ground. That explained where his hand had gone. *That Grim Wood ate my hand!*

His hand landed at the Djinn's cloven feet. From this distance it was hard to tell how much of it had been digested, but he needed to get it back if he ever wished to get out of the forest. All he had was his knife. One little knife against a full grown Djinn. Not an easy feat at full strength and he was weak, tired, and one-handed. There was something else he had, though. He had just been bested and wounded. He knew he was stronger than that, so now he had to prove it. He had lost his honor, and this was his chance to gain it back. By accomplishing the impossible, he could earn his right to live.

It made the first move. He ducked under its claw before it took his head off. The fast motion caused him to stumble and he fell backwards with a thud. He tried to lift himself up, but he had forgotten about his injury. The raw burnt flesh at the end of his arm stung as it impacted the dirt. A massive hoof was coming down with all of the creature's weight behind it. He narrowly rolled out from under it before its leg landed, almost grinding him into bone dust. He was making mistakes, too many of them. Still being alive at this point was sheer luck. He would have to adapt immediately if he wanted to make it out of this alive.

Time was running out. He didn't have the strength to do this for much longer. He couldn't run, the Djinn would hunt him down tirelessly. Djinn weren't too difficult to take down once someone learned how to, but his usual method would require an extra hand he didn't have. He had to think and he had to do it quickly. He dodged another strike, but the tip of one of its claws caught him. Suddenly, the plan formed itself in his head.

He didn't need two hands exactly. He needed one hand to grab, and another to hold the knife. So he waited for his moment; a lull in the pacing of the battle. When he saw it, he took his chance. He stuck the blade of his knife into a fallen tree, just enough to hold it still. He grabbed his left forearm firmly and prepared himself. He took his stub and punched it onto the handle as hard as he could. The handle slid between the bones of his arm. The pain was excruciating, but it had to be done. Once it was deep enough and secure in place, he pulled the knife out, and examined his weapon. *It'll have to do.*

Now he was ready. This would be over quickly. He continued to evade razor sharp claws flying through the air until he found himself behind the beast. Before it could orient itself again, he jumped onto its back and grabbed a tight hold on one of its wings. Keeping himself in place as it thrashed violently, he plunged his knife deep in its back where the scales met fur. A roar of pain shot from its lizard-like snout. He struck it again and again, each time causing himself almost as much pain as his victim. After the fourth or fifth stab, the creature went limp. It fell over, face first, and the tired old boy couldn't find the strength to get off its back.

It took another Grim Wood reaching for his severed hand a few feet away for him to get back to his feet. He was ready to fight for his hand back from the eerie tendrils of the tree, but the minute he got close, they receded. He had never seen that before. He had seen them give up before, but never without at least a little fight. He looked around and noticed that wasn't the only one, they were all moving further away from him. It was very strange, but in his current shape he didn't waste the effort to put much more thought into it. He picked up his hand. It was still in relatively good condition. All he wanted was to get back to his dugout and heal.

Six days passed by, but it felt like a lot longer. In that time, he tried everything he could think of to reattach his hand. The smell of rotting meat didn't do anything to raise his spirits. He was less than an hour from his Fulfillment, and he didn't know if it would work. His last ditch effort was to hope and pray.

When the moment came, he pressed the rotten edge of the hand into the scabbed place it once called home. The light within grew brighter. This was it. He knew what was supposed to happen. He knew what it would look like. The light would spiral out of the palm and encompass the whole body. There would be a warm sensation that would penetrate to the core.

After a few seconds, the boy would be a man, and he would be delivered back to Tuckkar and into the arms of his family. That didn't happen.

The light came from the hand as it should have, but it stopped there. The light curved around the hand and didn't so much as touch the rest of his arm. All he felt was a cold fear. Fear that he would have to live the rest of his life in the forest. After a few seconds, the hand was gone. His Birthright was gone. His future was gone.

He walked from his dugout an empty man. *Am I even a man? Without Fulfillment, what am I?* He didn't know. He didn't care. *Let the forest have me. I have nothing left. Gylum has forsaken me.* He went to a nearby Grim Wood. He laid himself before it, but just like before, it fled from him. So he walked further and found a pack of Zed Wolves enjoying a large Knixx Viper. *I will not fight you beasts. Take me from this world.* They looked up from their meal at him. They circled around him but they did nothing.

All but one returned to the viper. The one came up to him and brushed against him. *What is this? Why do they not attack? Am I too weak? Not a threat to them?* The one wolf at his side motioned his head towards the half eaten carcass, as if asking him to join. *No. That's not it. They see me as one of them. One stuck here, like them.* This was something new. Something never before experienced by man. Thoughts of suicide were replaced by a dream of what wonders this could bring. He would return to Tuckkar, but now it was going to be on his terms. He had a lifetime to find it, and an entire forest to help him do it.

-O-

Moryn sat at the bar in Tuckkar's smallest tavern, The Twisted Fang. He was so tired, tired of living a lie. He was tired of carrying out unspeakable orders given by a beast of a king. All he wanted was to drown in alcoholic bliss. "Another," he slurred. The barkeep looked at him with contempt. Whether it was because he recognized him as the heartless head of the royal guard or was just disgusted with his drunkenness, he couldn't tell, but the man brought over another bottle of Niku mead.

"Are you gonna need a glass for this one?" he asked with a mixture of hatred and sarcasm. Moryn's response was nonverbal. He grabbed it and took a swig followed by a hiccup and a wet burp. "I'll take that as a no." Then he left to tend to his other patrons.

Moryn was very drunk; however, years of living in the forest tended to make people extremely attentive to their surroundings. That kind of self-conditioning doesn't go away easily. He heard the doors behind him swing open and two sets of heavy feet stumbled inside. "How can they get away with this?" a deep voice raged.

"Calm down Mirek. There's nothing you can do now." The second voice said.

The two men sat at the bar one seat down from Moryn. The larger of the two must have been Mirek. He looked furious. "There has to be. Everybody else is just sitting back and doing nothing."

The second man looked around nervously and whispered back to Mirek. "Keep it down. If the wrong person heard you…"

"Then what? They would have me killed like they did my son? What gives them that right?" He stood up and his stool fell to the floor behind him. "No more! It's time we take our village back!" He was engaging the crowd now, and they were cheering.

"I would advise against that." Moryn said. He was fighting to keep his words clear. The whole tavern fell silent. Mirek and his friend's faces froze in fear. "Those castle guards are very well trained. Trust me."

Mirek looked around at the once supportive crowd. They looked a lot less so now, but still he seemed to find his resolve again. "My issue is neither with you Lord Moryn, nor your guards. My quarrel is with the king."

Moryn just laughed and took another mouthful of mead. "A quarrel with the king? Wow." He stood up and faced Mirek. "Look at you. What are you? A miner or a lumberer? What do you know of politics?" He walked closer, as straight and slowly as he could manage. "Now are things perfect right now? Far from it. But things are already in motion that you couldn't understand." Moryn was right in his face now. "So sit down and shut up."

Mirek's friend picked up the stool for him and he sat like he was asked. Moryn went back to his own seat with his bottle. He didn't feel like finishing it anymore. Just before he stood to leave, someone in the crowd spoke up. "You mean Athan, don't you?"

"What? What are you talking about? Who said that?" Moryn looked around the blurry faces. He couldn't tell.

A different voice cried out. "So the rumors are true? Athan broke out of the castle's dungeon?"

A third said, "Ya, I heard he's out in the forest right now. He's building his strength to challenge Rynok. He's going to use Rukor's Law and become our new king."

Moryn was worried now. They were partially right, but he didn't want them to put all their faith in Athan this early. It would be ages before he'd return from his search for the ancient Warlock. *If they look to him now, by the time he does return they'll have lost faith.* "Rumors and speculation. There is no truth to these." But it was too late. They had made up their minds.

Mirek rose up again. "If Athan is going to save us, we need to help him as much as we can." He moved to the door and faced the crowd. "I say we march on the castle! I say we send a message to our false king! We tell him his time is coming to an end! We will no longer…" His sentence was drowned out with the collective gasp of the tavern's patrons. A large bloody sword was sticking several feet out of Mirek's chest. He had enough time to look down at it before he fell limp.

The bearer of the weapon kicked Mirek's body off his blade and stepped inside. It was Rynok. *He must've been looking for me. How did he find me here though?* Moryn walked over. "I had it under control. That wasn't necessary."

"Treason only has one punishment."

"Funny how that punishment is being dealt out more and more these days." Moryn tried to stumble out the door past Rynok, but was stopped.

"You are drunk my friend, but you should still watch your tongue," Rynok warned him.

"I will." Moryn took Rynok's hand off his shoulder and walked out the door. "I promise you, I will."

As he stumbled away from The Twisted Fang, Rynok's

voice echoed through the street. "Effective immediately, a curfew is in effect! Everyone found in breach of this will be sentenced to confinement in the dungeon! Return to your homes!"

His lust for power had grown out of control. The worst part was this was yet another insane law that Moryn would be forced to enforce. He was too drunk, too tired, and too worn out to care anymore. All he knew was that Athan had to hurry up out there because Rynok was killing their village. He feared that in a few years, there wouldn't be a Tuckkar left to save.

CHAPTER 10: NOW WE'RE MAKING SOME PROGRESS

"The passage of time is a construct of mortals. For Gylum, past and future are present; all things exist at once. His plan for each of His people unfolds before His eye instantly, but those it unfolds for must be patient. His plan may take years, decades, even centuries to play out in the mortal realm."

– The Xyrith: 70: 33-35

  Athan rolled up his map. He had probably mapped out a quarter of the whole moon before he was finally able to find a landmark old enough for him to make reference to the ancient one. In these five and a half years, he had grown strong. Stronger than he had ever been before, and if he had to guess, he'd say he was stronger than even Rynok now.

  He packed up his tent and continued on his way. If he really pushed himself, this would be the last day of his voyage. According to his maps Blood Lake was only forty to forty-five more miles away; however, the information he had was vague as to the exact location of his target, just that he was somewhere in the area. Athan had been studying the map to look for anything he could use. The only thing of promise was a small cave a few miles to the east of the lake. It only appeared on one of the original maps he used to create the one he had now, so it wasn't guaranteed, but it was labeled as the Blue Cave. Unfortunately for Athan though, he was coming up on the lake from the west.

  As he walked, he still hadn't made up his mind whether he wanted to chance crossing the lake, or waste another week going the long way around. He needed more information before making such a call. He had never heard of this lake before Moryn brought the journal and maps. He had never read about it, and no one had ever mentioned it when retelling their times in the forest. That wasn't a good sign, and the name, *Blood* Lake didn't fill him with confidence either.

  Thirty miles to go. He wished he could get in touch with Moryn again. The first few years there wasn't much to tell, and Moryn had told him it was becoming increasingly difficult for him to get out with the curfew. On Athan's end, he was travelling further out and expanding his search, he would be gone for months at a time before returning with bad news. When he finally did find what he was looking for; he found that he was already much closer to the lake than Tuckkar. Part of him had wanted to go back just to give Moryn the good news, but he knew how bad things were back home. People were starting to give up hope that Athan would ever return, so he made the executive decision to head straight there. He didn't want to waste any more time than he already had.

Twenty more miles. Athan started doubting his mission. His people thought he was out there solely to gain his strength, and he had done that and then some. They knew nothing of this ancient Warlock. They had no idea his true intentions were to end the Birthright, to free them from the ritualistic torment they were more than okay to endure. *What if I just turned around now?* His people were suffering without him. *Do I really need to end the Birthright to make them happy?*

Ten miles left. *Yes, I have to do this.* The Birthright was a prison. It held them back from their true potential as a species. Without it they could grow, expand, and advance their society in ways he couldn't even imagine yet. It would just take a little bit longer, and then he could return to his people as the king that they needed, not just wanted.

Athan reached the lake and almost walked right into it. It was nearly impossible to see unless he looked close enough. The trees were growing out of the water in nearly the same thickness as the surrounding forest and the water was dark, very dark. Athan reached down and cupped some of it in his hand. It didn't feel right. While his hand was submerged, it felt very slippery. When he pulled his hand out, it quickly became sticky. *Blood.* Red droplets clung to his hand even after he poured the water out. *So the name is more literal that I thought.* It wasn't just blood though, there was enough water to thin it out, but it was definitely a lot of blood. *Where did it all come from? It would take every drop of blood from every soul in Tuckkar to fill a body of water a tenth this size.* He checked his map again. The lake was over a thousand square miles, so even that wouldn't come close.

Athan circled the lake about a mile and checked the water again. *Same.* He decided to set up camp for the night, and he would keep an eye out for anything that might explain what was going on with the lake. As the night passed, he saw many Knixx Vipers swim into the water and deep into the lake. He never saw any leave, but it was a big lake, they could have got out anywhere. His guess was that they were attracted to the smell of the blood, but even if they were being killed in the water that wouldn't account for the levels of blood. He saw Dao Wings swoop down for drinks of water and fly away unharmed. He even had to hide when a small pack of Zed Wolves came running out from the center of the lake along the tree tops.

By the time morning came, he had devised a theory. The best solution he could think of at the time for this phenomenon was just that blood was seeping into the water table from all the creatures that died and were killed. He had never heard of such a thing, but he was out of ideas to explain it. A nagging in the back of his mind still wasn't satisfied, so he had to investigate further. He was going to cross the lake and see if he could find a better theory.

He thought about building a raft but the trees were close enough to jump, and would make navigating a raft too difficult. Once he was well rested, he jumped up into the first tree.

-O-

Moryn, along with all the people of Tuckkar, waited impatiently in the throne room for Rynok to arrive. The members of the cabinet and the throne on one side, with a wall of guards separating them from the rest of the villagers. Unlike the last village meeting six years ago when the room was packed, Rukor's Law had thinned those numbers by almost half.

Moryn knew when the king entered the room by the angry uproar given by the people. Moryn greeted him with a fake smile and waited for him to take his seat. It was about time. He had been pushing Rynok to hold this meeting for over two years, but of course, stubborn old Rynok thought he knew what was best. He finally came around though, better late than never.

Rynok took his seat and raised his hand up to silence the crowd. They continued to ramble, and Rynok was not pleased. He signaled to the guards and they drew their weapons in perfect unison. Now they were quiet. "Years ago I said this day would come. When all others feared our population increase I stood unafraid, but alone. I said the day would come when Gylum would return balance to our numbers, and that time has come."

The people erupted again. "This is not the work of Gylum! This is the work of a weak king!" one voice cried.

"You did this to us with your population control and Rukor's Law! Gylum is not to blame, you are!" another man yelled.

Rynok got his guards to restore the silence. "Rukor's Law was created by a man just like all of you. My hand was forced when you failed to see as I see." Rynok paused. There were no outbursts this time. "Now, this time I ask you to have faith; not in me, not in my people, not even in your sons that have yet to return to us, but in Gylum." He closed his eyes and raised his arms out. "His plan for us is unfolding as He wishes it."

Surprisingly, this worked fairly well. A good percentage of the crowd calmed down and prayed with the king. Those that didn't were at least less rebellious than they had been when they got there, even if it was only slightly. The meeting ended less than an hour later, and Moryn felt good for the first time in a very, very long time.

The last to leave, Moryn walked out with Rynok. "I'm very pleased with how that went. You did well my Lord."

"Yes. Well, I had to come up with something. I could not have told them what is really going on out there."

Moryn stopped and looked at him questioningly. "What do you mean? You don't believe…"

"No. I believe as they do, but this thing that is happening to us; not a single Fulfillment in two years, and only a handful the two years before that. No. I know exactly who is to blame." The king looked at Moryn as if waiting for him to realize it himself. He had no clue, so the king threw him a bone. "You think it a coincidence all of this began not even a year after Athan's escape?"

"Athan?" Moryn knew it couldn't be Athan. He had been in contact with him up until about a year ago. He specifically mentioned that he hadn't crossed paths with a single child on Pilgrimage. There had to be another explanation, but he couldn't very well tell Rynok what he knew and how he knew it. He knew they needed to find and solve the true problem. If Rynok put all his effort into finding Athan, the real source would remain unchecked. "But why would he be targeting our children? And how could he get to all of them? No. There must be another explanation."

Rynok thought about it. Moryn hoped he gave him enough doubt to open this topic up for discussion with the cabinet before settling his mind. "What else could it be? My brother was always influential. He's building an army of our sons out there. We have to stop him before he gets any stronger."

"I don't know, and neither do you. Your judgment is clouded by your hatred. I understand, I do." Moryn tried to reach whatever part of the old Rynok still existed. "I know you lost everything, but please, all I ask is that you keep an open mind. Let us discuss this with the cabinet tonight."

"No! There is no need. We must find Athan!" Rynok grabbed the top of Moryn's chest piece and pulled him in roughly. "You have had years to do it and have nothing to show for it!"

"I'm sorry my Lord, but I've been through every book in that library. There's nothing there, I promise you." It was actually the truth. Moryn had been destroying everything he found after relaying the information to Athan. He didn't want to risk even a shred of it to fall into Rynok's hands.

Rynok threw him to the ground in anger. "I need to find him! I want him dead!" He stood over Moryn, his knuckles were turning bone white.

Moryn sat up as far as he could. Rynok was a strong man, that throw had hurt quite a bit. "I know you do. The man who killed Ivary deserves to die. I know." Moryn feared that might have been going too far. He didn't want Rynok to figure out he knew the truth, but he couldn't help getting that jab in to make Rynok remember who really killed his wife.

Rynok slouched, grief taking him over. It worked. He

was remembering what he did. Moryn didn't move though, he had to wait this out. Suddenly though, Rynok grabbed his head and his face contorted. "No. No. No. It wasn't me. I didn't do it. No."

"Rynok, it's okay." Moryn moved to comfort him.

Rynok smacked his hand away. "No!" He then slugged Moryn right across the face. "It is not okay!" He climbed on top of Moryn and began pounding his face into the marble floor, crying as he swung violently.

Moryn's nose was the first to break. Blood coated his face and flew onto the walls and floor around him with each blow. Next was his left cheekbone. His vision blurred from disorientation, then filled with red, and finally faded into blackness.

-O-

Paladin waited patiently. For the past hour Princess had been running an obstacle course he designed for her to test each and every area of survival and hunting he had taught her over the years. Should she pass, this would be her final test. It hadn't come a minute too late either. Paladin was only ten days away from Fulfillment, and she needed to be ready to take care of herself. *She sure is taking her sweet time.*

Not a moment later, she took a swan dive off a tree branch a few dozen feet high. Her perfect gold hair was rolled up into a tight bun to keep it out of the way. She had a new set of armor, one which contoured to her thin figure perfectly. It looked very much like her old armor; the same makeup, but this one she made herself. Her sword and round shield were fastened to her back while she fell through the air and landed gracefully in front of him. She looked up and smiled at him. "How'd I do?"

He tried not to look impressed. "You're late."

"What? You said I had an hour," she pouted.

"I said in under an hour. You were late." He moved around her.

She turned after him. "So what, you're going to knock me for one minute?"

"One minute in a fight is a lot longer than you think. One minute can feel like an eternity. We can try again tomorrow."

He could hear as she drew her sword and pulled her shield onto her arm. "How about we try again right now?"

He stopped and glanced back at her over his shoulder. "Are you sure you want to embarrass yourself again?"

She banged her sword against her shield to pump herself up. "That was months ago. I've learned a few tricks since then."

He placed his hand on his sword. He would go easy on her at first. He would keep the knife in its sheath. *No need to end this too quickly.* "Very well. Just remember…" He drew it with lightning speed and attacked. She blocked it with her shield. "You asked for it."

She threw him off and followed up with her sword. She kept it hidden behind her shield until the very last second. *Good, just like I taught her.* He spun out of the way and delivered a thrust right between her sword and the space behind her shield. She clamped the two together and caught him by the blade. She twisted and forced the hilt right out of his hand. His weapon flew across the battlefield and stuck into a tree. *I guess she does have a few tricks up her sleeve.*

She looked proud of herself, and he had to admit he was too. She swung at him a few more times, but he was too fast. *Come on, I'm too fast. What's your next move? How do you counter speed?* He wanted her to figure it out; he knew he had taught her that there was always a way. She jumped in the air and performed a spinning sword attack. He dodged the blade, but didn't prepare himself for her bringing her shield around to follow it. The cold hard face of her shield connected with the side of his head.

He was stunned, but not down. She tried to take advantage and slashed at him. He caught her by the arm and threw her across his body. He had her on the ground and pinned her arm. He raised his fist to strike, but she protected her face with her shield. He grabbed it to pry it out of the way. He pulled hard expecting resistance, but there was none. He fell backwards with the shield that was now free of her arm. Using her now freed left fist, and with him off balance, she struck him square in the face.

He released her and rolled backwards. She was a lot

stronger than she was a few years ago. His cheek swelled. They both got to their feet. She had her sword, he had her shield. He put it on his arm and taunted her to attack. She twirled her sword around beautifully. *Showoff.* So he made the first move. He used the shield as a weapon to bash, gripping it with both hands for stability. Without her shield, she looked worried. He had taught her a bit to fight with limited weapons or no weapons, but she was still far too dependent on what she knew best.

He kept up a relentless attack, and he got her on the defensive. She was backing up with every one of his attacks. Soon, he got her to lose balance completely and she fell back. He lifted the shield for one final blow. She deflected it to the side and brought the tip of her sword to his stomach, stopping just at the armor. "Gotcha."

"Did you?" He tapped the side of his knife against her neck. He had drawn it when she hadn't noticed, and had it been a real fight, would have opened her artery before she had known what happened.

He stood up and offered a hand to help her up. She refused. "So, let's hear it." She hopped to her feet. "What's the lecture going to be about today?"

"I don't lecture," he said as he handed her shield back to her. She just stood there looking sideways at him. "Okay, maybe I lecture a bit, but I do it so you learn and grow into a better warrior." They started walking back to the dwelling. "So that was very good, but you really need to learn to be more comfortable without your shield. There's no guarantee you'll always have it for every encounter."

"I know, and I'm working on that, but that wasn't all that was happening. I was trying to see if you would get overconfident and make a mistake if you thought you were winning," she explained.

"That could work, but remember the tide of battle often determines the victor. Instead of making a mistake, your enemy might find their second wind. It could make them stronger rather than reckless." He could see she was thinking on that hard. "Instead, the approach I took, while you never want to underestimate your opponent; you might try keeping one of your strongest attributes hidden from them. Once they learn your fighting style and are working on a counter, you can pull that last surprise out at the right moment; like I did with my knife. You didn't know I had it, so you couldn't defend against it."

"But wouldn't that…" she started to ask.

He cut her off with a swift hand gesture. He heard something; it was faint, but it was something. Using only hand signals, he told her to get down low with him. They were completely still, so quiet that he could hear her pulse beating. It took a moment, but he heard the noise again only slightly louder. *Something's coming this way.* He motioned for her to climb. Whatever was coming, it was on the forest floor.

She did as she was told, and she did it quietly just like he taught her. He followed swiftly behind her. They reached high enough that they would remain unseen, but could still see whatever would pass beneath them. The sound was unmistakable now. Something was running full sprint through the forest. When they saw it, it was a young boy right around six years old. The boy had some light armor, nothing like what the two of them had, and a very well-crafted bow and quiver slung over his shoulder. Paladin tried to see if there was anything behind him. *What's he running from. A Djinn? No.* There were no trees snapping like twigs behind him. He listened for the footsteps of his pursuers. There was more than one. If he had to guess, a pack of Zed Wolves, but something felt off about it.

Then he saw them. They weren't wolves, they weren't vipers, they were three other boys. All three were in their late teens. He looked up at Princess and she was already looking at him. She wanted to help him, but it was too risky. When the younger boy reached right under their position, he tripped and fell hard. He was gripping his knee, whether he just twisted it or broke it was unclear; but he wasn't going to be able to run anymore, and he certainly couldn't fight.

It didn't take long for the older three boys to reach and surround him. The young Archer tried to draw an arrow, but the largest of the three kicked the bow from his hands. Princess pulled her sword halfway from its sheath before Paladin told her to stop. He shook his head at her, but the defiant look she gave him didn't look good.

Paladin looked back down when he heard one of the boys speak. "Just give up kid. Come with us, or die here. The choice is yours." He didn't even have a chance to look back up, he just saw Princess falling towards the ground with weapons drawn.

Damn that girl. She's going to get herself killed. Unless he helped her, which is probably exactly what she wanted. Paladin jumped right after her. She landed first, right in front of the Archer. The older boys looked at each other; they had never seen a girl in the forest before. It was just the distraction they needed. She didn't wait for them to snap out of it, she lunged for the smallest of them. He defended himself and engaged her back. Paladin landed directly on the largest boy with both blades down. The boy was down before he even knew what happened.

Princess was doing very well for herself. She had her opponent on the defensive. She was faster, and she would be fine on her own. Paladin pulled out his blades and turned to the last remaining attacker. He was backing up in fear. Paladin took a single step in his direction and he turned and bolted out of there. *Coward.* Paladin turned around to the boy they had saved. The scared little Archer had recovered his bow and had an arrow drawn on Paladin. "Whoa, easy now. I'm not going to hurt you."

The boy glanced over to Princess still fighting. Paladin took the opportunity of him looking away to move closer. Archer spotted this move and drew the bow even further on him. "Don't move! J-just stay there." He shook nervously. His knee was buckling under him. He winced.

"Look, you're hurt. We saw you twist your knee, I promise, we just want to help." He held out his hands and bent down to put his weapons down. He tilted his head to speak to Princess but kept his eyes on Archer. "You okay over there?"

She was still fighting even though she should have finished him off already. He trained her better than that. "I got this! I'm fine!"

He set his weapons down and stepped back from them. "I have something that could help that knee, I'm just going to grab it." He reached for the small pack on his lower back.

"Slowly! Easy." Archer said. The pain in his knee was getting to him and his grip on the arrow was slipping. If he let go of the arrow, that could mean bad news for him.

Paladin pulled out a Knixx-skin wrapping and held it out to show Archer it wasn't a weapon. Suddenly Princess shouted out. "Got him!" They both looked over at her. Archer's hand slipped and the arrow went whizzing past Paladin's head.

"Oh Gylum! I'm so sorry. It slipped." He looked even more nervous now. He stumbled backwards.

Princess ran over, oblivious to what was going on between the two of them. "See. I told you I could handle it." She was trying to hide the fact that she was out of breath. She looked at the cowering Archer, and then hit Paladin. "What are you doing? You're scaring him!"

"B-but… H-he's the one…" He tried to explain it to her, but she wasn't listening.

She walked to him slowly and nonthreatening. "It's okay. We don't want to hurt you. Don't be afraid."

Archer's eyes widened and his jaw dropped now that he was getting a good look at her. "Y-you're a… a…"

"What? A girl? Yes, I am." She smiled and laughed. "It's okay, I get that a lot." She took the Knixx-skin wrap from Paladin and held it out to him. "Now are you going to let us help you or not?" He nodded and sat down with his bad knee out. "Good choice." She sat next to him and began wrapping his knee.

Paladin pulled out some Integro Roots and water. "I'll get some tea going. It'll help with the swelling." Archer nodded in appreciation and Princess mouthed the words *thank you*. He would need a Djeg leaf if he wanted to boil the water, so he went to search the bodies of the attackers. He searched the first one. Nothing. He moved on to the one Princess had fought. He had one on him, and good thing it hadn't ignited yet.

He turned all the way around before he realized something was wrong. He turned back. *Something's off. What is it?* There was something different about him, but Paladin was having a hard time seeing it. *Where's his Birthright?* That had to be it. He checked the boy's left hand; nothing but a scar. He felt the skin and it was hollow. There was no light because there was no Birthright. He went to check the other body. *Why wouldn't he have a Birthright? Maybe this Archer took it. Could that have been why they were chasing him?* He reached the other body. Same, no Birthright. *No. These scars are completely healed, they must be several days old at least, probably much longer. What was it that boy said to him? 'Come with us, or die here.' Why did they want to take him alive?*

Paladin didn't like having unanswered questions. Archer had to know what was going on, and he was going to tell Paladin everything he wanted to know. If he didn't, than that kid was going to wish that arrow hadn't missed.

CHAPTER 11: SOME RUMORS ARE TRUE, OTHERS ARE NOT

"In the forest, there is only oneself. There are no friends, no family, no loved ones. Once Fulfillment is reached, then these things can become a part of life. These things hold no importance in the life of a boy, but are one of the most valued treasures in the life of a man. For a man to forsake his loved ones is to forsake Gylum Himself."

— The Xyrith: 142: 13-17

Paladin stalked back to Archer where Princess was wrapping his knee. She must have seen the look in his eye because she jumped up and put herself between them. "What are you doing? What's wrong?"

Paladin could have just shoved her out of the way, but he stopped. He yelled at the boy over her. "Why were those boys chasing you? Huh? What did you do to them?"

Archer was afraid again. He started slinking away. "I d-don't know. I didn't do anything. I swear."

Princess was looking back and forth at them both. She tuned to Paladin first. "Easy now. Just calm down. You're just scaring him." She tuned to Archer and knelt down to him. "Now just tell us everything, from the beginning."

Archer eased up, and so did Paladin. He'd give her way a chance. Even if it didn't work, he could always go back to his way. The boy cleared his throat and started. "I don't know what happened. One second, I was tracking down some Zed Wolves, you know, for food. And then…" He hesitated.

"Then what? What happened to their Birthrights? Where are they? Did you take them?"

Princess looked at him confused. "What? What do you mean?"

"I mean that neither one of them have Birthrights. They've been cut out."

Archer perked his head up. "What? Are you sure?" He jumped to his feet and headed for the nearest body.

Paladin stopped him. "Whoa! Where do you think you're going?"

"I need to see for myself." He fought against Paladin for a good moment before he finally released him to let him go to the body. Archer picked up the left hand and ran his fingers across the scar. "And the other one was the same?"

"Yes. What does it mean? What do you know?"

Archer dropped the hand but remained sitting there. "It was four years ago. I was still young and came across a much older boy. He wanted my Birthright; Head of the Royal Guard is a pretty good one after all." Paladin looked at his hand; it certainly was. He glanced over at Princess. She held out her own and looked down at it. His father must have known hers. "I ran. He was so much older than me, I didn't know what else to do."

Paladin was getting impatient. "What does any of this have to do…"

Princess shot him a look to shut up. "Let him finish," she whispered.

"He tracked me for three days. I had barely slept and I was injured. He just about had me when…" He looked down at the body again. "When five other boys found him. I hid nearby, afraid to run, or even breath. So I stayed and watched the whole thing. Four of them had their Birthrights cut out, just like these guys, only they looked fresh. The fifth…" He turned to face the other two and held up his left hand. "He didn't have his left hand at all."

Both Paladin's and Princess's jaws dropped. *It couldn't be. That boy, the one that tried to take Princess's Birthright. He was eighteen all those years ago, there's no way he would still have been here in the forest.* Paladin feared the answer, but he had to know. "Was there anything else about him? Anything unusual?"

Archer nodded. "Ya, I didn't understand how it was possible, but he was old. He was…"

"Twenty." Princess finished for him. She must have had fewer doubts about it than he did.

Archer looked baffled at her. "Ya, how did you know that?"

Paladin put his hand on his sword. The same sword that took that hand. "We've met before."

"But how? He should have Fulfilled years ago. You told me that on your eighteenth birthday…" she started.

"That your Birthright is Fulfilled, yes; but if you don't have one, not even the hand? I don't know. I've never heard of that happening. It's possible." That would mean he was stuck here; stuck in the forest. Stuck in the most dangerous environment in the known universe. He couldn't even fathom how devastating that would be. And it was all his fault. He was the one who took his hand. He's the one who took his future.

"So it's our fault." She looked at the bodies on the ground. "This is all because of us."

He turned on her. "You don't know that. This could be anything."

"I'm afraid she's right," Archer said quietly.

"What do you know? How can you be sure of that?"

"I… I just am, okay. It's been going on for years. The man with one hand is reaping the children of the forest. The forest fears him, it respects him for that."

Paladin and Princess exchanged looks. He asked, "Where did you hear that? Have you seen him take more?"

"No. But the trees, they whisper to each other. I can hear them speak of him. But I only get glimpses, I can't always understand. I'm not as sensitive as my father. I wasn't even convinced it was true until now."

Paladin looked at the nearest tree. *Is that even possible? Could the trees really talk to each other?* "Why can't we hear them?"

"I don't know. It's a rare gift. I got it from my father, he from his."

"What does that matter?" Princess sounded angry. "What matters is that Gylum knows how many children this man has already reaped. We can't just sit back and allow this to continue. We're the ones that caused all of this. It's our responsibility to save them."

"Even if it is the same guy, that doesn't mean anything. He's still responsible for his own actions. That doesn't fall on us." She was doing it again. Just like what she had done with that Archer. Just like what she always did, she was always trying to help everybody. She didn't understand, that wasn't the way of the forest.

"Maybe it should. You saved me. You took responsibility for me."

Paladin changed the tone. He wasn't arguing anymore, he was pleading. "Exactly. You are my responsibility and in ten days I'll be gone, and you'll be on your own. I can't have you going on some suicide rescue mission. I need you to promise me you'll stay safe until it's your time." He walked over to her and held her head in his hands. "I'll be waiting for you in Tuckkar. Don't keep me waiting forever."

She nodded in agreement. She wasn't happy about it; he knew her well enough to know that, but for now at least, she would let it go. By the time they pulled away from each other, they noticed Archer limping away. She looked at him, and then at Paladin. He knew that look. "Please?"

"No," he replied. He knew she'd ask.

"But look at him. He's so cute. Can we keep him?"

"Hey!" Archer turned around. "I can take care of myself thank you very much."

"See, he's fine. Let's go." Paladin tried to pull her away but she resisted.

"You know, after you're gone, I sure would be much safer with the soon-to-be Head of the Royal Guard." She held up her Royalty Birthright.

Archer saw it and hobbled over. "Oh my, is that? You're a Princess?" He bowed. "Your Majesty." He looked around the forest and down at his hurt knee. "You know she's right. She would be safer with me." He was trying to play it off, but Paladin wasn't fooled. He just didn't want to be alone in his condition.

Paladin considered it. Archer's knee would be healed in a day or two. He could use those days to see if he was strong and noble enough to take his place as her new protector once he was gone. "Very well. This way, we aren't far."

They made their way back to the dwelling. At first she was trying to help Archer walk, but he refused. He didn't want to appear weak, but that only lasted a few minutes before he reluctantly accepted her aid. The three of them made it back safely and went inside to rest. It had been a long day for them all.

-O-

The boy looked behind him as he continued to run. There was no sign of the other boy who had just killed his fellow Hunter, the feminine looking boy with golden hair, or the young Archer they had been hunting. He felt safe enough to stop running, but he still moved with a quickness. *What happened back there? Who were those two? Were they working with the Archer? Did they lead us into a trap?* He had never seen anyone outside his camp working together before. He didn't know any of the answers, and quite frankly, he didn't want to. He would be completely happy if he never saw those three ever again.

He had a long walk ahead of him, plenty of time to dwell. He had run away like a coward. He left the youngest Hunter behind to face those two alone. What would they do to him when he returned with nothing to show for himself but weakness? Part of him didn't want to return at all, but that would never work. He knew better than most, *there is no hiding from… him.* Hunters like him were the lowest level of finding people he had at his disposal. He had to return. He had to pray for mercy.

Hunter was nearing the boarder of the camp. He looked around for the sentries, but they were nowhere to be seen. That's exactly what they were trained to do. Before he even heard a branch move, he was surrounded. "Show us your hand! Slowly!" One of them said; with full helmets it was difficult to tell which one.

He held out his left hand, showing that he lacked a Birthright. They lowered their weapons. "I'm a Hunter. The rest of my party has been killed. I must speak with him." They looked at each other questioningly. He could understand why. No hunting party had ever met more resistance than they could handle. That's why they hunted in threes; their prey, no matter how old, would be no match outnumbered.

Two of the sentries escorted him into the camp. The camp had grown significantly in the past three years since he was first taken. There were a lot more permanent structures and fewer portable tents. About half of the trees had been harvested for wood or food, and it made it a little more spacious. Wooden walkways, ladders, and pulleys ran around and between the trees on several different levels. Boys, young and old, moved throughout the camp in the hundreds. Even though he had never seen Tuckkar personally, his genetic knowledge let him know what it felt like to live in a community. It felt like home.

They reached the center of the camp, where the largest, and by far tallest, structure stood, Reaper's Palace. This one structure dwarfed everything surrounding it. They were heading for the very top, the highest point, even over the other trees; Reaper's throne room. As he entered on the ground floor, a cold chill rushed over his skin. Unlike the other huts and tents in the camp this building hadn't been built, it was grown. He didn't understand how or why, but Reaper had an unnatural connection to the forest. He could control the trees; he made them grow as he wished through sheer will. It wasn't just the trees, he could tame the beasts as well. Hunter had seen some of the more advanced hunting parties that actually rode Zed Wolves.

The mysterious power he held over the forest and its beasts extended to his people as well. Most of the children Hunter had helped reap over the course of his hunting career resisted heavily when they were first captured, but after a short audience with Reaper they stopped fighting. Even he never would have seen himself as a loyal follower before he went into that room for the first time. *Look at me now.*

He stepped onto the elevator, and it wasn't until after it already started ascending that he noticed he was alone. The two sentries had already begun heading back to their posts. As the elevator rose, his heart rate did as well. Every foot he climbed, he was nearing an uncertain fate. It was bad enough having to face Reaper, but to do it alone? If he hadn't been nervous before, he certainly was now.

The floor below him shuttered to a halt as it met the floor of Reaper's throne room. He stepped out into the light of the room. The elevator descended back down into the darkness as soon as his feet left its surface. There was a single spotlight in the center of the cavernous room. The surrounding areas were shrouded in shadow. He had an eerie feeling that he was being watched, almost like there were dozens upon dozens of eyes leering at him from the other side of the veil. The only thing he could see was the front portion of the throne, half blended in the light, half just beyond. A dark cloak fell down over what he could only assume were Reaper's legs.

"Speak." The voice filled the room, echoing around the walls. It felt as if he were everywhere in the room at once.

It chilled him to the core. Hunter tried to get words out, but none passed his lips. "I said, Speak!"

Hunter began groveling. "Y-yes my Lord. Um, the other members of my party. We were attacked. They're dead. I'm sorry, I'm so sorry."

Reaper was silent for a moment; the only sound in the room was Hunter's own sniveling. Then, he spoke again. "Yet you live. Did you vanquish your attacker then? I should hope so. There would be no reason for you not to stay with your men, to fight till the end."

His eyes widened and his heart raced even faster. It felt like it was about to burst. Reaper was going to kill him. He ran like a coward, he should have stayed, he shouldn't have left his friends to die alone like that. "B-but, we were out matched. They killed the oldest of us before we even knew what was happening. It was an ambush." Reaper's hand came into the light. He waved his hand and a massive older boy emerged with a heavy axe in hand. "N-no! Please! They were older than us. They were working together. It wasn't our fault!" Hunter crawled away on his back but another young man, even bigger and older than the first, came out from the dark behind him. He grabbed him and held him down as the first boy lifted his weapon. "We were caught off guard! The one with the golden hair! It wasn't my fault! Please!"

"Wait." Reaper held out his hand again. His men stood down. "What about the golden hair?"

The older boy ripped Hunter off the ground and back to his feet. He had no idea how he just saved himself, but he didn't really care. "Um, he was almost seventeen, but there was something strange other than just the hair. I don't know what it was, but something."

"Are you sure it was a 'he'? Could it have been a female?"

What? That was crazy, no girls lived in the forest. Everybody knew that. But hell if he was going to call Reaper crazy in his own throne room. "Um, well. I do remember thinking he was very, um, feminine looking. But how could that be?"

Reaper didn't answer him. He seemed to not care about Hunter anymore, he just snapped his fingers. "Mage!"

"Y-yes sir?" A thin, squirrely looking ten-year-old boy

stepped out in front of the throne. He shook uncontrollably, but he didn't think it was out of nerves it just seemed his character.

"What is the status of the Tracker?" Reaper was addressing his Mage. Hunter felt as if he were invisible now; forgotten. He was glad, but figured it would be better to stay still than risk being seen trying to leave.

"W-well, he survived the process, but, um, he didn't take as, um, well, as well as we hoped. He's unconscious for now, but should be good to go in a few days. A week at the most." He paused for a second, but then caught himself. "But Berserker! He has recovered completely. He's ready to go." He shook his head up and down excessively. He waited for praise.

"No, I want them alive. Alive isn't exactly his strong suit." Reaper was thinking. Not a single molecule in the room moved until he made his decision. "Alchemist!" He snapped his fingers again.

A heavily armored man broke through into the center of the room. A mask covered his mouth and nose, only his bright grey eyes where visible alongside the small patch of pale skin around them. The most outspoken characteristic that differed him from Reaper's average minions was his bandolier of Dao Wing bones. Upon closer look, the ordinarily hollow bones were filled with varying liquids and powders. He knelt before the throne. "Yes, my Lord?"

Reaper whistled, and then a loud cawing pierced the air from behind Hunter. A Dao Wing flew down and nearly took his head off as it passed him on the way to Reaper's arm. Reaper sat there and just looked at his bird. The bird was looking right back at him, as if it could read his thoughts. After a few short seconds, the bird took off again and blended into the darkness. The fading sound of its horrid cawing indicated it must have left through an unseen window and out into the forest.

Reaper's next words were his orders for the Alchemist. "I want you to follow the Wing. It will find them for you. Take them alive and bring them to me. Can you handle that?"

He stood and placed a hand on his bandolier. "I have just the thing. It will be done my Lord." He took off at full speed in the same direction as the Dao Wing. As soon as he left the spotlight, Hunter didn't hear a single noise from him; not a footstep, nothing.

There were no more distractions to keep him unnoticed now. He was still unclear as to whether he was going to live to leave that room, or be taken out in pieces. "S-so, you're not going to kill me?"

"Your information today was worth a great deal to me. I have no fear that you will never fail me again." Hunter scrambled back to his feet and bowed excessively. He turned and headed back to the elevator; the sound of it reaching his floor giving away its location in the pitch black. He stepped onto the platform and waited for it to move back down, as far away from that frightening room as it would take him. He felt a slight coldness in the back of his neck, and then nothing. His head hit the floor, but his feet hadn't moved. Reaper's words rang in his eardrums as the last flicker of brain activity faded. "Never again."

-O-

Princess opened her eyes. Paladin was asleep in his bed, and Archer was just outside the door curled up, also asleep. Paladin hadn't trusted him enough yet to let him stay inside, which worked perfectly for her. She had been practicing for years to sneak out without alerting Paladin; she had only managed to pull it off a small handful of times, but she thought she had the hang of it by now. She made it all the way out the door and listened closely to see if he had woken. His breathing remained consistent. She did it.

Now was the real hard part. She needed Archer to find wherever this *Reaper* character was held up, but waking him up without Paladin being disturbed was a tall order. She started by placing her hand over his mouth so he couldn't make a sound when he woke. She shook him gently until his eyes parted. She put her finger to her lips, he understood, and she released his mouth. She motioned for them to move and keep quiet. He looked around, probably wondering where Paladin was. She didn't answer him, just signaled to move again. He stopped looking and complied. It wasn't until they were well out of earshot that he finally whispered, "What's going on? Where are we going? And where is the big scary one?"

"If he's not going to help those children, then it's up to us. I need you to find where they're being held."

He stopped walking. He wasn't whispering anymore. "Whoa, what? What about what he said? The whole 'suicide rescue mission' thing. He's not wrong you know."

She was going to hush him, but they were far enough away by now. "But we need to do something. It's all my fault they…"

"You keep saying that. How is it your fault? What happened?"

He deserved to know. If she was going to ask him to take this major risk for her then he deserved to know everything. They started walking again and as they traveled, she told him her story. She told him about the day she was born, about how Paladin raised her ever since, the night the older boy tried to take her Birthright, how Paladin cut off his hand to save her, everything. By the time she was done, Archer needed a minute to process.

She was sure he was full of questions, but the first one he asked wasn't one she was expecting. "So, how much do you know about your father?"

Now she was the one who needed a minute. "Um, nothing really, just what he's told me. He was royalty obviously." She held up her hand with the Birthright. "And he killed my mother." She started tearing up. "And left me for dead out here." She regained control of herself. "You must remember him though, through your father, right?"

"I know of him. What do you know of genetic knowledge? You don't have it, do you?"

She shook her head. "No, and not a lot, just that you retain the memories of your father up until you're conceived."

"Not quite. It's not memories like you know them. Like, I have memories of living out here myself, but I know things from when my father grew up out here. I don't remember it, I just know it. Does that make any sense?"

She probably never could fully understand, but she just figured it was like how she knew how to speak or how to move. It just was. "Well, what do you know about him then? My father I mean."

"He used to be a good man, not the greatest king we ever had, but a good man. But then, in the later years, he wasn't such a good man anymore."

"What changed? If he was such a good man why did he..." She trailed off. She didn't want to actually say the words again. "What made him change?"

"I don't know. He didn't change until after the queen died. His younger brother, Athan, he forced your father's trusted servant to kill your mother and her unborn son. At least that's what he claimed happened. But you being here, if what you say happened that night is true, then..." He was afraid to finish his sentence, and she knew why.

"Then I'm the reason he killed my mother. I'm the reason he changed." She knew it was true. Somehow, she always knew, as if she did have a small piece of genetic knowledge after all. Paladin had always avoided talking about that night, and when he did, she always felt that he was keeping more details from her than he knew. She always thought he was just trying to spare her crying, but now she knew. He was trying to spare her from knowing that her being born a daughter instead of a son was the reason her mother died.

She broke down. She fell to her knees as her tears fell to the soil. Archer held her close, letting her cry into his shoulder. She let it all out, all of the tears she had ever held back to look strong in front of Paladin. She couldn't bear to hold them back any longer. After what seemed like hours, but was closer to only a few minutes, Archer started shaking her to stop. "Quiet. Hold on."

She wiped her face and looked at him. At first she thought he was just getting impatient with her, but that wasn't the case. He was scanning the treetops. "What is it?" He put his finger up asking for silence. *He's listening for something, but for what? Was something coming their way or was it the trees?* She saw a Dao Wing land on a branch fifty feet above their heads and caw at them. She readied her blade, but Archer stopped her. "What are you doing?" she hissed at him.

"It's not here to attack us." Just after he said it, the bird took off and flew back the way it came. "We have to go. Now!" He grabbed her hand and took off running.

"What do you mean? What's going on? It left." She

followed him, but she still wanted answers.

"It's one of his. That Hunter, the one that ran away, he must have reported back. He knows were out here." He pulled her arm harder, she ran faster to keep up. For a younger boy, he was fast.

"What does that mean? Is he going to send more Hunters?"

"No, probably not. Hunters are just the beginning. Just run. Run and pray we don't find out what's after Hunters."

CHAPTER 12: WE ALL MAKE MISTAKES

"It is often possible for His children to feel lost, as if they have fallen off their path. Fear not, for even when all seems lost, Gylum's all-seeing eye is always watching. He is the light that guides those in the dark, and at the end, it will be revealed, the darkness was always necessary for the light to exist."

–   The Xyrith: 67: 10-12

Rynok entered the castle's infirmary. He walked past a few beds of villagers that refused to follow the orders of some of his guards. By the looks of them, only about half would make it. *Maybe they are not as well trained as I thought.* He finally reached Moryn's bed. Moryn looked worse than he remembered. *He should be dead. He has been failing to find Athan for years.* No. He was his friend. He never should have done this to him. What had he done?

He took a seat on the empty bed beside Moryn. A forty-year-old guard walked over to Rynok. He had lighter armor than the rest of the guards, closer to what Moryn wore. It was Teed, the acting head of the royal guard for as long as Moryn was out of commission. "My Lord."

He stood at attention. It was very respectful of him, but it just served as a reminder of how Moryn was always more casual with him. Moryn was his friend. *Moryn was useless! I have no place for him anymore.* "Go to your men. Any men we can spare from the wall and the curfew patrols, assemble them into teams. I want the entire forest searched. My brother and our sons are out there. Find them."

"Yes sir!" He turned on a dime and left the room to loyally follow his order. Only the other patients, all of whom where unconscious or worse, a few nurses and, a doctor remained in the room.

"Get out," Rynok barked. They didn't need to be told twice. Everyone who wasn't in a bed dropped whatever they were doing and bolted from the room faster than if it had been on fire. *Good, now we are alone. Time to finish the job.* But he didn't move. He sat there in internal conflict.

"No, you are my friend. I need you." He cried over Moryn's body.

I don't need anyone! I am the king! I am above them all!

"You are all I have left. With Garm dead, Athan gone. Nimm and Ivary…" He placed his head in his hands.

Athan killed them! He is no brother to me anymore.

He screamed into his hands to muffle himself. "No he did not! Stop lying to yourself. I killed them!" He dropped his hands and whispered, "It was me. I killed them." He had never said the words out loud. He tried never to even think them. He pushed the truth so far back into his fractured mind, that most of the time he believed his own lie. But not right now. Not in this short moment of lucidity. "I am so sorry Moryn. Please forgive me."

Shut up! Someone could hear!

"I do not know why I did it. All I wanted was a son. What was I supposed to do? How could I face anyone with a daughter? I do not know how things got like this. Please! I need you back. I need you to help me fix this. To fix everything I have done."

No! Enough! Rynok screamed into his hands again, but not words. He was losing the internal struggle. He was winning the struggle. He didn't know where one fragment of his mind started and the next ended. *Who am I anymore?* The thing that stopped him was a squeak. He jumped to his feet. There it was again. He followed the direction of the noise to the furthest bed. The man had one eye open, but only because the other was wrapped in bandages. "You heard that I suppose?" Rynok asked; his voice chilling the room. The man shook his head, but he wasn't fooled.

No, there is no need to kill him. Where is he going to go? Who is he going to tell?

Rynok slowly unsheathed his sword. "That's not a risk I'm willing to take."

I can throw him into the dungeon. I've killed enough. No more blood. Please! But the tables were turned. His darkness was back in control. The voice of reason no longer had any influence on the outside world. It was nothing but what it was, a voice. A voice in his head that he no longer could hear. If he could, then he just didn't care.

"Goodbye." He was speaking to the villager, but it was just as meaningful to the last grain of good left within him. As the sword pierced flesh, both died forever.

-O-

Paladin got up. It was time for his perimeter check. Usually he would have checked on Princess, but tonight he wanted to make sure Archer was still there. Make sure he didn't take off with any of their belongings or anything else. He looked outside where he had left him. *Gone. Big surprise.* His knee would have been healed by this point, not one hundred percent, but well enough to survive on his own again.

He turned back inside to check on her, but he froze when he saw her bed empty. A thousand thoughts raced through his mind. *He's taken her! He killed her! I'm going to hunt him down!* Then one stuck in his head. He knew it was the right one. *She went to save the reaped children, and she dragged him along with her.* "Damn it!" He strapped his gear on and flew after her.

He wanted to just sprint after her so he could stop her before she got too close, but he didn't know which direction they went. He searched the area and found their tracks. *I taught her better than this. She knows how to cover her tracks. She wants me to find her.* The tracks were visible enough for him to follow, but not so easy as for him to gain on her very fast. He had to constantly check and make sure he didn't lose them.

At most, they had a two hour head start, but odds were it was closer to an hour. The further along he went the more time he had to think about the whole situation, and the more upset he got. *I can't believe she lied to me like that. I can't believe she deceived me. And that Archer, why didn't he stop her? Why didn't he alert me to what she was doing? He seemed like a smart enough kid; smart enough to know what she was doing was suicide. How can I justify leaving her in his care now?* If Archer was just going to allow her to do it and blindly follow her, he wasn't capable of caring for her like he thought.

Paladin found a spot where they had stopped, but for how long was unclear. It couldn't have been for them to rest, it was too close to where they left for either of them to need rest. There were no signs of a struggle either; at least none there. A few miles further, it was a different story. It was another spot where they had stopped, but when they took off again the tracks were deep and in a new direction. *They ran away! But what were they running from?* He looked around for any signs of a pursuer. There was nothing.

He followed their tracks much easier now, but that wasn't a good thing anymore. They were still together, *that's good*, but they were definitely running from something. He slid to a halt. *Where did they go?* The tracks just stopped. He turned back to the point they ended. There was nothing nearby. No trees closer than twenty feet, no streams for them to have followed, nothing at all to explain the trail running cold.

He was looking around frantically. He couldn't lose her, not like this. Then in the corner of his eye, he saw something drop from above him. He snatched it out of the air. It was a Dao Wing bone; just a bone. *What? Where…?* There was something else strange about it; it had a small hole in it. When he looked closer, he saw it was filled with a dark liquid. The liquid started to bubble. *That can't be good.*

He readied himself to throw it, but he was too late. The bone exploded in his hand and a light yellow gas plumed around him. He used his hands to try and fan the gas away, but it was already filling his lungs. He tried to hold his breath to stop more from entering his system, but the gas made him cough. He staggered out from the center of the cloud, but each step he took was slower and more of an effort. After a few feet, he strained to put his next foot out in front of him. Even with every ounce of strength, it wasn't enough and he fell crashing backwards into the muddy floor of the small clearing.

His body was no longer responding to what his brain told it to do. He was paralyzed. The memories of that day seventeen years ago rushed back to him. The fear he felt as he was helpless to stop that viper from killing him; all of it came back. He was just as weak and useless as he had been that night. If Princess or Archer found him, he would once again owe his life to another. He didn't want that, not again. He'd rather die. But the nagging question kept popping into his immobilized head. *How? How did this happen?* That bone, the gas, there was no way it was natural. Someone had done this to him, the question was *who?*

His eyes could still move, and with his head looking straight up he had a decent view of the treetops, but not the forest floor. *The bone came from above, over that way.* It was hard to see, but he saw a man standing on a branch high above. If he needed any more proof that he was the one responsible, the white bones crossing from shoulder to waist was it.

"Oh no!" Princess's voice cried out. "Oh, what happened? Get up!" Her voice was getting closer. Her words were uneven, she was running to him.

He tried to speak, to warn her to stay away, but his vocal cords wouldn't budge. *No! Stay back! It's a trap! Please!* He was helpless to stop her.

"What's wrong? Please get up. Don't leave me. Please. I'm sorry." She was crying over him. For all she knew, he was dead.

He had to watch in horror as the mysterious man above them dropped another one of his paralytic capsules down beside them. She looked at it when it exploded just like the first. She covered her mouth, but didn't try to run. She covered his mouth and nose and huddled with him. *No! Just leave me. Run! Save yourself.* A few breaths later, she fell completely still.

The man jumped down and walked up to them. He pulled down a mask that covered his nose and mouth to reveal a sly smirk. *Bastard.* He clearly couldn't take them in a fair fight, so he had resorted to dirty tricks. He lifted Paladin up onto his shoulders, and then picked her up in his arms. As he left the clearing, Paladin got a good look behind him. Archer was hiding behind a Niku tree and popped his head out. There was no way he could relay anything to the kid, so he just hoped he was smart enough to know what to do. *Follow us. Do whatever you can, but don't get caught.*

After a mile or two their captor reached a small group of other boys, mostly younger. They had a large wooden cart with a cage on top. They were hoisted into the cage and strapped up against the bars. They were forced to face outward and watch as the pair of Zed Wolves pulled them through the forest. At one point, Archer ran up ahead to show them he was still there, but it was dangerous of him. If they could see him, so could the others. The only thing they had going for them, was they weren't looking for him. That might just be the edge they needed. But regardless of anything else, Archer was their only chance. If he failed, there was no hope for them.

-O-

Athan had been making his way across the lake for hours now. Each time he landed on a new branch, Djeg leaves would shake loose and float to the lake below. They lit up like flares before quickly getting extinguished. Jumping from tree to tree was costing him a lot more energy than regular ground travel. The further into the center of the lake he got, the further apart the trees were; which was making it even more difficult. But he was well past the halfway mark, so instead of resting he figured he'd push through.

For quite some time now, he had seriously been reconsidering building a raft. He was expecting that as he neared the far shore the trees would start increasing in density again, but they weren't. It was really starting to take its toll on him, his pace was slowing, and his breathing was growing heavier and heavier with each leap. Sweat was dripping from his brow into the bloody waters below.

He stopped at the next tree. He was beat and needed to rest, even if only for a minute. He focused on controlling his breathing. After he had that under control, he checked his supplies. He finished the last of his water; there was only a mouthful left. He looked down. It was a shame, surrounded by water, but not a drop to drink. He wasn't too afraid though, he could last long enough to find fresh water when he landed back on solid ground.

He was almost ready to continue on ahead when something caught his eye. There were ripples in the water, but they dissipated quickly. *What was that? A Knixx Viper perhaps?* He made his jump to the next branch, but kept his eyes on the water. *There*, another ripple. He barely caught a glimpse, but there was definitely something there. Whatever it was, it looked white. He knew that he should have just kept moving because whatever it was, it couldn't be good. In this forest, it was probably better left alone, but curiosity got the better of him. It often did.

He scoured the red glass-like surface for anything. It took a minute, but he finally found it again. It was a bone.

What kind he was unsure, but it was just a large white bone covered in drops of red water. *That's it?* He almost turned away, but then the bone moved. It was gliding along the surface of the lake. As it circled his tree, it began protruding further and further from the lake. It started to take shape. It looked almost like a fin. Then more white broke through the crimson; it moved at the same speed and course as the fin. The pattern they made reminded him of a ribcage. He didn't think it was possible for any species of fish to live in blood like this.

Suddenly, it came to him. It was vague, as if the knowledge was coming from several generations before him, but it was there. *It's a Dragoon Fish.* He had a name now, but not much else. That wasn't good. *How am I supposed to fight something if I don't know any of its strengths or weaknesses?* What he did know though, it was getting close fast. It looked like he was on his own with this one; he'd have to learn on the fly.

He waited for it to get closer. He had to assume they could catch prey even if it was out of the water. As soon as it was close enough, he made the jump to the next tree. The fish broke the surface of the water and lunged at the spot he had been a few seconds before. In the air, Athan got a good look at the creature. It was covered in an external skeleton that looked to serve as a suit of bone armor. From mouth to tail, it was easily longer than seven feet, and almost as wide. Its circular mouth opened even wider than its body and was lined with dozens of rows of pointed teeth. It splashed a giant wave when it landed. The water splashed high in the air, igniting the leaves of half a dozen trees. The flames were far away, but he could feel the heat stinging his skin.

He wasn't going to stick around for it to make a second pass. He sprinted and jumped as fast as he could. He glanced over his shoulder as often as possible to keep an eye on it. It was gaining on him. As fast as he was, it was faster. He stopped to prepare himself for another dodge. The fish was nearing the point for him to jump again, but this time the fish didn't jump. In fact, it stopped moving all together. In that split moment of hesitation, Athan saw blood oozing out of the fish's body from several different areas. He hadn't wounded it yet, but it was bleeding. *That's it! That's where all the blood comes from.* They secreted blood into the water to attract prey, like the vipers he had seen before. *How many of these Dragoon Fish are in this lake?* He didn't want to find out. It finally made a move, but it wasn't moving closer. Instead, it just opened its mouth and a large four foot long harpooned shaped tooth flew from its mouth directly at him.

He narrowly missed it and watched as it impaled the trunk of the tree he was on. It was the creature's tongue. The barbed bone on the end was attached to a long fleshy tail that led back into the beast's mouth. He readied his knife; much smaller than it had been when he received it from years of re-sharpening. He tried to slice through its tongue, but it yanked on the tree and the trunk snapped somewhere below the surface. The tree fell towards the Dragoon Fish, bringing Athan along with it.

A metallic taste filled his mouth as he swallowed a gulp of water. The blood blinded him and all he could do was thrash in hope of finding the floating tree trunk and not the fish's stomach. Athan's hand found a hard surface. It was wood. He climbed onto the tree and wiped the blood from his eyes as best he could. He got one eye cleared just in time to see the gaping mouth only feet away from him. He rolled out of the way further down the log. The fish bit down and took half the tree with it in its mouth.

Athan rode what was left of the floating tree until he could reach a branch and climb out of the water. He lost sign of the Dragoon Fish, but more importantly, he had lost his bearings in the battle. He was in the center of the flames now; they were all around him. His skin on the verge of blistering, he scanned the horizon for something familiar. Then he saw it. Lit up from the fire, it was the shore. It was close; once there, he'd be out of the Dragoon Fish's reach and safe. He still didn't know where it had disappeared to though, so he moved carefully. He was fifty feet away. He moved faster. Thirty feet. *Almost there.* Ten feet. He could see dry land.

The fish broke the surface of the lake right in front of him. He was so close to shore but with that beast between them, it might as well have been a mile. It launched its tongue at him again, only this time it was too close for him to dodge. His armor did enough to deflect the razor sharp bone, but it was powerful enough to crack one of his ribs. He fell backwards, catching himself just before falling into the water below. His chest seared with pain, but he had to keep fighting. The fish started reeling its tongue back in, but slowly enough for Athan to be able to grab ahold of it just below the point it met with the boned tip. He held his knife firm, and in one mighty swipe he cleaved through it cleanly.

It quickly retracted what remained and blood shot out of its mouth. It writhed and squirmed before submerging again. It swam in an uneven line back into the center of the lake until it resurfaced about fifty feet back. It floated and turned upside down. It had bled out. It was dead. *There could be more.*

Athan couldn't rest just yet. He made the last drop from his tree onto the shore. He traveled in far enough to make sure he was out of range of anymore Dragoon Fish tongues, and fell to the ground in exhaustion. He would set up the necessary defenses and shelter in a while. For now, he was too tired. His cracked rib caused him sharp pain with each breath. He just needed to rest. He fought it, but it was hardly a fair fight. He passed out.

CHAPTER 13: FEAR THE REAPER

"Fear can be an ally or an enemy. It can cause one to freeze in the face of danger and accelerate defeat, or drive one's spirit to fight for survival and accomplish the seemingly impossible. The fear will always be present, how it's used is the real choice."

—　The Xyrith: 114: 52-54

There was nothing Paladin could do, so he spent the trip studying his enemies: how they operated, their armor and weapons; everything he could whether it seemed important or not. Most of the boys were young, between twelve and seventeen. The one who captured them was the only one past his Fulfillment age. Princess would appreciate that. The rest could still be saved.

Their armor and weapons were fairly well crafted; an added benefit of working as a large group. There was a very clear hierarchy, and they operated efficiently with one another, except for that older boy. The way he carried himself was unlike any of the others. The younger boys feared him more than Paladin did, that was clear. He must have been outside of the chain of command too, because he did whatever he wished and he never said a word to any of the others. He would continuously check the bones of his bandolier, making minute adjustments with spare chemicals from his pack. Paladin had never seen anything like it. It was far more than simple chemistry; he was an Alchemist.

After about four hours, they reached their destination. A team of well-armed men fell from their well hidden positions above. They prepared their weapons, but eased back when the men lifted their left hands. *Archer, I hope you're watching. I hope you know what to do.* The sentries jumped back up into their hiding spots. Even though he knew to look for them now, he still couldn't find them. They had been well trained. That didn't bode well for them.

They moved another hundred feet further when they finally broke into the man-made clearing. It was an expansive camp; huts and tents melded seamlessly with the trees and foliage. The walkways were filled with boys of all ages, from over eighteen to as young as one. They all moved with a purpose. None of them were relaxing or on break, they were either working or rushing off somewhere else; probably to do more work wherever they were headed. He figured with their numbers that this level of activity wouldn't be necessary. They must have been preparing for something.

As they passed through the camp, many of the boys stopped or slowed in their work to watch as they passed. Whether it was the fashion in which they were being brought in or the fact that they had never seen a girl before, he wasn't sure, maybe both. It didn't take long for Alchemist to put a stop to the unwanted crowd. One move for his bandolier and they turned back around real quick.

The cart stopped in front of what had to be the center of the camp. The largest building towered before them. The entourage disbanded and only Alchemist remained. He hopped onto the cart and took the Zed Wolves by the reins. The cart pulled into the structure. It was much darker than he expected and completely empty. The temperature inside dropped drastically and Paladin could see a plume of white with each breath. When he saw the second column of air beside him was much larger and quicker, he knew that Princess was scared. He wanted nothing more in that moment than to be able to tell her everything was going to be alright, even if it was a lie.

They stopped again, only for a moment. When they started moving again, they were moving up. They were on an elevator of some sort. He didn't know how he knew it, but he knew they were going all the way to the top. They were taken alive for a reason. Reaper wanted an audience with them. *What does he want? To gloat about his success despite what I did to him? To express his anger over it? Or does he just want the satisfaction of killing us himself?* Whatever the reason, he didn't like it.

They jolted to a halt. They were there. And there he was. He looked different from the last time he saw him. He was older of course, but there was something else. It was intangible, but it was definitely there. He had a presence about him, like an aura. He sat up straight in his throne and smirked at them. "Not so nice when someone gets the drop on you, now is it?"

If it's a fair fight you want, bring it on! He wished he could get the words out, but the effects still hadn't worn off. Whatever that gas was, it was stronger than ordinary Knixx venom.

He laughed. "Oh yes, I almost forgot. You can't talk. You can't do anything in fact. Brilliant concoction I must say, Alchemist, if you don't mind."

He bowed. "As you wish." The first words he had heard him say this whole time. He pulled out another bone and brought it underneath Paladin's nose. He cracked it and pulled it away quickly. Paladin felt a rush starting in his nose, running throughout his sinuses, and into his brain. It was spreading but as soon as Alchemist pulled it away, the sensation ended abruptly. Everything from the base of his neck and above was back under his control.

He stretched his neck out and loosened his jaw. "How about a rematch then? No more surprises. Just you and me."

Reaper laughed again. "Now why would I want to do that? I hold all of the power here. And besides, I've got something much more fun in store for you." His eyes shifted slightly. Paladin followed his new gaze. He was looking at Princess. "And her."

"You leave her out of this!" He tried to break free, but his body was still frozen. "This is between you and me. She has nothing to do with any of this!"

"She has everything to do with this!" He rose from his throne and Paladin suddenly felt afraid, more afraid than he knew he should be. "I was eight days away from Fulfillment. Eight!" He looked Paladin up and down and smirked. "Gylum has a twisted sense of humor, don't you think? It can't be a coincidence. Here you are, also eight days away. And now, here you are. My wish for vengeance finally at hand."

Paladin was the one laughing now. "Good choice of words." It wasn't the smartest choice antagonizing him like that, but anything to keep his focus away from her. "How is the hand by the way?"

Reaper didn't look angry. In fact, it didn't faze him one bit. "Glad you ask." He tilted his head to the left. "Mage!"

A younger boy stumbled over from the crowd watching in the darkness surrounding them. His arms were full, clutching bushels of strange looking plants and herbs Paladin had never seen before. "Y-yes my Lord?" He stopped by Reaper's side. A pair of deep red roots fell out of his grasp. He shifted quickly a few times trying to think of a way to bend down and pick them up without dropping everything else. He abandoned the idea and looked back up at Reaper. "Oops."

Reaper sighed. "Is everything ready for the infusion?"

He nodded vigorously, dropping a roll of vine in the process. "Yes sir!"

"Then what are you waiting for?" Reaper asked, impatience growing in his throat.

Mage jumped. "Oh, yes, yes, yes." He turned back to where he had come from. "H-hurry, bring it out! Bring everything!"

A pair of Reaper's men heaved out a stone table. On one end, a large mortar and pestle, on the other side, a severed Djinn hand. The clawed scaled hand was still dripping blood. It was fresh. They set the table down in front of Mage and he awkwardly climbed on top of it. He started throwing his plants and herbs into the mortar one or two at a time. He directed the larger boy to grind them very specifically. "Easy now. Slow it down," he would say or, "what are you doing? Look at that! Grind it evenly." He was a new man up there, confident. That was his domain. "Good. Stop! That's good."

"I thought you said it was ready." Reaper had been waiting the whole time Mage was preparing whatever it was he was doing. He didn't look happy.

"It has to be fresh. Hurry. Stand over there." He never took his eyes off of his powdered mixture. From the look on Reaper's face, he didn't appreciate an order from such a puny child but he made his way to the end with the Djinn claw anyway. "Now, for the key ingredient," Mage said, rubbing his hands together in excitement. "Bring them in!"

Paladin knew what it was before it left the shadows. There was only one thing it could be; it gave off an all too familiar blue glow. It wasn't just a single Birthright, but over a dozen of them. The light from the collected mass pierced through the wicker bowl like knives of light. The one holding the bowl brought it over and poured it into the mortar, but before all of them could fall inside, Reaper stopped him. "Wait."

Reaper walked over to the bowl; one Birthright remained. "But my Lord. We have to do it now," Mage pleaded. Reaper picked up the last Birthright and placed it on the table's surface. It rolled off and onto the floor. "What? We need to be exact or it won't work!" Mage was about to lose it.

"We'll just need another one then." Reaper turned to Paladin. "Won't we?" He moved so fast it was as if he glided over to him. He took out his knife. By the look of it, it was the same knife he had used to almost kill Princess that night. He pressed it to Paladin's left hand and dug out his Miner Birthright. He was not gentle about it. When it was in his hand, he leaned in and whispered through gritted teeth into his ear. "Remember this mercy. I've let you keep your hand. It's better than you deserve." He swiftly returned to his spot at the table and threw Paladin's Birthright in as the final one. "Now, proceed."

Mage wasn't going to wait a second longer. He heaved the large pestle himself and dropped it onto the Birthrights. The sound of shattering glass filled the still room. He picked up a bladder of dark liquid by his feet and poured it in as a blue vapor began pouring out over the lip. He started stirring the brew. The faster he stirred, the more vapor spilled out onto the surface of the table, and then onto the floor. He stopped and dove off the table. Before he hit the ground he shouted, "Now!" The two that had originally brought the table in now lifted on one end of the mortar, tipping the contents all across the surface of the table.

The liquid that came out didn't behave like any liquid Paladin had ever seen before. It was a bright luminescent cobalt, and it seemed to be flowing through an invisible channel that curled all across the table. It made its way to the severed beast hand and pooled in a floating sphere around it. Reaper prepared himself and brought his stub up to it. The magical liquid stretched out and took hold of it. "Yes! It's working!" Reaper cried out, followed by a menacing laughter that chilled to the bone. The potion exploded in blinding light, and then infused itself into Reaper's wrist and the hand. It was gone, but what it left behind was unbelievable.

Reaper lifted his left arm, only now there was a hand at the other end. The Djinn's hand. He marveled at it as he moved the clawed fingers around as if they were his own. The scales blended into his own flesh halfway up his forearm. The two were now one. "Finally," he whispered to himself. He turned to Paladin. "Now you see. For years I was so angry. Angry for being stuck here, for losing my future. But don't you see it now? This is my destiny, it always was." He must have only now realized Princess was still paralyzed, because he called Alchemist back. "Could you please? I'd love to hear what she has to say for herself now."

Alchemist freed her with another crack of the bone, but he let her recover completely. She immediately started fighting against her restraints. "You bastard! When I get down from here I'll kill you myself!"

Reaper clapped his hands, being careful not to cut himself with his new razor tipped fingers. "Ah, much more fight in you now. I like it." His chuckle trailed off and his expression went back to stone cold seriousness. "Now, as I was saying, I should really be thanking you. If I had never crossed paths with the two of you, I know the life I'd be living right now. Don't get me wrong, a Councilman Birthright was not a bad one, but this." He threw out his arms to gesture at everything he had accomplished. "Out here I am unparalleled. Out here even the beasts and the trees do my bidding. Out here, I am king!"

"You're nothing but a monster! All you're doing is depriving everyone else what you lost!" she snarled at him.

He came face-to-face with her. "I'm not depriving them anything. I'm giving them everything they could want. They have security here; no more fighting for survival every waking moment. No more fear of falling asleep and dropping their guard. Now it's not perfect yet, but soon when we find it, we'll have everything else." He raised the tip of his new forefinger to her palm. "And then I'll Fulfill my destiny."

She screamed as he pressed into her flesh. Her Birthright fell into his right hand and he examined it. It was the same look of bliss he had the first time he held it in his hands, only this time, Paladin was helpless to stop him. Reaper pulled out a chain from under his robes and set the Birthright inside a vacant pendent. It fit perfectly. He really had been waiting a long time for that moment.

"You're talking about Tuckkar." Paladin guessed, but he tried to sound confident. It made sense. "That's what you're looking for. You talk about being okay with all of this, but all you really want is to go home."

"It's hard to keep the moral of men without the promise of women, and present company excluded, Tuckkar is the only place to find them." Reaper spun around looking at all of his devout followers. "So, yes. I do need to return to Tuckkar, but it is no home to me. The forest is my home now." He turned back to Princess and ran the back of his beast hand along her cheek. "But every king needs his queen."

She quivered away from him, but she had nowhere to go. "You stay away from her!" Paladin fought with every fiber to break free and tear him limb from limb. He could start to feel more of his body freeing itself from its paralysis, mostly in his extremities, but he could do little more than twitch a finger or two.

Reaper walked slowly over to Paladin. "No, you don't get it. I'm not going to force her to do anything." He grabbed Paladin under the chin with his normal hand. "Because when I'm finished with her, she will die for me." Paladin spat in his face. That got his message across as well as any words could have. Reaper whipped his face off smiling. "Lieutenant!"

A very lean looking boy came out and stopped at his side. He was the same age and build as Paladin, only a day older and a few inches taller. "Yes sir?"

"Could you cut our guest here down please? Take her my private quarters. I'll be there shortly." He glared deep into Paladin's eyes as he said it. Paladin wanted to look away. He wanted to turn to Princess and reassure her that everything would be okay; that he would save her from him, but that gaze. It leered into his very soul. As the Lieutenant was dragging her away, he could hear her voice crying out for him. She was begging and pleading, but it sounded muffled. The world outside the small bubble between him and Reaper seemed to be falling away. Soon nothing else existed but the two of them. He felt like even without the paralysis, he would have been unable to move anyway.

Is this what he does to his followers? Is this why they follow him so faithfully? It was so powerful. *But how? How is he doing this?* Pretty soon the questions faded into acceptance. He was falling, and he didn't know how to fight it. He didn't even know if he could. Just as he was about to teeter over the brink, a lifesaving memory flickered into his mind. It was her laugh; Princess's laugh, the most beautiful thing he had ever known in this world. With that one thought, he began to snowball it with more and more. Before long, the world started to rush back to him, and Reaper became the one losing focus. Paladin knew he would never be able to fight that off again, so he prayed that Reaper wouldn't try again. "Is that it? That the best you got?" He tried to hide his exhaustion.

Now Reaper was mad. "It makes no difference. If you don't want to do things the easy way." He backed away and signaled for Alchemist to come back. "We have more entertaining ways to deal with your kind." Alchemist used another one of his chemical weapons on Paladin. This time, the cloud of vapor was a silky silver color. Paladin didn't fight this time. He knew there was no stopping it. His moment would come, but it was not now. His eyelids started feeling heavy, very heavy. He hadn't felt this tired since his first few days with Princess. The sleeping gas started turning dark, or it was his eyes, he wasn't sure. But the last thing he heard was Reaper's voice addressing his people. "Spread the word. I want everyone at Crater Field in the morning. They won't want to miss it." After that, there was nothing but dreams.

CHAPTER 14: INTO THE LION'S DEN

"Any of His gifted children can charge into a battle they have foresight into. The real courage lies in facing the unknown and never blinking an eye. It is only when forced to make split-second reactions, assess danger as it comes, and adapt to sudden changes, that the average warrior rises up and joins the ranks of the exceptional."

– The Xyrith: 111: 4-8

Athan was well rested now. He had taken a day after the near fatal battle with the Dragoon Fish to recover his strength. His map was ruined from the bloody water, but it wouldn't have been too helpful anyway. He knew he was in the general area of the Blue Cave. It was near the lake on the same side as he was on now. It would just be a matter of searching, and compared to what he was used to, this would be nothing.

He salvaged what supplies he could. It wasn't much because the Djeg leaves burned out pretty much everything in his pack. As he started his systematic search of the area, he stocked up on the necessities. The first day of searching yielded little success, so he set up his mobile shelter for the night.

With a lot of bad luck, it took him three days to find the entrance to the cave. The opening was well hidden. He probably would have passed it by if he hadn't noticed the dim blue lights twinkling from within. He crept up to the opening and peered inside. If this was indeed where the ancient Warlock was, there was no telling what else was within.

The inside looked more like the sky than it did a hole in the ground. The sea of darkness was permeated with specks of light like little aquamarine stars. They made it difficult to judge the size of the cavern. Wherever the walls were, they blended into the dark so well he couldn't tell if they were right in front of him or miles away.

Once Athan felt like he had surveyed the area well enough, there was nothing left he could do but continue ahead. He took the first step inside. He was careful; he wasn't even sure there was a floor. Half of him expected that there would be nothing to step onto and he would fall into the abyss; however, his foot did find a solid surface below him. He took a second step, but something was stopping him from crossing the threshold.

It was a strange sensation. There was nothing physically stopping him, but when he tried to pass there was an unseen force pulling back on his waist. His arms, legs, and everything else were unaffected; it was only the one part of him that felt it. After several attempts to overcome it, he took a step back to try and figure out the strange phenomenon.

He examined the edge of the cave's entrance. It was ordinary rock. He chipped away at a corner of it, but found nothing beneath. He considered looking at it differently; not what was causing it, but why it was targeting his waist specifically. He looked down at the knife on his hip. He drew it and examined it. *I wonder. Could it be?* He tried walking into the cave again, only this time, his waist was able to pass through uninhibited. Now the force was pulling on his hand. *It's the knife. It won't let my weapon pass.* He dropped the knife and his hand was freed from the ghostly grasp and he now stood completely inside.

He stood there looking at his weapon lying in the dirt. He considered his options carefully. *I could try to figure a way to counteract the magic field.* It was entirely possible that couldn't be done. *Or I can just continue on ahead; it would be the quickest solution.* The last thing he wanted was to venture into a mysterious cave with nothing to defend himself with, but it was beginning to look like he would have to.

Athan lit up a torch. Now with the flames licking the rocks of the ceiling, he could see the sources of the twinkling lights up close. They were smooth as glass and rounded, like marbles imbedded in the walls. He knew what they were; they were Birthrights. There were thousands of them. He walked further into the cave and there didn't seem to be an end to them. All the way down the cave each and every one was the same, they were blank.

Athan grew more and more nervous with each step further into the cave as the entrance behind him appeared smaller and smaller with distance. At the same time, his hopes that his search was nearing an end were raised. The odds of this being the place he had been looking for, the home of the one responsible for the Birthright, was almost guaranteed at this point. He had no doubts that it wouldn't be easy though. The field at the entrance was sure to be only the beginning.

-O-

His eyes were still closed, but Paladin could hear the roar of thousands of individual voices from every direction. He felt dusty rocks beneath his hands and knees as he eased himself up. He opened his eyes, but was still in a daze from the sleeping gas. As he moved his eyes, the spotted torches that burned in the distance around him grew tails behind them. Everything else blurred into one soup of confusing images.

He took a moment to collect himself. He slowed his breathing and strained to make his eyes focus. It was working, things were starting to take shape. The floor around him bowed upward, gradually at first and then turned sharply upwards. He was at the base of a giant bowl of rock. *Crater Field? I remember him saying something about a Crater Field.* He was alone for hundreds of feet in each direction, but further up the walls of the crater there was a massive crowd huddled among stadium-like seating.

Paladin reached for his blades, but only found air. His weapons weren't the only thing he was missing. His armor too was gone, replaced with a light cloth tunic. He was feeling more helpless than he had in a long time. His only saving grace was he could move now. As long as he could move he stood a chance; however small it may be.

Paladin surveyed the arena, looking for anything of use. The crater was deep and wide, the walls of it were all but vertical for over eighty feet before they met the stands. It was difficult to tell from this distance, but they appeared to be too smooth for climbing bare handed; not that it mattered with the overwhelming audience that would see his every move.

Paladin abandoned looking for an escape route. Now he was watching the crowd. Boys of all ages littered the stands. They were screaming and chanting; beating their swords to shields, pounding their spears into the ground, or just shaking whatever other types of weapons they had into the air. As he spun looking at their uniformed mass, he came across one section that was clearly set apart.

Giant pillars of bone and rope held up a darkened

perch overlooking the field below. Paladin faced it with a strong hatred in his heart. There was no doubt, the ominous architecture spoke for itself. Reaper was in there. The troops quelled the moment Reaper stepped out and onto the balcony of his private skybox. The dim glow of the stolen Birthright around his neck glinted in Paladin's angry eyes. When he spoke, his voice thundered across the immense space at a level he didn't think possible. "Welcome my children! For all of your hard work and dedication to the cause, I have quite the treat for you here today!"

The crowd erupted in applause once again. Paladin stood his ground. If he was to be publicly executed here in front of everybody, he would do so without fear, and not without one hell of a fight. He still had no clue what Reaper had in store for him, but he wished and prayed Reaper would have the stones to do it himself. Nothing would give him more pleasure than to get a rematch with him; whether it would be fair for him or not.

Paladin took his opportunity in a lull of the surrounding cheers. "Where is she? What have you done with her?" He yelled as loud as he could, but his voice paled in comparison; it barely reached the edge of the crater. Some of the boys laughed. The smirk Reaper shot him however, hinted more respect than anything else. As much as they may have hated each other for their own personal reasons, they had to respect one another. Reaper raised his claw and waved out behind him.

The moment the golden hair became visible over the ledge, Paladin's heart rose. She was still alive, but the more she came into view, the more his thoughts turned sour. He had been unconscious for five hours. For five hours she had been alone with Reaper, and the memory of less than five minutes with him still gave him shivers. He had to brace himself for the possibility that the Princess walking out to stand with Reaper was no longer a prisoner, but just one more of his indoctrinated masses. Just thinking it broke his spirit more than anything else Reaper could have put him through.

Princess continued to glide towards the edge of the platform. Her head came into view first. Her beautiful hair was combed up in an elegant braid among small brightly colored stones. Her straight face gave no indication of whether she was able to resist Reaper's influence or not, but so far it wasn't promising. Next, her slender shoulders emerged. They were bare; only thin straps draped over them holding up a Knixx-skin dress. Paladin finally found his saving grace when the dark metal shackles binding her wrists glinted against the dark scales of the gown. *She did it. She resisted. I knew she could.*

Paladin's will was renewed. If she had fought all night, he could fight now. He shouted back up; this time with more confidence. "Just stay there! I will come for you!" This time, almost everyone in the crowd laughed. He still didn't know what was awaiting him in this arena, but he could bet they did. He knew that whatever it would be, no matter how many had stood in his place before and failed, he would not.

With the raising of one hand, Reaper silenced the entirety of his masses. He turned to Princess. "Yesterday marked the beginning of a new era for us all! We gained our first victory against Tuckkar! And believe me when I tell you, it will not be our last!" With this, the stands erupted into thunderous applause. Reaper looked on with immense joy as his followers celebrated. He allowed their cries to die out on their own before continuing. "Now, this victory did not come cheap! Years of blood and sweat! The lives of two of our mighty Hunters! It even cost me my hand!" Reaper paused to give a moment of silence for his people to mourn the loss of their own. "The years we have devoted can never be returned to us! The men we lost will never be returned to us! Even my lost hand was not returned to me!" He raised his beast hand. "It was replaced with an iron fist! An iron fist that I will use to strike down justice upon this moon! Justice against our fathers that sent us out here to fight and die, so we would grow strong for them! But no more! Soon we will use that strength, not for them, but against them!" Again Reaper's minions broke into deafening applause. Paladin watched helpless and small from the center of the field.

Silence fell again and Reaper waved his hand behind him another time. "But those days are still ahead of us! Today we pass judgment upon this boy before you!" Two large thrones rolled into view and stopped at the edge. Reaper took his seat, and a large fifteen year old guard forced Princess into the other. Reaper gazed into Paladin's eyes from atop his perch. "For the crime of murder, I find you guilty! Sentence: five rounds in Crater Field, unarmed! Survive all five rounds and you earn the freedom of a life! Whose life you choose, that is up to you!"

Five rounds? That's all? Without weapons or armor it would be more difficult, but he had faced enough tough situations that he should be more than capable of defeating five rounds of Reaper's forces. It was the fact that it would only save one of them that worried him. *Once I win and free her, then what? Will he honor the deal? Will he give me another five rounds or just kill me out of spite?* Paladin shook the negative thoughts from his mind. He would worry later; for now, he needed one hundred percent concentration. He didn't want to take any chances.

Reaper waited to get his attention again. "And by the way, no one has ever survived past round two." He then stood and outstretched his arms. "Let the first round begin!"

Dust clouds erupted in the near distance all around him. He widened his stance in a defensive position. His hands reached at the empty air where his weapons should have been. It was an instinctive reaction, one that he would have to rid himself of if he wanted to survive. He couldn't afford even a slight hesitation in battle. He would have to be perfect in every move if he wanted to make it out alive.

He collected himself. First, without weapons or armor a defensive position would be useless. Until he knew what he was facing, he couldn't risk an attack either. He rose onto the balls of his feet and prepared himself for a quick evasion. Now whatever came at him he would be ready to dodge, but that wasn't enough. He had to know what was in the arena with him now. It had been minutes since the start of the round and he still hadn't seen any movement. It was too long. The rustling of sand tickled the back of his ears, so he spun around quickly. There was nothing but disturbed dust now. He didn't have anyone to watch his back anymore; another weakness he had allowed to develop without realizing. The past number of months, Princess had been capable of fighting by his side. It had made him soft. It was just another bad habit he would need to break.

If he couldn't see them, he would have to deduce what

he was fighting based on the style in which they hunted. He'd never seen anything hunt in an area as large and flat as the crater which could make it more difficult, but not impossible. It wasn't a Shade; there was enough light emanating from Gylum and its rings to light the field, and nothing to cast a shadow for it to hide this well. Djinn were too large, and Dao Wings wouldn't be at ground level. It could be a pack of Zed Wolves, the tactics fit, but he would have seen the red glow of at least one of their eyes by this point. That left Knixx Vipers.

What was Reaper thinking? Knixx Vipers? If that was all he could muster up for the first round, this would be easier than he thought. Paladin thought back to the puffs of dust. There had been twelve of them in all, so odds were there were twelve vipers. He started to see where things might get tricky, but it was still nothing he couldn't handle. Knixx Vipers couldn't work together, but given everything he had seen in his short time within Reaper's camp that probably wasn't the case here. From what he saw they were working similar to the pack mentality of Zed Wolves, so he would have to incorporate this into his attack plan.

Paladin waited. He wanted them to make the first move. There were still too many unknowns. *If they're trained to work together, what else are they capable of? They already have me surrounded, so what are they waiting for? Are they waiting for me to make the first move too? Why? Do they want to judge my capabilities same as I want to judge theirs? Or do they have a trap set for me just waiting to be sprung?* He weighed his options for a moment. *If it is a trap, what better way to draw them out than setting it off?*

He wasn't going in half-cocked; he just wanted it to look that way. He had all his senses working in overdrive and every muscle in his body primed to twitch even before the first sign of danger. He moved a few feet when he came face-to-face with the first snake. It was coiled back, ready to strike, but waiting. *It's a decoy. I go in for the kill, leaving myself defenseless.* There wouldn't be any behind the decoy; too easy for him to see coming. They wouldn't be able to attack him from directly behind quickly enough either. If they tried, he would hear. That left the possibility of being flanked from the left or right, probably both. More of a hunch than anything else, he was fairly sure they would only have one, two at the most, attack from each side. In a trap like this, less is more. That still left between seven to nine of them unaccounted for. *As soon as their plan falls apart, there's no telling how they'll react.*

The time for planning was over. He knew what he had to do, and he trusted his training and experience enough to know that he could adapt on the fly. He made his move. It lunged at him like it would in any normal circumstance. If it had been a normal situation, Paladin would have caught it just below the base of the skull and wrung its neck, but not this time. While one hand did grab the base of its head, his other grabbed its body halfway down to the tail. He spun it around his body, wrapping himself with the viper. Any other day, this would have been a fatal mistake, however, when four other Knixx Vipers dug their fangs into multiple points along its body like a living shield, it wasn't able to constrict him any longer.

Paladin dropped the paralyzed body of the viper around his legs and stomped on the closest of the flanking snakes, crushing its skull beneath his heel. The other three still had their fangs stuck in the tough tissue of the decoy viper, giving Paladin time to deliver back-to-back open palmed strikes to each one in lightning fast succession. *Five down, seven to go.*

Angry hissing filled his ears from all directions. It was soon drowned out by cheering from the crowd. As much as they wanted to see him die, they wanted a good show beforehand. *I'll give them a show alright.* Paladin tore off a few strips from his tunic, wrapping them tightly around his hands. He bent down and stuck his hand into the open mouth of the first viper, ripping out both of its large fangs. He readied them, one in each hand, in an attack stance. Blood and venom soaked through the thin cloth and dripped down his fingers.

The remaining enemies began launching themselves from their hidden positions. They had lost their element of surprise, and they were starting to break down as a team. The loss of coordination meant they were easy pickings for him now. It took less than a minute for the final viper to fall lifeless at his feet. The fang in his left hand had snapped in half during the battle; it was useless. Paladin discarded it among the carcasses.

More roaring came from the onlookers, only this time

a small percentage of them were booing. It didn't matter though. He wasn't there to entertain. His only goal was survival, for her sake. He returned to the center of the crater and looked defiantly back at Reaper. Then Princess caught his eye. Her hands had been unshackled and tied to each of the throne's arms. She couldn't clap for him, but her glinting white smile and the happy tearing in her bright blue eyes expressed her joy more than anything else she could have done or said.

Reaper rose. He only gave three slow claps. "Very well done! Round one complete!" He closed his eyes and stretched out his arms. "Clear the field!"

Before Paladin could so much as move away from the littered bodies, the ground rumbled beneath his bare feet. The dirt shook around the fallen foes. Paladin jumped out of the way, landing on the ground clear of the tremors. Just as he turned back to see what exactly was happening, he saw the thin tendrils of Grim Wood roots burst out from the surface he had been standing on moments earlier. *What? Where are they coming from? The closest trees are outside the crater.* He looked back at Reaper. He still had his eyes closed, and seemed to be concentrating very hard. Paladin knew that Reaper had an unnatural ability over the natural, but he had no idea it was that strong.

Paladin was still lying on the ground in awe long after the Grim roots had finished their meal, and Reaper had returned to his seat. "Open the gate! Let the second round begin!"

No resting then. What does he have for me now? A small portion of the far wall began to crumble. There was a large gate built into the rock, and it rose slowly with a rumble and the clanking of thick chains. There would not be as much guess work this round, not if he could face his next challenge head on like this. It wasn't necessarily a good thing; whatever this next round lacked in surprise, it would surely be made up in a different area. After all, Reaper had said, 'No one has ever survived past round two.'

The stone door came to an abrupt halt at its apex, casting a dark shadow over the cave beyond. Paladin was still, the only muscles moving were the ones in his hand as his grip tightened on his only shred of defending himself. The stands disappeared from his mind; they didn't matter right now. The dim glow of red eyes were the first to break the blackness. One pair, then a second. Two more, four more, twenty eyes in all. *Ten Zed's? That'll be tough, but shouldn't be a problem.* It was only when the rest of their massive bulks entered the light that he realized what twist this round had. Each wolf had shining silver armor plating covering from the base of the horns, over the body, and down the legs. The armor was expertly crafted. The plates were thick and contoured, enabling maximum protection without limiting movement. The joints overlapped, covering any weak points that would usually reside there.

There wasn't time to strategize. The wolf in front, the Alpha, barked orders. Two wolves darted out of the formation and arched out in opposite directions to flank him from both sides at once. If he stayed where he was, they would converge on him simultaneously and he wouldn't stand a chance. He took off straight for the one to his right. He had no defense; not without armor. From here on out it would be full offense. The wolf lunged when he got close. Paladin jumped higher. He took one of the top horns in one hand and dug his fang into the side of its head. He landed on his feet, but when he tried to pull the makeshift weapon out, it didn't give way. There was no time. The second beast had caught up and was almost on him. As much as he hated to, he had to abandon it.

He released the fang just in time to catch the other wolf by the horns. His toes dug into the course dirt, sliding at least twenty feet before forcing the beast to a halt. The wolf's legs were pushing against the ground in place. It was taking every ounce of his strength to hold it still. He couldn't hold it there forever, not with eight more of its pack right beside them. He quickly changed his momentum and instead of pushing he pulled down, forcing the beast's head straight into the ground. Paladin twisted his hands with all his might, and was satisfied with the sound of vertebrae snapping.

The Alpha snarled with rage for his fallen brothers. It held back keeping two at its side, but let the remaining five brake formation and circle out slowly. They moved around until they had Paladin surrounded. Once again, he took initiative and went on the offensive. He picked one out at random and charged. All five moved to converge on him, but they weren't fast enough. Paladin caught the armor of his target and heaved it above his head before launching it into two of its nearest brothers. *That's three down, but not out.* It would only buy him a short moment, but that was all he needed. He made quick work of the two still standing, snapping both of their necks at the same time with each hand. The others were back on their feet and growling at him. The silvery drool hanging low from their jowls glinted as it dripped, turning the dirt to mud at their feet. It took significantly longer and more energy than he would have liked, but one by one they were bested.

Paladin was tired, dead tired, but there was no way he was going to show it. Not to the Alpha Zed Wolf, not to Reaper, not even to Princess. What he showed them was quite the contrary. He taunted them. The two behind the Alpha started howling, mourning the fallen. It barked at them in anger. They whimpered in fear of him, but shortly got back in line. There was a fire in its eyes; Paladin could tell there was something different about this one. It wasn't just the size. He was at least fifty percent larger than the others. It wasn't just the control he held. The pristine shine of his armor indicated that he hadn't seen any combat since he had been held in the arena, or if he had he did so unscathed. If no one had ever survived past this round he never would have had to, but that didn't mean he was any less experienced. It didn't mean he was any less deadly.

The Alpha dug his feet in deep and sprinted towards him. The two behind him tried to keep up, but they fell behind. He had hoped to save him for last. Taking down a wolf this powerful would take all of his effort in his current state. He charged at the wolf as well, like playing chicken with a carriage. He hoped the beast had been watching him, learning his tactics. He was counting on it. When they were moments from colliding, instead of clashing head on as he had been doing before, he slid to the ground and passed clean underneath its legs. It slid to a halt and turned back around without missing a beat, but it was too late. Paladin was already engaged in fighting the last of his pack.

Paladin used every second of his head-start to finish them both off. It took him too long though. By the time he turned back to face the Alpha, he couldn't dodge him in time.

One of its upper horns caught him in the chest and tossed him a dozen feet into the air. He heard the snap of a rib, but with his level of adrenaline he felt nothing. He considered himself lucky because it was only one rib, and it didn't puncture his lung.

Paladin was in the air long enough for the Alpha to position itself underneath him, ready to snatch him and finish him. He reoriented himself as he fell and caught onto its horns with both hands, keeping himself from falling into the powerful jaws and yellow teeth below. It wasn't much of a victory though. The wolf shook his head hard to the side, causing Paladin to lose his grip and fly halfway across the field. He bounced and rolled through the course dirt for a quarter of a mile before grinding to a stop.

Now he could feel it; the cracked rib, the cuts and bruises, the aches and pains. Every inch of his body hurt, and every fiber of his being begged him to give in and welcome the sweet release of death. But while his body may have been broken, his will was not. He knew despite everything, he must prevail; not for himself, but for her. He rose slowly to his knees. He glanced up to see once more what he was fighting for. She sat there in a golden throne, made prison. Her golden hair littered with jewels shined like a giant star, but most importantly, there was her face. Her beautiful, blemish-free, pale-skinned face. There was no look of worry or fear. It was faith. Faith in him, and in his ability to overcome any obstacle. She had known him all her life. She knew him better than he knew himself. It wasn't that she *believed* he could do it, she *knew* that he was capable of winning.

The Alpha was back. It towered over Paladin, still on his knees. It stopped, almost hesitant to make its final killing blow; as if afraid he still had some fight left in him. It was right to be afraid because when it finally made its strike, Paladin stopped it dead in its tracks. Before the beast even knew what had happened, Paladin rose to his feet, snapped one of its horns off cleanly in two, and plunged it down into the exposed skin of the neck, just before it met the armor. The wolf squirmed, so he pushed harder on the horn until he felt it pierce its heart and other vital organs. It fell in a heap, dark blood oozing out over his hands and onto the ground at his feet. He stumbled backwards away from the massive carcass, as the mixed cheers of the crowd thundered around him.

Paladin fell to his knees. He didn't care anymore about hiding his weakness. If he expected any success for the next three rounds, he would need some rest; even if it was only for a minute. He closed his eyes and focused on controlling his breathing, trying to get his heart rate down while the Grim Woods cleared the playing field again. The sound of branches moving and bending, and meat getting sucked into dirt was very off-putting, but he had nothing to fear from them. Reaper promised his boys a show; he wouldn't pull a cheap shot like that in front of them. "Let the third round begin!" With Reaper's words he opened his eyes, but he remained on the ground. He was going to use every second he could to rest.

The ground trembled into his knees and up throughout his body. He looked into the dark cave that the Zed Wolves had come from. His heart sank when he saw the hulking figure of a Djinn stride into the crater. *Not a Djinn. Without a weapon, how am I supposed to kill a Djinn?* He desperately scanned the area again for something of use. He knew it was in vain, but he didn't know what else to do. He looked back at his new foe and rose to his feet. He took a step forward but froze in fear when a second, even larger Djinn broke into view. *No way. It's impossible.* But it was the third and final one that caused him to fall back down to his knees. They stood side by side by side, claws flexing, wings rising and falling with each deep breath. They roared in unison. Even from a hundred feet away, the rush of hot breath blew his tunic back and filled his nostrils with the rotten stench of their last kill. *I'm so sorry Princess. I tried. I'm sorry.*

CHAPTER 15: REST IS FOR THE WEAK

"Gylum demands strength. Anytime a child of His is not training, fighting, or killing, it is time wasted. Anything short of one hundred percent commitment is an offense to Gylum, and they hold no place within His domain. If one cannot defend oneself, they are worthy of only one thing, and that is death."

- The Xyrith: 66: 100-103

Moryn opened his eyes. He tried at least; his left eye was swollen shut. He wanted to see his left side, but his neck hurt when he tried to turn it. He was still dazed, he couldn't quite remember what had happened to him. Hazy memories started flooding back at random. At first, he was fighting what he was remembering. *No. It's not possible. Rynok would never.* But the longer he fought, the clearer the memories became. The old Rynok, the one he had known long ago, never would have done this to him, but Rynok had changed. Moryn was convinced. In fact, he was surprised it hadn't happened sooner. He was surprised he was left alive at all.

He lifted his arms. They weren't bound. Either Rynok didn't know the extent of his betrayal, or he never expected him to wake up. He pulled needles out of his arms and sat up. It wasn't easy. Over half of his ribs were either cracked or outright shattered. His hip had been dislocated and put back in, and he was pretty sure one of his kidneys had ruptured. He spun around and placed his feet on the cold stone ground.

"What are you doing?" Rynok's voice cried out as he rushed into the room. He caught Moryn before he could hit the ground. His legs couldn't support his weight.

"Get off me. I'm fine." Moryn's voice whistled as he said the words through broken teeth. He knew it was a lie. He was far from fine, but he would never admit to that.

"Please Moryn. How long have we known each other? You are the only true friend I have left. There is no need to pretend with me. You need rest."

The nerve of him. There was no one but Rynok to blame for that. So much of him wanted to come clean and call him out on everything, but now was not the time to show his hand. He had been out for a while but he was fairly certain Athan had not made his return in that time, so he held his tongue. He just nodded his head and let Rynok help him back into the bed.

Teed entered the room. He was a good man, one of Moryn's best guards. Part of him had always wanted to bring him in on the plan to overthrow Rynok, but he had always been one of the few that believed wholeheartedly in Rynok's rule. So as much as he wanted to share his burden now that Garm was gone, he couldn't know for certain where Teed would place his allegiance. Teed reported to Rynok with a sharp snap to attention. "Sir! Search parties Echo and Foxtrot are assembled and ready to move."

Rynok put him at ease. "Very good. Send them out immediately. There is no time to waste."

Teed snapped again. "Yes sir!"

He turned and stared towards the door. Moryn sat up as far as he could comfortably. "Wait. W-what do you mean?" Teed turned back. He was looking nervously between Moryn and Rynok. Moryn decided to go easy on the kid, so he redirected his question to Rynok. "Rynok. What are you up to?"

Rynok looked at him for a moment, then turned slightly to Teed. "A moment, please." He didn't even wait for Rynok to finish his sentence. He was gone in a flash. Rynok slowly walked over and sat on the edge of Moryn's bed. He was a large man, it wasn't comfortable for either of them. "You should not worry yourself. Teed, while he may not be you, is very capable."

"I know he is. I'm the one who trained him, but I'm back now. I need to know what is going on with my men." Anger was filling his voice, but he was unsure how much of it was discernible from pain.

"That is irrelevant right now. You need to rest, you are not fully healed yet." Rynok placed his hand on Moryn's, but Moryn pulled away quickly.

"Have you forgotten why I'm in here? You have no right to…" Moryn hissed.

Rynok stood and raised his hand as if to strike him again, but he didn't. "I think it is you who has forgotten! For too many years Athan has been out there in the Immortal Forest! I asked you for one thing! One thing! To find him, and you have produced nothing!" He walked a few steps away and then turned back. "Teed has done more to find my brother in six days than you ever did in six years."

Moryn's voice was all rage now. Traces of pain could no longer be heard. "Maybe there's nothing to find! You've been so blinded by your hatred for Athan that you are not willing to listen to reason! So what? What's your plan? Send out search parties looking for him? That will never work! You'll be upsetting the natural order of the Pilgrimage, and for what? If he's dead, his bones are long turned to dust. If he's alive, he'll be more than capable of avoiding a small search group." He sat up all the way. "All you'll be doing is wasting time, resources, maybe even lives. Please don't do this," he begged.

Rynok came back over and sat down again. "If you already knew what I was doing, then why did you ask?"

"I was hoping it wasn't true." Moryn lowered his head. "There are a lot of things recently that I've hoped weren't true."

Rynok put his hand gingerly on Moryn's shoulder. "Look. You are still my oldest and most trusted friend, and I value your input. I really do." But then his eyebrows narrowed. "But if you ever question my methods again," his grip tightened to a painful squeeze. "I will not hesitate to finish the job." Rynok's spit flew through the air following each word. He relaxed his death grip and swiftly exited the infirmary.

Moryn fell back down into his lumpy mattress. His now broken collar bone was hardly noticeable among the sea of pain he found himself in. Any shred of hope he had hidden away in the deepest darkest regions for Rynok's soul, the one that he had clung to even after everything else faded away, was finally gone. Until that moment he himself didn't even know it was there, but he could feel it as it left. He watched as the doctor came in and gave him an injection. The pain fell away almost as quickly and the clear liquid entered his bloodstream. His eyelids began to sag lower and lower over his eyes. His heartbeat grew louder, but also slower. Before very long, he slipped back into blissful unconsciousness.

-O-

Princess's heart nearly stopped when she saw the three Djinn make their way across the crater floor. She had been fully confident in his abilities up to this point, but three Djinn? Even she had a hard time believing he could overcome such insurmountable odds. She looked back at Paladin. He was just sitting there on his knees; no hope, no fight left in him. She knew it was because of her that he found the strength he needed to finish the last wolf, and she knew she would have to do it again. The question was how.

The same trick wouldn't work again. Even if he did look back up at her, she couldn't give him something he didn't already have. *Or can I?* She looked around Reaper's loft. *Something. Anything. A weapon. Some armor. Anything.* And then she saw it. In the back behind the small handful of Reaper's guards stood a rack containing Paladin's twin blades. They were sitting out like a trophy on display. *That bastard! He's not even dead yet and you're already acting like you've won.*

She checked her chains. She didn't want to make any noise that would alert them of her intentions, but she had to see how well they would hold up. They were solid. There was no chance she could break free. The only weak spot was a latch on either side, but they were at the base of the throne out of her reach.

She realized she hadn't been watching Paladin for several minutes. She spun back forward; the whole time terrible thoughts of what might have happened to him filled her mind. She was relieved to see him still alive, but that was the only good thing from what she saw. He was flying around the arena. Mostly he was dodging strikes from the three beasts, all working together in perfect horrifying harmony. Every once in a while they would land a blow, causing Paladin to hurl through the air. Despite the beating he was taking, he was still going. He was moving with a level of endurance that he wouldn't be able to maintain for much longer.

He can't hold on forever. If I'm going to do something, I have to do it soon. She looked back at the weapons behind her. She almost looked back at the field when she heard the crowd cheering, but did a double take. There was something different in the back of the room. She scanned the room trying to figure it out. *There's an extra guard.* Before there were only three, but now there were four. The fourth one was easy to distinguish, given that he was easily two feet shorter than any of the others.

The tiny guard moved. He lifted his mask and revealed his face. *The Archer? It is! But what's he doing there? How did he get in here?* He quickly replaced the mask and motioned for her to look away. As her gaze affixed on the battle below once again, her ears stung with a deafening roar from the crowd. Paladin had done the impossible. He stood over one of the Djinn now dead. She had missed how he had done it, but she could clearly see that the beasts own clawed hand was now impaled into its own chest cavity. Princess glanced sideways at Reaper. His jaw tightened and the knuckles on his right hand turned white. He definitely never expected Paladin to survive this long; it made her smile.

It took a minute, but the audience finally fell back to their anticipating silence. The battle waged on, but the burst of momentum he had gained from the first kill faded quickly. Princess gasped when she noticed that the back of his tunic was sopping wet with blood. There were five gaping lacerations running down his back; taking down the first Djinn had cost him dearly.

Suddenly, there was a tug on her chains. She pried her tearing eyes away from Paladin and the arena to find Archer unlatching her restraints. Princess had been so entranced in watching Paladin's fight, she had forgotten all about Archer. He placed his finger over his lips, telling her to keep quiet. She nodded and went back to acting as normal as possible. She calmly turned and looked behind her to where the guards had been before only to find them all collapsed in a heap. Archer must have really taken them by surprise, because he was half the size of even the smallest and she never heard so much as a peep from them. Something else caught her eye. Paladin's blades had been removed from their display.

By the time she looked back down, Archer was gone. She wanted to look around to see where he had gone, but she didn't want to risk catching Reaper's attention. Wherever he had gone, he needed to make his move now. Paladin was in real trouble. The bigger of the Djinn had him in its grasp and he wasn't even struggling; he was on the verge of passing out. The creature spiked him down into the dirt at its feet. The rock cracked outward in a spider web around him.

Just before the heavy cloven foot of the creature came crushing down, it got distracted by the shining glint of Paladin's sword sticking into the dirt beside it. Archer was standing at the edge of the balcony with Paladin's knife still in his hand. He clearly wasn't trying to hide his presence from Reaper any longer. He turned to Reaper and held up the blade. "Show's over."

Reaper looked at Archer, then her, then to his dead guards behind him. When he faced back around, he cracked a smile. "I don't know who you are kid, but trust me…" Reaper flung himself from his throne and picked Archer off his feet by the throat. It happened so fast that if she had blinked she surely would have missed it entirely. "The show is just beginning." Archer winced as the razor sharp claw tightened around his neck, blood slowly dripping down the stolen armor. Reaper pulled him in close, and then threw him out over the edge and into the arena with Paladin.

"No!" She came halfway out of her seat as she yelled after him, but stopped herself. Now that her shackles were unlatched she could have easily gone after him, but she had to remember that Reaper still didn't know. It was an advantage she wasn't ready to reveal just yet. He approached her slowly.

"Oh, don't worry my dear." He ran a bloody claw gently under her chin. "This will be over very shortly." She pulled her head away from him in disgust.

He went back to the edge and looked down. Paladin was standing over the badly mangled bodies of the last two Djinn. With his sword back, he had been able to make quick work of them. Paladin limped his way over to Archer, who had survived the fall, but just barely. "You can keep your weapons for this next round. They won't do you any good anyway." Princess was really worried now. After seeing the first three rounds, she feared what the next two could possibly be if they were going to continue this trend of escalation. She coiled up one of her chains and readied to make her move. "Let the fourth round…" Reaper stopped mid-sentence and fell to the ground. The unlatched end of her shackles fell to the ground with blood and hair clinging to it.

She froze in disbelief. She couldn't believe she got him.

Is he dead? She wondered to herself, but a grunt told her he was just hurt. She looked desperately for a way out, but the only option was the single door at the back of the room which led away from Paladin and into an army of Reaper's troops.

As if just thinking it summoned them, half a dozen of his men broke through the door and circled out around her. Now there really was no escape. She backed away until she nearly slipped off the edge.

"Princess!" Paladin's voice cried out to her. She looked down at him. He was trying to stand as tall and strong as he could for her, but she knew better. He was in terrible pain, but he would be damned if he was going to show it, especially to her. "Jump!"

Is he out of his mind? Archer was much tougher than she was and he nearly died; there was no way she could survive a drop like that.

She conveyed her reluctance through her body language, and Paladin had to have seen it. "Trust me!" Then, even over the incredible distance, all other sounds seemed to fade away and they gazed into each other's eyes and suddenly, it was as if he was right there next to her. "Trust me," he said again softly.

She closed her eyes and stepped out. The rush of wind across her body, the clinking of the chains as they trailed behind, the outraged hollers from the stands as the boys began charging into the crater, none of it mattered to her in that moment. She felt warm strong arms wrap around her and seconds later, a gentle jolt as they landed down together. She opened her eyes to see Paladin's face right above hers. "Told you."

"Um, sorry to break up this little moment you're having, but…" Archer looked around at the thousands of men charging towards them from both sides. They were bottlenecking at the only two points where the stands were low enough for them to jump down safely, but they were still coming in fast. "We should really start moving." He started off for the gate that held the wolves and Djinn. "There's a way out through here."

They were getting close to the entrance of the cavern, and the mob was getting closer to cutting off their exit. It would be close, but they would make it. Princess felt a lance of burning pain race over her forearm. A series of Dao Wing feathers stuck into the ground in front of them, one of them with droplets of her blood on its edge. She was lucky though, it had just been a graze. The bird that fired them swooped over their heads, and came to rest on Alchemist's shoulder. She didn't know how he got there so fast, but he now stood between them and their only way out.

"This one's mine," Paladin hissed. He took his second blade back from Archer and sprinted out ahead. Alchemist pulled out one of his powder-filled bones and readied it, but he was no match for Paladin without the element of surprise. Paladin didn't even wait until he got into striking range. Instead, he threw his knife with enough force to penetrate Alchemist's armor. It struck him right in the chest missing the bone bandolier, but not the heart. The Dao Wing took off abandoning its dead master, but not fast enough to avoid being sliced in half. Paladin then took hold of his knife's hilt buried deep into Alchemist's ribs, grabbed hold of the bandolier, and kicked its owner's lifeless body off his blade in a single, fluid motion. She had seen him kill before, countless times, but this one was different. He killed out of anger and rage; it frightened her a little.

Princess and Archer were seconds from catching up with Paladin again. He was examining Alchemist's bandolier. When they reached him, Archer kept going, but she stopped. "What are you doing? We have to go!" she pleaded.

"It's no use if they just follow us. We have stop them, buy some time." He was rummaging through the bones frantically. "That's it!" He held up a portion with five bones in a row with thinly rolled Djeg leaves sticking out one side. He dipped them through the blood coating his tunic. They ignited and burned slowly downward with sparks flaring outward. He heaved the whole belt up into the air and wrapped it around one of the two thick chains holding the stone door above the cavern's entrance.

"Okay, let's go!" She turned and rushed to catch up with Archer who was impatiently waiting just a few dozen feet ahead.

He faced them, but didn't take a step. She slowed

down and looked at him, but he avoided her gaze. Instead, he looked past her to Archer. "Get her out of here. Keep her safe."

"What?" she asked. She started to head back to him when her arm was caught. It was Archer. He had a tight grip on her elbow and shot a regretful nod back at Paladin. She looked back at him too. He twirled his swords and faced the oncoming army of thousands. "Wait! No!" She fought to run to him, but Archer was too strong. He was pulling her further and further away. "No! Please! You don't have to do this! Come with us!" Tears poured down her face, her words choked up and broken by sobs.

"I'm sorry. I'm so sorry." She could hear it in his voice too, Archer wasn't any happier about this than she was. They were over a hundred feet into the cave when Reaper's troops finally clashed with Paladin. He was outnumbered and out matched, but he slowed them down significantly.

Princess finally freed her arm and took off sprinting back to Paladin. He continued to hold them back long enough for Alchemist's explosives to detonate and rain rock, dust, and ash over the men still inside the arena. The explosion shook the cave, but she didn't stop. One side of the stone door drooped low, but she could still see him fighting. She was only a dozen feet away now. She was going to make it. She didn't know what she would do or how she could help, but it didn't matter. All that mattered was that they would be together; the way it always had been, the way it should be. But seconds later the second chain holding up the other side gave way under the strain. It came crashing down, and the force of the door swinging back down at full speed knocked Princess off her feet.

"No!" She rose to her feet and ran to the sealed door. She pounded her fists against the door until they bled. Archer pulled her away and into his chest. She sobbed and started hitting him. It wasn't his fault, she knew that, but she had to let it out. She knew that if he hadn't stayed, Reaper's army would have got through, but she didn't care. That didn't make it any easier for her to accept.

Archer pulled her out to arm's length and wiped her cheeks. "I'm sorry, but we have to keep moving. They'll be coming around after us any minute now."

She nodded. *There's nothing I can do for him now. He would want us to keep moving, we can't let his sacrifice be in vain.* They ran. Archer led her through the cave; he had scoped it out before he snuck inside. When they reached the forest he uncovered a hidden cache with all of their gear: his regular armor, bow, quiver, her armor, sword, and shield. "But, how did you get these? They took everything when we were captured."

"It wasn't hard. They discarded all of it outside the camp before coming here this morning. Well, everything except his swords. I wondered why, but now…" Archer trailed off when he noticed what she was looking at. She picked up Paladin's chest plate. Archer had brought it there with the rest. He was expecting all of them to make it out alive. Seeing his armor like this, without him in it, tore the wound right back open. Archer put his hand on hers and lowered the chest plate down, out of sight. "You have to suit up. There will be time to mourn later." He held out his hand. There was a chain hanging from whatever was inside his fist. He placed it in her hands. "And don't forget about this."

When he pulled his hand away the sparkling blue glow of her Birthright residing within Reaper's amulet glinted in her eyes. "Y-you… But how?"

"I snagged it off him when he threw me. Hurt like hell, but I'd say it was worth it." He took Paladin's armor from her. "Now, hurry up. We can't stay here."

He tucked the armor away under some roots and then quickly got out of the enemy disguise and into his own clothes. She finished getting dressed before him. She looked down at the familiar design. She had always loved how her armor matched Paladin's, but not anymore. Now it was a constant reminder. When he finished, he waited an extra moment to listen. He said he could hear footsteps coming. His hearing, like Paladin's, was much more attune than hers so she trusted him. He took her by her bandaged left hand, the faint glow of her freshly restored Birthright shone between their fingers, and he led her away from the approaching forces. They disappeared into the forest together.

CHAPTER 16: DON'T PANIC

"The moments before death reveal the true nature of a soul. To face the end of mortality with either courage, or fear in one's heart can make all the difference in the eyes of Gylum. A faithful life can be tarnished, as can an outcast be redeemed."

–   The Xyrith: 144: 79-81

Athan had been walking through the dark cave for hours with nothing but the tiny twinkling stones to keep him company. There were no discernible markings of any kind, just the same eerily dark backdrop for what seemed like forever. He was starting to wonder if he was even moving at all, as if maybe the walls were just moving around him and he was stuck walking in place between them. He decided to test this theory. He broke off one of the stones at random, which was much more difficult without a knife, and chucked it through the cave ahead of him.

The glinting gem flew about a hundred feet and started bouncing along the hard cave floor. After a few more feet, it hit a solid wall and ricocheted off to the left and disappeared. Athan was surprised. *What was that? Where did it go? Around a corner?* After hours traveling through the cave there hadn't been so much as a slight curve in the path, at least none significant enough for him to notice, but now there appeared to be a clear left turn ahead of him. Hopefully it meant that he was nearing his final destination.

Athan rushed ahead, but had to slow down when he got close. Whatever wall was in front of him blended in as well as everything else around him, so he didn't want to run face first into it. He stretched his hand out as he neared where he believed it was. Athan was thankful he did, because even when his hand was touching it he still found it hard to believe it was there. When he looked down to his left, he saw the blue stone he had thrown.

He walked over to it and picked it up. It wasn't until he stood up that he realized he wasn't in the tight confines of the cave anymore, but a decent sized cavern. The only way he was able to tell the difference, was a series of torches lining the walls. Ten feet off the ground and circling the room they illuminated the walls, showing it to be easily fifty feet in diameter. Unlike the rest of the cave he had seen so far, the stone in this room was a bright silver. He was surprised it took him as long as it did to notice the difference.

Athan slowly walked inside, gazing at the wonder of the cavern. The brilliant blue glow behind him was almost completely drowned out by the torches, but the intricacy of the carved out room more than made up for it. Between each torch stood a cylindrical pillar imbedded in the wall curving upwards to a central point, forming a dome out of rock. At the far end was a large slab of rock which was obviously a door, but there were no apparent ways of opening it.

He approached the center of the room, where there stood a pedestal. Upon the pedestal stood a small crystal goblet full of a bright golden liquid. He surveyed the room, but there was nothing else of interest. He stared at it as he passed questioningly around it and over to the large door. He pushed against it. Nothing. He tried wedging his fingers in the cracks to pry it open. Nothing; it wouldn't budge. After a moment, he abandoned his attempts.

He went back to the pedestal. Whatever he needed to do, it was there. He circled around it, hesitant to touch it at first. The type of stone and design was reminiscent of the Altar of Pilgrimage. He reached out his index finger and ran it along the corner. *Smooth as glass.* He proceeded to run both hands up and down feeling for a switch or button, anything that could open the door. Nothing.

There was nothing left to inspect except for the goblet and its luminescent liquid. He took hold of the cup, and carefully raised it from its resting place. Nothing happened, but now he could see that underneath it there was a recessed section in the tabletop where it had been. Suddenly, the cave shook and the recessed plate moved upward. The door started to open as well, but the moment the plate rose further than flush with the surface around it the door slammed shut again.

He replaced the goblet and it lowered back down with the same result, the door started opening until it sank past the point of being flush. The third time around, Athan placed his hand on the moving inner stone and held it in place, and it worked. The door opened all the way revealing a descending stairwell. He took his hand away and made his move towards the door, but as soon as he did it snapped shut with a loud thud; way too fast for him to even consider making a run for it.

He took a moment to consider his options. *The goblet is too heavy to hold it where it needs to be but without it, it raises too high. There's nothing else in here to hold it in place.* Then suddenly it hit him, the cup is only too heavy because it's full. He took the crystal base and tipped it over away from the pedestal, but not a drop passed the rim. He watched as it sloshed around, but it was as if there was an invisible seal over the top of it keeping the drink inside.

Athan set it back down. *This will be more difficult than I thought.* He ran his fingers along the rim and felt nothing, no indication of what held the liquid within. He dipped his hand inside and cupped some of it in his hand. It felt thick and creamy to the touch. He pulled his hand out trying to scoop the liquid out one handful at a time, but as soon as his hand left the cup's interior, the golden drink slid off his hand and remained inside yet again. Athan was getting frustrated now, he was running out of ideas. The only viable option he had yet to try was also the most unthinkable. *I have to drink it. I have to drink it all.*

Athan paced the cavern trying to convince himself that it wasn't necessary, but he already knew it was the only way. *There's no telling what it will do to you. It could kill you.* It was possible, but not likely. He knew that color after all, and from more than just the hair color of his family. The only other place this specific hue was found was in the Yuma Berry. While somewhat rare, most men knew about them, if not from personal experience then through their genetic knowledge. Yuma Berries attract prey with their bright beautiful color and sweet taste, but have a potentially fatal side effect. Their juice causes vivid hallucinations for anywhere from a minute to several hours, depending on the concentration. Whatever this potion was, Yuma juice was certainly a major ingredient, and at this level, he could easily feel the effects for days.

Athan patted his pouches, desperate for any ideas that could spare him. He felt his empty weapon holster and fear crept up on him again. While he had gained a great deal of strength over the years living in the forest again, he still liked the security of having something. He stopped when his hand touched the pocket of Integro roots, and he quickly tugged them out. He separated out a majority of the roots and began grinding them to powder. He added a bit of water to make it into a thick paste. Athan took the small remaining stack and a few Djeg leaves to boil up some Integro tea. When both were ready, he took one last breath to settle his nerves.

He started with the paste. While usually used for external wounds, he put it in his mouth and swished it around until his teeth and tongue were thoroughly coated in the stuff and forced the rest of the thick sludge down his throat. Any protection he could get from the Yuma potion would be worth it. He placed the tea close enough so he could find it and drink it the moment he finished, in case the hallucinations started sooner than he could expect. Now was the time. He lifted the goblet, placed the smooth crystal of the rim to his lips, closed his eyes, and tipped the bottom towards the ceiling.

-O-

Princess placed both hands against a tree as she stopped. She was dripping with sweat, and her breathing was on the brink of wheezing. They had been running nonstop for almost twenty-six hours. Archer had been forcing her to keep moving, and by the looks of him, forcing himself too. He stopped beside her and his face scrunched up in pain. He wiped the sweat from his forehead and eyes. When he opened his eyes again, he looked back the way they had come. She knew what he was about to say; the same thing he had been saying for the past twenty hours when she first started getting winded, but she cut him off before he could get the first word out. "No. We're far enough away now. We need to rest. They won't find us, at least not yet."

Archer looked at her. He had the same defiant face he always did when she would ask him to rest, but it faded after a moment and he turned to lean on a tree. "Ya, I suppose you're right." He unslung a bladder of water and took a quick swig before handing it to her. "But just for a few hours, four, maybe five. If they're using Zeds to track us, they won't be far behind."

She took the water and drank a small mouthful. Under normal circumstances she wouldn't be worried. She had been trained to cover her tracks, even at the speed they had been moving, but this was not a normal circumstance. There was an army hunting them, and they had resources she had never believed could be possible. "Ya, but how? I mean tamed beasts? That paralyzing gas? Have you ever heard of such things?"

Archer held out his hand to get the bladder back. He remained silent except the sound of him gulping down more water. He set it aside and started massaging his legs. He finally answered, "No, never. Whatever this is, nothing like this has ever happened before."

She had already known that, she just didn't want to accept it, but he had just removed all doubt. She tilted her head back and rested it against the tree. She stood there just staring through the branches, getting her breathing and heart rate back to normal. Then it hit her. *The trees!* She didn't want to get her hopes too high, but they were definitely raised. "What about the trees? What can you hear from them?"

He looked at her for a second, still as a rock. He lowered his head. She hoped he was listening to them; it was either that or he was about to tell her something she didn't want to hear. "Whatever... Whatever power that Reaper holds over the forest," he paused again, "they're scared of it, of him. They aren't talking. I'm sorry, I can't tell you anything else."

Her hopes plummeted. "So," she didn't want to finish her question. She didn't want to hear the answer she knew was coming, but a part of her needed to ask. "So you wouldn't know what happened to…"

"No, not for sure, but that doesn't mean he's dead." Archer cut her off before she could finish, and she was glad. Just saying the words would have hurt too much for her to handle. "He's strong, you know that better than anyone."

"But the Reaper. He wanted him dead, and that was before we escaped. What's to stop him now?" Tears were welling up in her eyes.

Archer got up and placed a hand on her shoulder. "The Reaper is still just a man, a man with power yes, but still just a man. Trust me, my father knew…" He hesitated. He was about to mention her father. She really wished he wouldn't but it was too late, the damage had been done. Archer continued trying to be more vague. "People like that, with power like that, only want one thing: more power. By now, he knows that your friend is stronger than anyone else he has under his control. He'll want to try to control that strength before anything."

Part of her was glowing with the thought that Paladin could still be alive but if that was true, then the fate Reaper would have in store for him was worse than death. She jumped to her feet. "If that's true, we can't just abandon him. We have to go back."

Archer caught her arm as she tried to go past him. "No, we are going to respect his dying wish. We're going to get you as far away as possible as fast as possible."

"You don't know he's dead! You said yourself..."

"And you don't know he's alive! I gave him my word I would keep you safe! I will not go back on that." Despite him being a foot shorter than her, she felt like he towered over her. It wasn't in an angry way though. His eyes screamed that he wanted nothing more than to march right back in there by her side, but his honor was overpowering his personal feelings.

She wasn't happy about it, but she backed off. Images of Paladin being beaten and tortured flashed in her mind. Her own memories of the night in Reaper's quarters came back; the power of persuasion he held, the difficulty of fighting off such a force. *Is that what he's going through right now? How long can he fight something like that?* She always knew Paladin was strong in body, but how strong was his mind? She wasn't as certain. She had to stop thinking about it; it hurt too much. "I'm hungry."

Archer was just as glad of the subject change. "I'll go hunt down something for us." He pulled off his bow and held it tight to his chest. "You stay here, set up a small shelter. Keep it as simple as possible, when we move on we can't leave a single trace we were here."

She was already used to thinking like that. For most of the others in the forest, leaving things like a rope or remnants of a fire were not a big deal because the only things hunting them weren't intelligent enough to see things like that. Paladin, however, had taught her differently. He never wanted to risk anyone searching for them, whether their intent was hostel or not. He wanted to keep her Birthright as well hidden as he could. "Ya, I don't suppose there are very many left out here."

Archer was already halfway out of sight when he stopped, and without looking back, "There's nobody left." He glanced up at one of the trees. "That was the last thing I heard before the silence." Then he continued on, disappearing into the forest.

-O-

His eyes opened slowly. *Where am I? How did I...? What happened?* Memories returned slowly, one by one and out of order. They were still hazy, but became clearer with each passing moment. *T-there was an explosion. Did that knock me out? No, no it was far enough away.* He blinked his eyes, all he saw was darkness. *I can't see. Am I blind? What else happened? Think damn it!* He tried to reach his eyes, but his hands were held steadfast by strong thick bands. As he struggled, he felt a slight stabbing in his side. *My rib! I remember breaking it, but I can't remember how. It's almost healed, about a day, or a day and a half?* Soon he realized that there was nothing wrong with his eyes, they were blindfolded.

"He's awake, sir," said a small cracking voice. *Damn it! They know I'm awake. Wait. Where do I know that voice from?*

"Perfect timing." Now this voice he would know anywhere; it was Reaper. "Bring him in."

He braced himself, waiting for someone to grab him and drag him over to where Reaper's voice was coming from, but no one did. Instead, he heard the sound of small shuffling feet scurry away in the other direction. *The Mage. That's whose voice that was. One of the Reaper's henchmen, just like...* The memory of Alchemist triggered, along with the satisfaction that came from plunging a blade through his heart.

Another minute passed without anyone disturbing him, so he returned to focusing on clearing up his clouded memories. *What else happened after the explosion?* Fragments started popping up. The door sagging, then the snap of the second chain. The rush of wind blowing the thick layer of dust that coated the rock up into the air. The shroud covered the thousands in the field. *They were screaming. Why were they screaming? It was just dust. Wait, no. There was something in the dust.* It was from

Alchemist's bandolier. When it exploded all of his mixtures, potions and powders rained down over the men. He remembered running, turning back to see. Plumes of black, grey, green, and gold permeated through the brown dust. Men and boys were getting caught up, suffering from the various effects of Alchemist's concoctions. Some froze, paralyzed in place. Others began melting into red sludge; a terrible sight to see. A few started swatting the air around them as if fighting off an invisible attacker.

Mage's shuffling feet returned. "You called for me, my Lord?" said a new, third voice. There was a cold stillness to it and whoever it belonged to, he was extremely stealthy. If he hadn't spoken, he wouldn't have known he even entered the room. *'He's awake.'* They weren't talking about me. Maybe they don't know I'm awake yet. Maybe they don't care.

"Yes," Reaper replied, "but first, how are you adjusting?"

"Better than I could have ever dreamed. Honestly, I don't know how I ever lived without it."

"Good, very good. Then I have a job for you." The sound of Reaper getting out of his chair and walking towards him carried through the still room. "I've lost something. Something very dear to me." The footsteps got nearer. "I want you to do what you do best. I want you to track it down, and return it to me."

"That shouldn't be a problem my Lord," the stealthy man replied.

"No, I don't suppose it will be." Reaper's feet vibrated through the floor. He was right on top of him now. "But don't underestimate her." Suddenly the world came into view as the blindfold was ripped off his head. Reaper held out his claw, grinding the razor-sharp edges together. "She's already slipped between my fingers twice now." Reaper glared into his eyes. "It won't happen again."

"You're never going to find her. She's gotta be on the other side of the moon by now." Paladin sneered with false confidence. Truth was he knew her well enough to know that she would more than likely do something stupid, like try to rescue him and get herself caught. *She's better off thinking I'm dead.*

Reaper laughed. "Silly boy. It doesn't matter how far

she runs. Do you see that man right there?" Standing over him, right next to Reaper, was a dark figure that must have belonged to the voice he heard; the Tracker Reaper would send after Princess. He stood a miniscule five ten, was very thin like the runners in Tuckkar, and his head was covered in a dark hood.

Paladin looked him up and down. "Ya, what makes this one so special? More cheap tricks? You'll have to do better than that."

Reaper circled around over to the little Mage hiding by the wall. "No, no. No more cheap tricks for you." Reaper ran his index claw under Mage's chin. He shivered, but didn't move any more than that. "You see, I spent a long time with only my one hand, thanks to you of course. A lot longer than was really necessary. Now why do you think that is?" He paused and waited for an answer.

"I don't know," Paladin growled. He didn't want to play into Reaper's games.

"Magic has been lost from this world for a long time. In the Ghor of old it was common practice, relatively easy, but not anymore. It takes patience, creativity, and most of all, trial and error." He flicked his claw and left Mage with nothing more than a tiny bloodless scratch. Mage nearly fainted. Reaper returned his attention to Paladin and Tracker. "So you can understand why I would not be the first in line to volunteer for such a thing."

"You're more of a sick bastard than I thought."

Reaper laughed again. "I doubt that. I have no misconceptions about your feelings towards me; regardless, after several unfortunate failures my clever little Mage finally managed to get it right. He figured out how to harness the magic of the Birthrights and imbue men with traits of beasts."

"So you're saying there are others out there with claws for hands?" Paladin wanted to know what they were up against, but not without a jab of sarcasm.

"Not quite." Reaper motioned to Tracker, and then he proceeded to remove his dark hood. "I don't know how much you know about the anatomy of a Knixx Viper, but they don't see like you or I do. They see heat, anything warm lights up like a Djeg leaf." As soon as the hood came off, he could see it. The man's eyes were solid black with a glint to them. The skin around his eyes blended seamlessly from black scales to pale skin. His nose was flattened, making his face look more snake than man. "So believe me when I say: It doesn't matter how far she runs. He will find her, and he will return her to me."

Paladin was frozen in shock. He couldn't believe what he had just seen. Tracker pulled the hood back over his face and sped out of the room, and despite the speed he was going he didn't make a single sound. No footsteps, no breaths, nothing. Now he was really worried. He had trained her well, and she had Archer with her, but he feared they would be no match for that Tracker.

Reaper must have sensed his doubts. "Don't worry. He will take good care of her. I don't want her harmed any more than you do." The fact that he believed in what he was saying sickened him. "But it will probably take a few days," Reaper leaned in close, a terrifying grin crossing his face. "So we'll just have to find some way to pass the time." Reaper dove into his mind, just as he did the night before the arena. Only this time, it wasn't for a few minutes. This time, it lasted for days.

CHAPTER 17: MAGIC IS AN UNFAIR ADVANTAGE

"In the creation of man, Gylum was so proud and loving of His People, He granted them the use of magic. In time, He grew to regret His choice, for mankind was unwise and abusive in its use. Gylum ripped magic from the people of Ghor, but remnants lingered. He hoped that in time, man would learn to harness it once again, but not repeat the mistakes of their ancestors."

– The Xyrith: 2: 14-17

Princess sat up with a start. She was cold with sweat and panting hard. She had just woken from yet another nightmare. It had been three days since they left Crater Field, and every time she closed her eyes she relived those final moments. She saw Paladin, the only person she had ever known, the person she had never been without, vanish from her life forever. She hadn't had nightmares in years, and it was all thanks to Paladin helping her overcome her fears. With him gone she felt weak again, like she did when she was a child.

She looked over to where Archer was sitting watch. His back was to her, bow at the ready, exactly as he had been when she went to sleep. She got up and walked over to him. "How long was I asleep?"

"Two hours, seventeen minutes. That's a new record." She didn't notice until she got close, but his hands were shaking slightly.

"I can take the next watch. I couldn't sleep anymore even if I tried." She unsheathed her sword. She doubted she would need it, but Archer seemed nervous; she hoped it would help ease him.

"You dreamed about him again. You were talking in your sleep." He still held his weapon steadfast.

She decided to ignore his comment. "You should really get some sleep."

"I slept yesterday." He finally lowered his bow and slung it over his shoulder. "And if you're not sleeping anymore, we should keep moving." He started moving without so much as a glance back.

She chased after him, annoyed. "What? You don't trust me? Don't think I can keep watch?"

Archer laughed, "'Trust'? Not really something people say out here." He stopped and turned to her. His smirk faded and he looked serious. "I 'trust' you just fine, it's not that." He hesitated. He had probably never spoken to another living person; it couldn't have been easy for him to open up, but he did. "It's the silence. I've spent my whole life listening to the forest. I could hear the trees talk to each other, talk to me, guide me to food, water and safety. I would fall asleep to their stories, wake up to their songs. Living that long with something just to lose it, do you have any…" He froze mid-sentence. He must have noticed the tears welling up in her eyes. "I'm so sorry. I didn't mean…"

"No, it's fine." She wiped her eyes. "But I think it's safe to say I know how you feel. He was…"

"You don't have to talk about him. If it hurts too much, I understand." He had regret in his eyes. He must have felt terrible for the way he was talking, as if she couldn't relate, but she had underestimated him also. Although it did hurt, she wanted to help him take his mind off his own loss, even if it was just for a short time.

"No, I want to. I think he would want me to." She took a second to make sure that when she spoke, it wouldn't come out choked up. "He used to tell me stories every night, I couldn't sleep unless he did. He had an older sister so he knew a lot of good books, the ones his father had read to her. On special occasions he would retell the greater battles of his ancestors; those were some of my favorite." A smile broke out across her face. "He had a way of making the terrifying nature of the forest beautiful and magical.
Sometimes he would catch me playing. I'd have a stick and try reliving the battles against imaginary monsters. He would have to remind me of how dangerous it really was. Then it would be straight back to my lessons." Her smile faded away again.

There was an awkward silence that Archer finally broke. "What kind of lessons? Like combat?"

"Not at first, when I was young it was mostly survival. All the stuff usually covered with genetic knowledge. Strengths and weaknesses of all the plant and animal life, shelters and tracking, the Xyrith, that kind of stuff."

"So you believe in the Xyrith?" he asked.

She was caught off guard. She didn't know there was such a thing as not believing. "Of course. Don't you?"

"Well, ya I do, or I did." Archer started mumbling and tripping over his own words. He took a second to shut up and regain his bearings. "It's something I get from my father. He spent his whole life believing every word of the Xyrith with all his heart, but…" He was searching for the right words. "But more recently, after seeing the way the king was ruling, and thinking about what your uncle Athan believed… Your uncle was a smart man, young, but far smarter than anyone else in the cabinet. He believed in science and reasoning over blind faith. He was trying to advance our people, while believing that the Xyrith kept us stunted and fixed in our ways." He paused again. He looked around at the forest before resuming eye contact. "But none of that matters anymore. He was locked away in the dungeon. Things in Tuckkar were getting worse by the day, I couldn't even imagine what it's like there now. And with these children being reaped, so many that never returned. Who knows how long it will take to bounce back from this, if it's even possible."

She opened her mouth to argue with him, but didn't know what she could say. He was right. She had never really thought about it. In another year, she would reach Fulfillment and return to Tuckkar. *What then?* No one knew she was even alive; worse, no one even knew she had ever been born. It wasn't until she met Archer that she knew things in the village were so bad, and that was how it had been over six years ago. *How bad are things now? How bad will they be when I Fulfill? Will there even be a village to return to?* There were just too many variables on top of an already bad situation, but it wasn't something new for her. She had lived her whole life in the dark. "We have hope," she finally said.

"'Hope'? Another word you don't hear very often."

"Think about it. Ghor is a dangerous world; whether you believe in the Xyrith or not, you can't deny that. And yet, after everything, after only the most fierce and deadly creatures have survived this long, we remain. I might not have the same inherent strength or knowledge as you, but what I do know is that we are far stronger than you're giving us credit for. If we can survive the depths of the forest at birth, then by Gylum we can find our way through this crisis."

Archer thought about her words for a moment. "But what you speak of is physical strength. When was the last time our people faced any threat that couldn't be solved with the swing of a sword? Maybe if someone like your uncle Athan was king, we might, and I stress the word *might*, have a chance, but I just don't see it."

"Well then that's what we need to do. When I go back, I'll usurp my father and make sure he's freed."

"It won't be that easy. My father has been trying to accomplish that very thing since before you were born."

"If that's the case, then maybe he's already succeeded. Maybe my uncle is already free."

-O-

Athan opened his eyes. While he knew only four days had passed, the vivid hallucinations he had been suffering from all that time made it seem like years. He was lying on his back, but not on the hard rocky floor of the cavern he was in before. He was on a soft wooden table in a decent sized workshop. If he had to guess, he was still in the same network of caves deep underground, but the walls of the workshop were smooth and flat with even corners. For the first time in four days, what he saw looked real.

Dusty and rotten wooden shelves coated the walls, and every inch of every shelf had been utilized. There were jars with amber liquid surrounding strange unrecognizable plants, organs, or whatever. Boxes of straw and weeds, some housing rocks or gems, others with depressions as if they once did as well. Smaller glass jars of powders and grains, racks of spoons and ladles, cups and bowls of wood or stone in decreasing sizes, all and more lining the shelves in a cluttered yet organized mess.

Something wasn't right though. He couldn't move his hands or feet. Looking at them, there were no restraints, at least none he could see.

"Ah. Waken ye is." A shaky quiet voice rolled through the room, but Athan saw no one.

"Who is that? Who's there? Come out and face me like

a man."

The voice crackled a laugh, interrupted very shortly by a sickly cough. "No, no. Be no need for violence." The man finally stepped out from behind one of the shelves. His back arched higher than his head. His feeble hands with elongated and twisted fingers had an uneasy grip on a thin walking stick. It wasn't much, but it didn't need to hold very much weight. "The visions, gone is them?"

The man spoke very odd making it difficult to understand him, but he got enough of it. "Yes. Given of course that you yourself are not one of them."

"No. If ye visions gone, ye be free." He waved his hand, and Athan's limbs were released from whatever invisible force had been holding him. He sat up and rubbed his wrists, still confused. "Ye were being a danger. Hurt yeself, hurt I ye could of."

"Yes. I wasn't quite myself. Are you… Are you the ancient Warlock?" Athan looked around the room again, looking for a door. There were none.

He laughed that laugh again. "Warlock? Aye. Ancient? That's a new one."

"Did you bring me here?"

"No. Ye stumbled in. Just ye." The Warlock began searching through the jars on a particular section of shelf. He lifted a very thick, broken lens to his white cloudy eyes.

"Do you know why I've come?" Athan rose off the table. He stood a clear two feet over the Warlock. He continued searching through his wares, seemingly uninterested in anything Athan was saying. "I've come for…"

"Knowledge or information. Ye know for which?" He selected a small vial containing a black liquid. He put it back with a shake of his head.

Athan thought for a moment. *What is this? A riddle? A trick of some kind?* "Knowledge."

"Wrong!" The Warlock turned to Athan and the room shuttered around them. "Knowledge not given, earn it ye must. Ye be seeking information, nothing more." He resumed his search along the shelf. It was as if nothing had happened at all. Athan, however, was still very startled.

"Information, then."

"Ah. Thank ye. Difference important." He selected another vial, about the same size only it was filled with a black powder. He examined it with his handheld lens and looked satisfied with it. He took it and started walking away at his crawling pace. "Always two things. One right. One wrong. No more. No less."

"Yes, well anyway, I've come for… information… about the Birthrights. Something's changed. Something's wrong." He followed the ancient Warlock a ways, but had to stop as he moved so slowly.

He chuckled, followed once again with his unhealthy cough. "Aye, always against it I was, but no more options they said."

Athan rushed around to the front of the Warlock. "Wait, I thought you were the one responsible for the Birthright."

"Aye, it's true. Responsible, but not happy about." He stuck out the stick as high as he could lift it, about knee level, and tried to push Athan out of his way. Athan moved for him.

"Then you can undo it? Put things back to how they were before?"

The Warlock reached a cast iron pot and opened the vile in his hand. "Knowledge? Aye. Strength? No." He poured half the bottle inside and then set the rest to the side. He tapped the side of the pot with his hand and the contents began stirring themselves. Slow at first, but soon it was fast enough to cause a vortex nearly reaching the bottom in the center, and almost breaching the rim on the outside.

"But this. You possess a power no one else does. Your magic…"

"Weak. Useless." The mixture began turning a deep blood red, and as it slowed down it became thicker and thicker until it was a sticky sludge. "Why ye wish this?"

"It's an outdated practice. For whatever purpose you created it, it's no longer necessary. We are a strong people. We deserve to be a free people. The Birthright is…"

"A prison," the Warlock finished. "Aye. Too right ye are."

"Then you'll help me? Will you tell me how to end it?" He looked into the bowl. The red sludge was beginning to boil and bubble.

The Warlock snapped his fingers and the potion erupted out of the bowl. Gray smoke plumbed out and coursed through the air as if it had a mind of its own. It wrapped around Athan and forced its way up his nostrils and down his throat, filling his lungs with a burning sensation. He tried to fight it, but it was too late. It already had hold of him completely. He fell to the ground, trying not to breathe in any more of the smoke but reflexively gasped for air. The ancient Warlock leaned over him, a shadowy figure through the smoke. "Aye. But ye won't like it."

-O-

They had a good one day head start over him, but their trail was still glowing with residual heat. Benefit of a cold world. If he hadn't undergone the imbuing process and received the thermal sensors, he never would have been able to track down the escaped girl and her young friend. Even as Reaper's finest Tracker, they were very skilled in concealment.

Tracker had been traveling by Zed Wolf for two days. They must have been traveling extremely fast if he hadn't caught up with them so far. There was a lot about these kids that he didn't quite understand. He had been a part of Reaper's army for a long time, almost from the beginning. In all that time no one outside of them had ever worked together, and only a handful had ever resisted to the point of being thrown into the arena. He wished he had been awake to see it. From the stories going around camp, it was hard to believe anyone could've survived passed round two, let alone the third. He was extremely grateful that the man in question was already captured, and not one of the two he was out there to acquire.

Tracker started thinking about his intended targets. *Is it really true? Am I really tracking down a girl?* That alone raised more questions than he could wrap his mind around. It was better for him to just not think about it. Thinking wasn't in his job description, at least not in that sense. He kicked his heels into the wolf's side to make it pick up the pace. He was getting close, very close, he could feel it. Another hour or two at top speed and he would be right on top of them, and when that happened he had a few surprises in store for them.

Trotting along right behind him was a second wolf. On its back was a fifty pound bag of tools and equipment; everything he would need to set up countless snares and traps. It would also come in handy when trying to transport back two additional bodies. He couldn't remember how many kids he had trapped over the years, he had lost count. Trapping beasts was easy, they were smart, but men were far smarter. There was a strange satisfaction in outsmarting another human, it was intensely addictive.

Just as he predicted, ninety minutes later he was close enough to see their body heat through the foliage. They were moving at a relatively slow pace. *Good.* They had their guard down. He broke off to circle out ahead of them. He took into account their pace, how long it would take him to set his traps, the terrain ahead of them, and the possibility of them altering course. He got to work.

Making and concealing traps was like second nature to him at this point. After ten minutes he already had five staggered snares, two pitfalls, and three nets. He continued to build in a wide arch, until he came around full circle with his targets inside. Now it was just a matter of time.

He stayed low, quiet, and out of sight, just watching as the two bright red and yellow figures neared the first of his pitfalls. Unfortunately, the need to capture them alive made that type of trap much less effective. He lined the bottom with smooth, but uneven rocks. It wouldn't kill them, but there was a decent chance they could twist or snap an ankle. Regardless, they would be hurt and easier to capture, but on guard. It wasn't ideal, but this wasn't his first time. He wasn't worried.

Twenty feet. He would have vengeance for all his fallen brothers soon. Fifteen feet. His beast beneath him crept closer, ready to move in when it was time. Ten feet. They stopped. *What are they doing? Just a few more steps. Come on.*

"Wait a second." The boy with the bow and quiver around his shoulder whispered, just barely loud enough for him to hear.

"What? Did you hear something?" The girl whispered. Her voice was beautiful, unlike anything he had ever heard before. He wished he could see what she looked like, but all he saw was a blob of warm colors. It was probably a good thing; he didn't want to get too distracted.

"No. Nothing. But something's not right." He took a step backwards. "I think we should double back."

Damn it! Guess we have to do this the hard way. He kicked the wolf in the ribs. It took off and pounced in front of them, where their backs now faced his array of traps. If they wouldn't go willingly he'd have to herd them where he wanted them. He pulled out his twin Zed leather whips and unraveled them at his sides. In that short amount of time, Archer had already drawn an arrow.

"Stay behind me!" Archer cried as he released his grip, sending an arrow directly at Tracker's chest. With a crack, the arrow snapped in half and rained to the ground on either side of him. He brought his second whip around and caught the upper limb of Archer's bow. They both had strong holds, so it wasn't until a loud crack along Archer's knuckles gave Tracker the upper hand.

Tracker flung the bow up into the high branches of a nearby tree. "There's no escape. Just come quietly and you won't be harmed." He knew they'd refuse, but he figured he'd try anyway.

"Over my dead body," Princess snarled. She stepped out in front of Archer, sword and shield at the ready. "You made a huge mistake coming after us."

"Very well." He hopped off his wolf. With Archer unarmed, and his only opposition a weak seventeen year old girl. He could do this one handed. "You may have survived this long out here, but this time your precious protector isn't here to save you."

"I don't need him to beat you. I'm stronger than you can imagine." Tracker laughed. "Go get your bow. I'll handle him," she said over her shoulder, but never broke eye contact.

Tracker glanced over to the tree with the bow. One of his snares was right at its base. He was okay with letting Archer go for it. He looked back at Princess. "Well, even if that's true," He grabbed his hood and pulled it back, revealing his snake-like face to her, "then we both underestimated each other."

She took a few startled steps backwards in reaction to his twisted face. She punched a hole through the cover of his pitfall, but she didn't fall in. She looked around frantically, the wind scared out of her from the near drop. "Look out for traps!" she shouted to Archer, but it was too late. Just as he reacted to her, his foot was already being ripped out from underneath him.

"Like I said, no one left to save the little old Princess." He circled around her until her back was to another one of his traps, then he started advancing; unleashing a flurry of lashes, one after the other. He kept her at a decent range making her sword useless. All she could do was block with her shield. She was good and her reflexes were fast, but he was just toying with her. Every few strikes she stepped back trying to brace herself. Exactly what he wanted.

She was only another two steps away from his trap when she stopped moving back. He pushed harder; he had to drive her back. Suddenly, she opened up her guard and let one of his whips wrap her armored forearm. She wrapped it further around her arm and grabbed it tight. She pulled, spun, and using her shield to form a pivot point, yanked the handle right from his hand. *Unexpected.*

She charged at him, another action he never would have guessed from her. He used his only remaining whip to try and slow her advance, but she blocked each strike until she was inside his effective range. He jumped up and into a tree, narrowly escaping her blade. She had him on the defensive. He couldn't believe it. She was right, he had severely underestimated her. However, he knew where all his traps were, he could still lure her into one. It would actually be easier if she was the one on the offensive.

He jumped back to the forest floor a good twenty feet away from her. "Okay, you wanna play? Let's play." He hooked her leg and pulled hard. She fell to her back and he lunged at her, arching high through light branches. He unsheathed a knife from his thigh, usually only used for cutting rope and cord. She pulled her shield up just in time. He landed on it and bounced off back into the trees.

He easily could have landed on his feet, but he was going to keep working his angle. He rolled, making fake grunting noises and stopped at the base of a Niku tree. Princess jumped to her feet and immediately charged, right into another trap. Her eyes darted to the falling counterweight as it shifted. She knew what was going to happen, but he knew it was already too late for her to do anything about it. He rose with a triumphant smile on his face, but lost it almost as quickly.

She swung her sword up and cut the snare before it had even reached its apex and she landed gracefully back on her two feet. *Damn she's good.* He was so caught off by it, he almost forgot to defend himself when she got close. She jabbed with her sword right towards his chest. Tracker gripped his whip with both hands about a foot apart and caught her wrist with the leather like a rope. He twisted and she dropped it with a painful scream. Before he could do anything else from his position, she bashed him in the back of the head with the side of her shield.

Tracker stumbled back a little, dazed but still alert. He could feel the blood dripping down his neck. He spotted her reaching for her sword. He cracked the whip at her outstretched hand, forming a thick laceration below the knuckles. She stepped away from it, her face twisted in pain. The two of them circled each other, neither making the first move. Neither of them had to. After a few steps, she made a wrong step and walked right into yet another one of his traps.

He sat there for a moment watching her struggle. Without her sword there was no way for her to cut herself down. Not for a lack of trying though. She tried using the edge of her shield, and when that failed, she dropped it to save her arm strength. He was getting bored of watching the blood flow to her head. Her head was glowing brighter as her feet and legs grew cooler.

He rolled up his whip and put it back on his hip. He walked over to her slowly, his noseless face even with hers. She swung her fists at him, but he caught them both and held her steadfast. "Easy now. Easy. You look so ungrateful. I would've thought you'd love the chance to be reunited with your knight in shining armor."

"You mean… He's still alive?" She choked the words out.

"Well, he was when I left. Anything's possible. Master was very cross with him after all." Tracker released one of her fists to deliver a blow right to her cheek. She fell limp. She was out cold. "Now let's get you back to where you belong."

CHAPTER 18: KEEP YOUR ENEMIES CLOSER

"More knowledge can be gained from a single foe than from a dozen allies. Only through the study of the Immortal Forest and its beasts can one surely overcome them. The same is true for all under Gylum's watchful eye; however, be wary, that which is being studied can often do the same right back."

‒ The Xyrith: 127: 33-36

Paladin gasped for breath as he regained consciousness. Reaper had given up on trying to break into his mind two days earlier. He realized Paladin would never break, so he had just resorted back to good old fashioned torture. There were never any questions asked. All he would do was talk to him, almost as if they were friends. He took a sick pleasure from it. Paladin was only one more day away from his eighteenth birthday, but without his Birthright he would be stuck there. Stuck with Reaper forever.

"Oh good. Welcome back among the living." Reaper circled around from behind where he was chained up. Paladin had been hanging by his wrists with only the tips of his toes reaching the ground since he returned from the arena. Since Tracker left to recapture Princess and Archer. That was five days ago. Blood, both old and dried as well as fresh, traced tracks down his outstretched arms.

"Cut the small talk. Just get on with it," he said as strongly as he could, but he was beginning to wear down.

"Oh, look at you. So eager. Well, sorry to disappoint, but the fun will have to wait for now." Reaper turned his back. "Lieutenant! Mage! Bring it in!"

The two entered the room from the far side and crossed over to join them. Lieutenant was holding a nice sized wicker box. The dim blue glow indicated it was full of the stolen Birthrights of his people. The Mage was pushing a massive wooden table on wheels. Due to his small stature, he was grunting and panting with exertion. At first, all he could see on the table was the same mortar and pestle the Mage had used to give Reaper his new hand, but it wasn't until the table came to rest right in front of him that he could finally see the whole tabletop. It was covered in a large detailed map of Ghor.

"Just a few more minutes master. Everything is in place," Mage said as soon as he caught his breath.

"I'm aware. Thank you," Reaper responded condescendingly. He turned to his Lieutenant. "Are you ready old friend?"

"Ready as I'll ever be." They extended their forearms out and bashed them against one another. "But are you certain my Lord? I could be of so much more use here. There has to be…"

"There's no one else I trust," Reaper interrupted.

"Of course. I won't let you down." He stood up straighter and opened the box. There were at least a dozen Birthrights inside. They were all different kinds: Blacksmith, Leather Tanner, Wall Guard, Runner, and… Miner.

"You must be asking yourself…" Reaper picked up the Miner Birthright, "who's was it? A brother? A cousin? Was he even related to you at all?" He brought it over and held it by the points of his claws. "What would you give to have your future back?"

Paladin lifted his head up high to face Reaper. "My future has already been decided. I will not steal another's."

"Oh look at you. So noble. So righteous. A white knight in a dark world." He twisted the Birthright in his hand, examining every inch. "Miner. Not the most glorious life one could live." He looked back at Paladin. "I never understood. You had the perfect life right in front of you for years. And I'm sure in your travels you must have come across others; boys with better Birthrights than this. So why not take them? What stopped you from claiming a better life?"

Paladin sagged his head again. "You would never understand." He remembered that night so many years ago. The helpless feeling he had as he knew he was about to die. The anger at himself for falling victim to such a low level beast. The look of disgust on his saviors face as he rejected his Birthright. Those memories had haunted him all his life, but this time was different. There was a strange sense of familiarity. He couldn't quite put his finger on it, but it was nagging at the back of his mind.

Reaper, still holding the Birthright, extended the claw of his pinky finger and placed it under his chin. He eased

Paladin's head up and then grabbed the viper skull hanging around his neck. "After all this time, you still wear it?"

What? How does he know? Paladin had a dozen more questions, but remained defiantly silent.

"If I had known then what I know now, I would've let this little bastard have you."

Reaper turned and walked back to his Lieutenant, but Paladin wasn't focused on anything happening around him. *What? Wait, no. It can't be.* He strained to remember; the first time he had ever intentionally relived that day. Seventeen years was a long time, the face in his head was that of a child, but he tried to imagine how he would look now. The boy that saved him was six years older than he was. Reaper was six years older than he was. "I-it was you."

Reaper threw his hands up. "Alas! He's got it. But in all honesty, I'm not even angry anymore, not like the first four or five years. I mean, just look around you. Look at what I have built here. And it's all thanks to you. So really, I should be thankful."

"Well, you're welcome. I can think of a few ways you could repay me."

Reaper laughed. "Nice try, but I'm not that grateful. I still despise you quite severely." He kept his eyes on Paladin, but tilted his head to Mage. "How are we doing on time?"

"We should really get started. W-we're going to be cutting it close." He looked very timid, as if he had wanted to say something earlier but was afraid to interrupt.

"What are you waiting for then? Get started!" Reaper raised his hand and Mage cowered. He hopped onto the table and started mixing the contents of the mortar. Reaper turned to Lieutenant. "Are you ready? How does it feel?"

"Nothing yet. It's a little strange after so long without it though. It doesn't feel natural anymore." He held out his left hand and stretched out his fingers. A fresh scar across his palm covered a Wall Guard Birthright.

Lieutenant handed the box of Birthrights off to Reaper. He carried it over to Mage, who was now ready to add them to his potion. He hesitated before dumping them in. "Last chance. We have one too many. Any of them could be yours if you want them." Paladin responded with silence. "As you wish." He poured the whole box in. The only Birthrights remaining were the one still in his grasp, and the Lieutenants. "They're going to have questions." He was directing the question towards Lieutenant.

The sound of breaking glass echoed through the room as Mage lifted and dropped the pestle repeatedly. "I know the cover story forwards and backwards. I'd never reveal our plans. You can trust me."

Mage tossed it aside and began stirring again. "The water! Add it now!" he commanded. Reaper emptied a bladder into the bowl. "Good. Good."

"I know my friend. You more than anyone."

Mage stirred faster and faster. He looked up at them. "Almost. Bring me the cup." Reaper did as he was asked. The cup was rather large, about a liter and a half, and carved out of wood. Mage snatched the cup and dipped it into the potion.

"Wait. I feel something," Lieutenant said, holding his arms out and looking over his own body.

"Now! He must drink it now!" Mage cried. Reaper rushed the cup over to Lieutenant and he chugged it immediately.

The cup landed on the ground, accompanied by droplets of blood. After Reaper had given him the potion, he had plunged his claw deep into the side of his abdomen. "But I can't take any chances."

A bright blue light started growing up and around his left arm. Lieutenant staggered backwards, the blood pouring much faster once Reaper pulled his arm back. "B-but, my Lord. Why?" Once the light reached his shoulder, it branched out. It extended down his torso, across his chest, and up his neck. He was still alive; he had to be for the process to work, but the wound was clearly fatal. He would survive the Fulfillment only to bleed out on the other side. The light burned through the dark room like no other light Paladin had ever seen before.

"It's nothing personal. I just couldn't wait any longer. I'm sure you understand." Mage was frozen in shock. Reaper turned on him violently. "What are you waiting for?" Mage snapped out of it and moved around to the outside of the table. With all his might, he lifted one end of the large stone bowl, tipping the remaining half of the liquid across the tabletop. The liquid was black as it came out, but as it coursed its way over every line on the parchment it began to glow the same hue as the Lieutenant.

Nothing remained but a twinkling bright light in the shape of a human. It fell to its knees and before it could finish falling to the ground, winked out of existence. It was over. His Fulfillment was complete. His body, seconds from death, was now somewhere inside the village of Tuckkar.

"Did it work?" Reaper asked Mage. Paladin had been so busy watching the Fulfillment, he hadn't noticed what was happening on the table right next to him.

"I think so, yes. I think it worked!" Mage squealed in excitement. The map that had once rested flat on the surface was now spinning a foot above, folded in on itself making a perfect sphere. The glowing potion receded from the ink lines and started to swirl around the miniature representation of Ghor. The spiral grew smaller and smaller as its center moved slowly in a straight line across the surface. "Just a few more seconds! Then we'll have it!" he said, even more bubbly.

"That's how you're going to find Tuckkar? You're tracking his Fulfillment, aren't you?" Paladin already knew the answer.

The mystical spiral was almost gone; moments away from becoming a single point. Reaper kept his eyes intensely fixed on it. "I've had my men search every inch of this moon looking for it. Wherever it's hiding, this will find it once and for all." A single flashing blue point finally came to rest three quarters of the way north, disappearing and reappearing as the rotation took it around and around. "Where is that? How far from here? What direction is it?" Reaper was spitting out the questions with more and more aggression each time.

Mage examined the globe. He would study the point, following it as it passed each time, and examine the other landmarks between each revolution. "No, this can't be right. It can't," he whispered to himself, but they both heard.

"Speak up boy! Tell me where it is now or I'll…" Reaper raised his claw.

"It's here! It's here!" he cowered. "It's right here."

"I can see that you idiot! Where in relation to the camp?"

"That's what I mean. Where we are right now, the camp. That's where it's showing us." There was a silence as Reaper contemplated what was just said. Mage was shaking behind the map, hoping it would protect him from Reaper if he decided to take it out on him.

"That's impossible. Let me see." Reaper stormed over to the table and examined it for himself.

"See, there's the Altar to the west. And Crater Field to the south. I'm telling you, it's saying that your Lieutenant is right here."

Reaper flipped the table six feet high and twenty feet across the room. The map lost its magic and fell in a heap nearby. "Then it was something wrong with your spell!" he raged at Mage where he landed after being flown from the table.

"No! No! My calculations were precise! It couldn't be…" He slinked away, still on his back.

"Was it? So tell me: was that light supposed to be flashing like that? Huh?" He demanded.

"Well, um, not really. But that doesn't mean…" His sentence was cut off when Reaper lifted him over his head by one of his ankles. "Please! We'll just try again! Please! It's not an exact science! You know that. Please!" Tears ran up his forehead as he dangled upside down.

Reaper looked over at Paladin, then back to Mage. "You have one more chance. Double, triple, quadruple check your numbers if you have to." He dropped him to the ground hard and stalked over to Paladin, picking up the Miner Birthright he dropped earlier as he crossed the room. He sliced open his palm and stuffed the Birthright into Paladin's hand. "You have until tomorrow." The words were meant for Mage, but the meaning was meant for him. In twenty-seven hours, fourteen minutes, and forty-three seconds, his fate would be the same as Lieutenant's.

-O-

Moryn limped down the hallway to his office, the one Teed undoubtedly occupied now that he had taken over his duties. He really shouldn't have been up and walking around.

He wasn't finished healing yet, not by a mile, but he would rather die than lay around as his men were sent on such a pointless mission that could result in any number of deaths. He knew his men were strong; that wasn't his worry. It was what he didn't know that scared him. Something was definitely happening out in the forest and until they knew what, the forest was the last place he wanted his men to be.

He reached the office and went inside. Teed was sitting in Moryn's chair signing a messy stack of parchment. He looked stressed. He was a good kid, but all of this was way over his head. Teed was very jumpy. He dropped his pen when he saw Moryn at the door. "W-what are you doing up? The doctor said…"

"That I'll be fine," he finished for him, "just a little sooner than he thought." Moryn closed the door behind him. He used that moment with his face away from Teed to momentarily allow his pain to show. After letting it out, he was fine to face him again. "So, where are we on finding Athan?"

Teed stood up. "Here, would you like to sit?"

"I'm fine damn it!" Moryn took a second to calm himself. He just hated being treated like he was weak. "Now, last I heard you said something about teams Foxtrot and Echo."

Teed looked around the room nervously as if looking for something to change the subject, but found nothing. "Yes. They were sent out to the northeast and southwest last night."

"Ah, I see. I assume you've already got teams out there," he said, digging for information.

"Yes, four of them, one searching each direction. We sent them out about two weeks ago, but they are starting to run thin."

"Right, so you plan to send two more, cover the rest? How many men is each team made of anyway?" This was where he grew a little nervous. He knew exactly how many guards he had. He knew each and every one of them personally. Most importantly, he knew how many wall guards he could lose while still maintaining a safe perimeter, and it wasn't very many.

"They're six man teams."

"What? You're telling me, thirty-six of my men are out

searching the forest for one man? That's nearly a third of our ranks. And you want to send out another twelve? How am I supposed to defend our walls without my men?" Moryn was furious. Even though the words were coming from Teed, he knew who was really behind this. Rynok had crossed the line so many times in so many ways, but this was in a class all of its own. "What did he say to make you agree to this? What did he promise you?"

Teed looked at the door. He had a nervous look on his face ever since Moryn arrived, but it just increased tenfold. "After… After what happened to you."

"You mean after what he did to me."

"Yes, after that," he paused. "After that, he put Fadek in charge." He lowered his head mournfully.

Moryn already knew the rest somehow, but he asked anyway. "Where's Fadek now? What happened Teed?"

"He refused to assemble the search parties. He knew you would never agree to it." His head was still down.

"What happened to him Teed? I need to know."

He lifted his head, his eyes glossy with the tears he held back. "He's dead sir. He wasn't as strong as you. He didn't survive what the king did to him."

Moryn's knees felt weak. Fadek was one of his strongest and finest soldiers. "I think I'll take that seat now." He got halfway to the chair when the door opened behind him.

"I need a status update on…" Rynok entered, but stopped halfway through the door when he spotted Moryn. "Did not expect to see you here."

"Rynok. I'm glad you're here." A blatant lie. "I must speak with you about your search. Please just hear me out."

Rynok entered the rest of the room and slammed the door. "Why do you insist on debating this? Athan is a threat to this entire village!"

"You are a threat to this village!" He regretted it as soon as it left his lips, but it was too late to take it back now. He just had to salvage it as best he could. "You're leaving our wall defenseless. If he makes it past our men, if anything does, we won't stand a chance. We need them on the wall, where they have the upper hand and the numbers." Even he was surprised at how well he turned that around.

Rynok's expression told another story. He looked as if Moryn had just spat in his face. "I would sooner watch all of Tuckkar burn than allow Athan another day to gain his strength. As long as he lives, we are all in danger."

"You're supposed to hold the wellbeing of the village above all else. How can you stand there and defend your personal vendetta over the lives of your people?" Moryn's blood boiled. He didn't care about holding his tongue anymore.

"How can you defend that treasonous scum?" Rynok was hovering inches over Moryn's face now.

"I'm not defending anyone!" Moryn replied, standing as straight as ever. Whatever pain he might have been in earlier was eliminated by rage.

"That is not what I am hearing. How do I know you have not been covering for Athan all along? It would certainly explain your absolute failure in finding him."

He was right, wholly and completely. Nothing would have given Moryn more satisfaction than to confess everything right then and there. To see the look on Rynok's face as his last remaining *friend* betrayed him, just like all the others, but it still wasn't the time. "You really have lost your mind. Out of every soul in the world, I would be the last to betray you. You know this." He knew better but prayed Rynok was still blind enough to believe it was true.

Rynok didn't speak. He stood there, still nose to nose with Moryn breathing heavily; his breath rancid. After a moment, the door to the office flew open. Burmin, one of Rynok's councilmen, leaned inside panting heavily. "There you are my Lord."

"Not now! I'm in the middle of something." Rynok snarled at him and then returned to face Moryn.

"But sir! There's been a Fulfillment."

All three of them dropped their expressions for a shared look of complete shock.

"What?" They said in unison.

"Over at Milla's hut. I don't know anything else, but word is spreading like wildfire."

Moryn looked at Teed. "Milla? He's one of ours."

"We have to go!" Teed dropped everything and rushed to the door.

Moryn went to follow him, but Rynok stopped him. "We are not done here. Teed!" He stopped dead in his tracks and turned back around. "Take Moryn back to the infirmary. Make sure someone stays with him this time." Rynok grabbed Moryn by the elbow hard. "I will be by to visit you shortly. We can resume out little talk there."

Teed reluctantly came over and took hold of Moryn. "I'm sorry," he whispered in his ear.

"It's okay," he whispered back. "You're damn right we'll finish this." He watched Rynok leave the room, following closely behind Burmin to go find out more about the Fulfillment; the first one in years. Then he left and headed for the infirmary with Teed. After learning of Fadek's fate, he wasn't going to do anything to put anyone else on Rynok's bad side if he could help it.

CHAPTER 19: THINGS ARE NOT ALWAYS AS THEY SEEM

"Gylum's knowledge of the universe is absolute. Lies, trickery, the unknown, these only exist for man. Whereas a child is given physical strength freely, mental strength must be taken. It is a choice all must make: to seek out the truth for oneself, or to accept the lies delivered by those wishing to perpetuate ignorance."

– The Xyrith: 68: 14-17

Athan took a deep breath, and for the first time since the Warlock's potion attacked him, it was clear and clean. Something was wrong though, he wasn't in the cave anymore. He was back in Tuckkar, in the throne room of the castle. Strangers stood around him facing the throne, where a slender man with the same golden hair as himself sat in deep thought. *What? Who are these people? I haven't been away that long.*

Athan paced around the group of men. He finally noticed that each and every one of them were talking and arguing, but no sound reached his ears. That wasn't the only thing off about them. They didn't seem to care at all that he was there. He waved his hand in front of one man's face, and still nothing. It was as if he wasn't even there at all.

"Silence!" bellowed the man in the throne. It was the only sound Athan had heard since he mysteriously showed up in the room. Even though he hadn't been able to hear the others, he knew they had ceased their arguing, because all eyes were on the man in the throne and all mouths were shut. "There will be no more debating, arguing, or discussion. We are enacting the Birthright, and that's that. Now bring me the Warlock! This war has gone long enough!"

Athan had a million questions but before he could even try to say anything, the room fell around him. He was alone in darkness for a long moment. It reminded him of the way he felt in the dungeon when he was dead. Thankfully, it ended as soon as it came. The forest came rushing up from far below his feet. He stood on the edge of a clearing, it looked like the same place where he knew the Altar of Pilgrimage to be but it wasn't there. The clearing was empty except a handful of men.

"Are you sure this will work my Lord?" Another unknown man said to the blonde man from the throne room. "I mean, we've never seen anything like this before." The man's hands didn't have a single callous. It was as if he had never fought a day in his life.

"I've had my best men working on it. It will work. It has to. We're getting our people back," he said softly.

Time began speeding up. All the men left, returned, and traversed the clearing in fast forward. Gradually, the eleven stone pillars grew as men labored away beneath them. Athan had his suspicions, but now he knew for certain. He was reliving memories of the past. The events he was watching were from the Ghor of old. The blonde man had to be a former King, one of his own ancestors; the one who ordered the Birthright into existence. He was still unclear as to why it was necessary, but he remembered hearing the word *war* and that was enough.

Once the pillars were complete, time slowed back to normal. The ancient king stood with his back to its edge, several dozen soldiers before him. "The bridge is complete. Find our people and find the Warlock. We can't enact the final stage without him. Most importantly, stay safe out there." The soldiers filed into the clearing through the largest gap; the same one that the road to and from Tuckkar ran through in present day. As soon as they entered, they rounded the nearest pillar and disappeared behind it. Dozens of men crossed behind it, but never came out the other side. Athan circled around himself where he saw them marching into the forest, but when he returned to the same spot he was in before, he saw nothing.

He was thoroughly confused. He rubbed his eyes trying to stop them from playing tricks on him. He was struggling to find a rational scientific explanation for it. Before he could investigate further, time jumped again. The Altar appeared in its place, the king and a handful of men around it. "It's done my Lord. The Altar is linked."

"And you're sure it will work?" The king replied.

"There's only one way to know for certain." He glanced down the road. A bright chariot slid to a halt just past the stone pillars and a man exited the driver's seat. He went to the back and helped out a pregnant woman. She was breathing heavily; she was in labor.

"This isn't right! Something's wrong! It shouldn't feel like this!" the woman cried.

"It's alright honey. That's just the pull of the Altar. Everything will be alright." He soothed and kissed the woman. It must have been his wife. He rubbed her belly before she got on top of the smooth stone. "Everything will be alright. You're going to be the first, my son. You'll be a pioneer."

With the help of her driver, she started pushing. The king and his cabinet walked away, giving her space. "Are you sure this is necessary my Lord? He'll grow up without magic. How will he survive without magic?" One cabinet member asked, the others nodded in agreement.

"The forest will make him strong, he will have no need for magic now."

"But he'll become king someday. Surely we can make an exception for…"

"There will be no exceptions. That's the whole point. Magic is too dangerous a weapon to wield. You all should know this more than most. You saw what one man can do. The destruction that he caused." The king paused to look at his wife. His son was almost with him. He turned back to his men. "We're creating a safer world for our children."

"By allowing them to grow up in the wild?" The same man interjected.

"By sparing them from the dangers caused from having too much power."

"So because of one man you're depriving every generation after us of their birthright?"

"I think you're forgetting that one man nearly ended all life as we know it. He split the world in half. He massacred whole cities. So yes. I will do whatever it takes to keep that from happening again." He looked back to the Altar. The driver was holding a small baby boy. The boy jumped out of the man's arms and walked towards his father. "I'm not depriving them of anything. I'm simply giving them a new Birthright. Allowing them to grow up independent of the influence of others. To build character from strength. Protecting them from knowing the loss of a loved one before they're capable of coping."

The newborn turned and sprinted off into the forest. As soon as he disappeared, the world fell out around Athan once again. When he opened his eyes, he was back on the table in the Warlock's cave.

"I assume questions?" the Warlock asked. He was cleaning up the mixing bowl he used to brew the potion. "Given ye answers, but more questions ye have, no?"

Athan shot up to a sitting position. "That was a lot to take in. Everything I've read. Everything I thought I knew. Not even close."

"Aye. Information ye had, not knowledge. Important difference. I told ye." The Warlock made his way back to Athan. "First question?"

He had to think. There were so many, he wasn't sure which one he want to ask first. The most unnerving came to mind. "The pillars around the Altar. There was something off about it. The king called it a bridge or something."

"Aye. The man they spoke of. Recall the 'splitting of the world' part?" Athan nodded. The Warlock pointed to a globe of Ghor in the corner "See. This Ghor as it looked in my time. Something missing, see?"

Athan got up and went over to it. He spun it around. It was very similar to the ancient map he had pieced together years ago. He had it memorized fairly well, but his was missing pieces. Eventually he noticed it. "Crater Field. It's not here."

"Precisely. Observe." He waved his hand and mumbled some incomprehensible ancient language. The surface of the globe sprung to life. The miniature trees were moving as if wind was blowing between them, and animals were moving among them. A long slender arm grew from the globe's base in a large arch. When it reached out to about Athan's eyelevel, a small irregularly shaped ball formed on the end. It spun as the arm shrank, pulling the ball towards the surface of the globe.

"Is that a meteor?" Athan asked as he watched.

"Close to. Before, just a rock in Gylum's rings. Harmless, until summoned. Ye remember the one spoken of? Aye, him. A single city, there, then not there." The representation of the meteor made impact with Ghor, and the surface erupted. As the shockwave spread outward, the globe cracked in half. The two sides parted, and retook their size and shape. Now there were two exact replicas of Ghor, side by side, each coated in dust and ash.

"What just happened? I don't understand."

"Not literal. Figurative representation." The Warlock stepped around the back of the spheres. "Impact so severe, shook the very depths of our realm. Fractured it. Two realms created. One on top of another. Half of all things in one. Other in other. Only two places bridge the realms. One made of man." He showed as the forest was cleared and the pillars were erected on one of the globes. Once it was finished it lit up like a flare. The same clearing with the same pillars appeared on the second globe once the light faded. "Location where parents return from way they came, back to their realm. Child goes other way, not way they came, enter other realm. Realm of the Pilgrimage."

As crazy as it sounded, it would account for the fact that he had never crossed paths with any children on Pilgrimage, a fact that had always bothered him. Athan stumbled a few steps backwards and rested his weight on the table. He had learned so much in such a short amount of time. So many things that were millions of miles away from anything that he'd thought he'd known before. "How is that possible?"

"All things possible. Rarely easy, but possible."

Athan rubbed his face with both hands. He stared blankly at a random spot on the wall. "What am I to do? I'm so lost."

The Warlock walked over to him and placed his boney hand on Athan's. "New information not need to mean new goal. Why ye come here? What ye looking for?"

He looked at the old man's face. The blank eyes glaring into his. "Um, I wanted to end the Birthright. But now…"

"Aye! Then end the Birthright ye shall. Ye have seen it. The source of its magic."

He wasn't quite sure what he meant. *I've seen it? I saw a lot. The source? What's the source?* "The Altar?"

"Aye."

"If the Altar is destroyed, the connection will be broken?"

"Aye. Stillbirths, Pilgrimage. All gone. Return to

normal."

Athan returned to the twin globes. He looked at the tiny Altar on each one. The maps had caught up to present day. The wear and tear of time showed on the stone pillars, but the Altar remained pristine. "But how? It can't be that easy. It must be protected or something."

"Your journey now. No more help I can give ye. Rest I must. Go ye must." He started easing himself down. There was what Athan had assumed was a rug beneath him, but it must have been the Warlock's bed. "No strength left. Not much for having guests." He chuckled sickly.

"Wait. No. Just one last thing. I just need this one last thing," Athan pleaded, but it was too late. The Warlock was already snoring. He didn't even bother trying any harder. He took a sweeping glance around the room. "How do I even get out of this place," he whispered to himself. No sooner one of the walls split open revealing an inclining corridor. *Well, that was easier than I thought.*

He grabbed for his map, but remembered it wasn't there. Before leaving he searched the room for another one. He found one rolled up behind the globe which had resumed back to its ancient and still surface. He left for the door, but just as he passed its threshold, he doubled back. A glinting piece of metal caught his eye. Garm's knife, as worn down and nearly dull as it had been when he abandoned it outside, was resting on a table a few feet away. *How did this get here?* He didn't really care, all he cared about was that he had it back. It was all he had left to remember his old friend and mentor by. He tucked it in the back of his belt and continued through the door.

It was certainly a different path than the one he used to enter. He never passed the chamber with the goblet, or the tunnel that had led to it. Instead, it was a straight, simple, boring climb all the way to the surface. *Why couldn't I have found this tunnel first?*

Athan unrolled the new map. He would have to find out exactly where he exited, it could've been anywhere. He had been traveling underground for quite some time with no reference point for direction. It wasn't easy; even though it was complete, it was still severely outdated. There were no signs of Tuckkar, or any other ancient cities his vision mentioned had existed. Tuckkar could easily be on the exact opposite side of Ghor for all he knew.

After an hour of walking without incident, Athan froze. There was a noise up ahead. A rustling sound, the sound of a struggle. *What is it? A Zed Wolf killing a Knixx Viper? A Djinn killing a Zed Wolf?* There was only one way to know for sure. Athan crept around the last remaining tree blocking his view from the sound. Something was off, if it had been a fight, the victor would have eaten and left quickly, but the sound continued. It sounded familiar, but it couldn't be, not after what he had just learned. But it was.

A small child, no older than six months, stood over a dead Knixx Viper. He was skinning it for food, for clothing, it didn't really matter, because it should've been impossible. *How can this be? Children grow up in a separate realm.* It still sounded crazy to him, even more so when he found himself saying it to himself, but he still knew that the Warlock wasn't lying about it.

The child turned and spotted Athan. He readied his little blade, prepared to defend his kill. It wasn't until Athan stepped out the rest of the way that the child realized how outmatched he truly was. The boy snarled and turned to leave. He wasn't running from fear, it was simply the smart thing to do.

Athan took advantage, he took the viper and cooked it for dinner. He wasn't going to just let the Grim Woods have it, they could have the bones. As he ate he replayed the conversation with the Warlock over and over in his mind looking for something to explain what happened. *Wait! He said, 'Only two places bridge the realms.' If one of those places is the clearing around the Altar 'One made of man,' then the other must be natural. But what could cause a natural bridge?*

He checked his map first but without Crater Field on it, it was no good to test his theory. He closed his eyes. He pictured the maps of Ghor from the cave as best as he could recall. He tried to remember where it had been. When he had it clear in his mind, he traced an imaginary line through the planet to the point on the other side. He had an extremely good memory, but he was pushing it quite a bit. If he was right, it was about fifty or so miles north of Blood Lake. About the same distance and direction that the Blue Cave had taken him.

It was marginally off, but since all he had was guesswork and estimation he was satisfied. *The Warlock's cave is the second bridge.* Just like the children that embark on Pilgrimage, he had not left the same way he had gone in. Just like them, he was now on the other side.

-O-

Paladin had got his first good night's sleep in over a week. He guessed Reaper had enough in store for him later that day to make up for the time lost. Either that, or Reaper needed some sleep himself. He was still strung up so it wasn't perfect, but it was bearable.

The room was empty. They must have all left for the night. If he was the first one awake, he wouldn't let this extra time go to waste. He checked his chains. They were too thick, even for him. He surveyed the area, checking for anything that could help him escape. There wasn't much. He was on the top story of the massive tower, nothing above him but a circular catwalk. The catwalk didn't look incredibly strong, and it was the only thing supporting his chains.

His feet could barely reach the floor, so it was difficult for him to gain leverage to pull. He lifted himself up with his arms and dropped down hard. The supports of the catwalk groaned, but didn't give way. He repeated it over and over. The shackles cut deeper into his wrists and his arms were weak from lack of blood flow, but he persisted. He knew he had to. He only had thirty minutes left until his Fulfillment, and there was no way Reaper would let that slip his mind.

"Having fun?" Reaper's voice carried through the room, but Paladin saw no one. "How's that working for you?"

He stopped and just hung there. "Can you blame me for trying?"

Reaper finally stepped into view. He came around from behind Paladin. He wondered how long he had been standing there, watching him. "You'd be surprised what I can do."

"Why don't you cut me down and beat me in a fair fight? Let's see if you can do that." Paladin chuckled weakly.

"It would be anything but fair."

"That's what you think. Without your army, without

your beasts, what are you? I've defeated them, I can defeat you."

Reaper smirked. "Not all of them. Get the lights!" he shouted over his shoulder. Every light shut off in a sweeping wave around the room. Everything was completely pitch black for only a moment. Then, eight spotlights illuminated a large circle around them. Reaper and his men stepped into the ring of light. Only Paladin remained in darkness. "Beastmaster! Bring it in!" A door opened. The creaking of wheels rolled in. "You remember, in the arena? I said there were five rounds." A large cart rolled out, a ninth spotlight following it as it rolled. The box atop shuttered and shook fiercely. The cart stood six feet tall and five feet across. "Say hello to round four." Eerie sounds came from the sealed wood, sounds he hadn't heard in a long time, but sounds he would never forget.

"A Shade?" *How's that possible?* Shades weren't like other beasts in the forest. If he tamed one, then he truly would be unstoppable. Then he realized it was in a cage, and it was fighting to be free. It must not have been under his control like the others, just a captive like him. "But how?"

"Shades don't do very well in the light. Once you know that, it's simply a matter of herding it wherever you wish." Reaper walked up to the box, still shaking violently, and placed his hand on it. "Then it's simply a matter of keeping the light on."

"So, what's your plan then? Are you going to track me to Tuckkar, or feed me to that thing? Huh? Cause you can't do both, and you're running out of time to make up your mind." Only fifteen minutes remained, they both knew that.

"That may be true, but I realized something as I slept last night. The thought of passing up a chance to see you torn to pieces by my little pet here is just too unbearable." Mage brought his cart out into the light, all his ingredients at the ready. "But I'm finished underestimating you. Should you somehow survive, however unlikely, then I shall have the best of both worlds."

"You're a madman! But it makes no difference. You may have me, but you will never lay your hands on her. Never!" As if Gylum Himself was mocking him, the door flew open and Tracker walked through not a second later. There were two prisoners tied up behind him.

No! It's impossible! Please! No! But it was. He saw Archer, his hands bound behind his back, and Tracker pulling him by a thick cable. Princess was on a wagon he was dragging behind him. Her hands and legs were all bound together, lying on her stomach, head in a dark bag. Maybe it was easier not seeing her face, her bright blue eyes, or golden blonde hair. He had longed to see her again, but not like this. Never like this.

"Ah, thank you! You have brought me my prize." Reaper walked over to greet Tracker proudly. "They didn't give you too much trouble, did they?" Tracker shook his head and returned the greeting with a padded forearm. Reaper walked over to her and pet her head through the bag. "It's okay my dear. You're back where you belong."

As Reaper put his filthy hands all over her, Tracker walked over to Paladin. He was prepared to hear the snake-faced bastard gloat or rub his triumph it in his face, but remained silent. The only noises that came from him were footsteps. *Wait. There's something different.* Tracker was shorter than he remembered. When he got close, Paladin could swear he saw a dim shimmer of gold from beneath the hood. *No. It can't be. Could it?* He looked away, back to Reaper. "That Shade of yours! The longer you keep it, the more likely it'll get loose on you, and the angrier it'll be when it does."

Reaper looked away from Princess. "Don't you worry about that. Unlike you, I know how to take care of my own." He grabbed a handful of the bag covering her head.

"I wouldn't be so sure of that," Paladin whispered low. The bag came off, but instead of the Princess's beautiful face, the scaly Tracker was underneath.

"Now!" Princess shouted as she removed Tracker's hood, drawing her weapons from under his cloak that had disguised her so well.

"What?" Reaper had the biggest look of shock Paladin had ever seen. Archer took his bow from the wagon, his hands not as tightly bound as they were all led to believe.

"The lights!" she cried to Archer. He picked up immediately, aiming for one after the other. Princess struck the chains above his hands, but they were too strong for her blade.

"After them! Get them now!" Reaper shouted, covered

in darkness as broken glass rained over him. Archer swept the room quickly, only two lights remained. He missed the next one's bulb, but hit the support around it. The light shifted to cover Paladin and Princess, where she killed three of Reaper's men in quick succession. "Stop them!" he yelled again.

Archer flew into the light to join Paladin. His next arrow was already drawn towards the last one, the one keeping the Shade in its corporeal form. The only thing keeping it in its cage. "Stop this." He released his drawstring.

As the light died, a deafening roar covered the room. It wasn't just the sound echoing around them, the Shade was moving. As it circled around them in their protective column of light, terrified screams followed. Each scream was quickly silenced with a soft rattle. The roar died down, but the cries of men and boys continued, accompanied by the light ringing of metal weapons falling to the wooden floor.

"Get the lights! Turn them back on! Now!" Reaper's voice broke over everything else. He was still alive, but even he couldn't kill a Shade. The dim lights that had filled the room before Reaper's Beastmaster brought in the Shade started coming back to life in the same succession as they went out before. When they caught up to the Shade it was enough to force it back to its corporeal form, but not bright enough to frighten it away. It was still ripping through Reaper's troops like butter. When Reaper was the only living soul left outside the safety of the spotlight, the Shade set its empty eyes on him. It swept a zigzag across the bloodstained floor to him. *This is it. I'll finally be done with him.*

It leaped at him, but he caught it right out of the air. His claw was dug deep inside the bulk of its mass. It struggled against him, lashing out with tendrils of shadow, leaving cuts in his clothes and lacerations along his exposed skin. He clenched his fist and there was a loud popping noise. The Shade turned into a vortex that in less than a second, swirled into a single point at the heart, right where Reaper's fist was. The point grew a bright white and then disappeared as quickly as it had come. Reaper had just killed a Shade. "You're going to pay for that," he snarled at Archer.

"Run." Paladin commanded.

"Not until you're…" Princess interjected with a

longing in her eyes. The look said she never wanted to leave him again, even for a second.

"Just go!" He didn't want to beg, so he let his eyes do it for him. She nodded and turned. He switched to Archer. "Just get her out of here." He nodded. The same nod he had seen each time he had asked the same question. The same nod he knew he could trust.

"Berserker!" Reaper roared. No later, the door and wall surrounding it blasted to splinters. The smoke cleared as Archer and Princess reached opposite sides of the room. Paladin could feel the floorboards rock beneath his toes. A hulking figure started to emerge from the smoke. *A Djinn? They can handle a Djinn.* But what appeared was not what he expected at all. Its legs ended in feet, not hooves, they were covered in the same scales as the upper body. Not only that but everything, every inch of its humanoid body, was covered in scales. In fact, it was human.

"Yes master." His deep voice reverberated, shaking the very walls.

"Kill the little one. The girl is mine." He acted like Paladin wasn't even there. As long as he was chained up, he might as well not have been. But it didn't matter, in four more minutes he wouldn't be.

They both charged towards their respective targets. Archer tried to help by firing at Reaper, but Berserker blocked them. He didn't bother to catch them or swat them down, he simply allowed them to bounce off his armor-hard skin. Archer knew he couldn't do much to fight the Berserker, so he quickly scaled the wall and went up to the rafters. Three more minutes.

Berserker jumped, just short of him. He landed hard, cracking the floor. "Be careful you fool. You'll bring this whole place down." Reaper was taking his sweet time stalking Princess. "Let him be for now. I'll deal with him soon enough. Just keep those arrows back."

Berserker grunted up at Archer. He wanted to crush him, it was in his eyes, but he obeyed his orders. Two minutes left.

"Do something!" Princess cried out. She hid her fear well, but Paladin knew her voice well enough to detect the deception.

Archer shot another arrow, just as ineffective. "Like what? I'm out of ideas here!"

Reaper finally made his move. She narrowly dodged and rolled further away. "Shoot the chains! Do something!"

Archer did, but the arrow was just as useless as her sword had been before. "They're too thick! It's not working!"

One minute left. He started to feel the tingle. His left palm warmed. "It's time! I'm about to go, but I can't! Not now!"

Princess turned to him, completely ignoring her attackers. "What? No! You have to go."

"Look out!" Paladin shouted. She looked, but caught a blow to the jaw from Reaper. "No!" He turned back to Archer, the light of his Birthright glowing brighter. "Do it! Nothing else matters right now! Just do it!" The light crawled down his bloody arm. Twenty seconds longer, and he would be gone forever. He would have a home back in Tuckkar, the ultimate dream for anyone, but not if it meant leaving her to die.

Archer drew the last arrow of the quiver on his back, after that he would be mostly useless until he could reach another one on the wagon. "Are you sure?" He looked over to Princess crawling backwards on the ground, Reaper looming over her. The colossal Berserker at his side.

Paladin's sightline became blocked by the light of his Fulfillment. He was fading away, he could feel the magic pulling him out of the room. "Now!"

He couldn't see anything but blinding light. Even with his eyes closed, all around and throughout him was pure magical energy. His hearing was unaffected though, and he heard a whistle in the air. The sound of wood, steel, and feather flying through air. It was a direct hit! The point of the arrowhead hit his Birthright, and the wood slid through his palm, stopping a foot and a half down, clean through his hand. Shattering glass fell to the floor behind him.

He brought his hand down to his chest and gripped it tightly. *Wait! My hands?* His eyes were still closed, but he knew he had been chained up in Reaper's camp. *Was Archer too late? Am I in Tuckkar? I was supposed to protect her!*

"What?" It was Reaper's voice. "How is that possible?" Paladin finally opened his eyes. He was still in the same spot as before, still in Reaper's tower, but his hands were free. The chains swung above him fully intact. The shackles were still fastened tight, but empty. If he was in the middle of the teleportation process, it might have just been enough for him to phase out of the iron. He couldn't think of another way. Truthfully, it didn't matter, all that did was he was still with Princess, and now he was free.

CHAPTER 20: DETERMINATION AND CONFRONTATION

"In the Ghor of old, there were hundreds of animal species. As time drew on, the weaker ones died off, and the stronger became stronger. One of the last, one of the weakest, was near extinction when, suddenly, backed into a corner with no place left to go, they rose up and overcame the fiercest of the beasts. From that day on, mankind was never weak again, for whenever the odds are against them, they prevail."

– The Xyrith: 9: 32-35

Moryn paced around the infirmary. Three more weeks had passed and still no word from Rynok or anyone, for that matter. The only people he had seen in all that time were a handful of patients all of which were too afraid to speak to him, and three of his royal guards that had been posted outside the door the whole time. They were his men and he knew them well, but these particular three held higher loyalty to Rynok than they did Moryn.

Most of his nerves about Rynok finding out about his betrayal, about being tortured and killed, had slowly been shoved out of the way by his curiosity. *The first Fulfillment in years. Who was it? Does he know what's happening out there in the forest?* He needed to talk to him. It was all he could think about.

The sound of shifting armor rang from the hall. The guards had snapped to attention, which meant only one thing. "At ease." Rynok's voice followed. Moryn moved to the door to confront him as soon as he entered, arms crossed over his chest. "Ah! Good to see you up and about old friend."

"Cut the small talk. What do you know?" He was being very offensive. He knew it and he didn't care.

"Right. Straight to business, then? You always did work too hard." Moryn just readjusted his folded arms, showing him just how impatient he was. Rynok seemed to catch it that time. "Fine, your way then." He snapped his fingers, calling one of his guards into the room. Under different circumstances he would have easily been able to take him out, but when they were in that armor, they were nearly unstoppable. "Why don't you have a seat?"

"I'll stand." But it hadn't been a question. Rynok shot

a look to his guard and he forced Moryn to sit down on the bed behind him.

"That's better." Rynok sat down across from him. "Now, I have a few questions for you. I suggest you answer as honestly as you can."

Moryn had some questions of his own. "Who Fulfilled? What did he say about the forest? What's happening out there?"

"You do not ask the questions here, I do. Now let us go back a ways. To right before Garm's betrayal."

"That doesn't sound like a question to me." His tactics had made a complete one-eighty. Instead of doing whatever he could to keep peace, he was doing anything and everything short of an outright confession to piss him off.

It was working, Rynok's knuckles were turning white. "The question is: In all your time with him, did he do or say anything that indicated his plan? You were one of his close friends after all."

"I'm a patriot. If someone, anyone, wanted to threaten the safety of Tuckkar or its people, then I would do everything I could to stop them. No matter how close they were, no matter how high a position they held." *And I'm not talking about Garm.*

"Are you certain? There is no reason to cover for him."

"I know. Have you forgotten who killed him?" It still hurt to think about it let alone to say it out loud, but he hid it away from the surface. "Because I haven't."

"Sometimes sacrifices need to be made. He had already been caught. Maybe you killed him to keep him quiet."

"Why are we even discussing this? You've clearly already made up your mind. You think I'm guilty, of what I'm not sure, but you've convinced yourself so entirely it doesn't matter what I say or do, you will never change your mind." He knew Rynok well enough. He had lost his mind, he saw enemies and conspiracy's everywhere. Albeit, most of the time he was right, he never had actual proof. All he had was pure paranoia.

"Is that a confession?"

Moryn stood up with rage. "How thick are you? No!

I'm not confessing because I've done nothing wrong! Why don't you just skip ahead and kill me already? Put me out of the misery of having to put up with this campaign of yours."

The guard extended his blades, but Rynok held out his hand having him stand down. "I'm not going to kill you Moryn, you don't get off that easy." He stood up and walked around Moryn. "Have you ever visited the dungeon? Taken a good look at the men that have been down there for a year? Two? Ten?"

Moryn feared the dungeon. Rynok knew that, he knew better than anyone. It was one of the main reasons Garm was the one that actually freed Athan, rather than him. He had nearly had a panic attack the last time he had gone down there. "You know I have."

"Then you're familiar with the effect it has on the mind? How even the most strong-willed minds can deteriorate. Our species was never meant to be confined."

The guard rested his gauntleted hand on Moryn's shoulder. He stood up, he was done fighting. "Was it not your brother that reminded you? We've been contained within the boarder walls of Tuckkar for millennia. You're just changing one prison for another and quite frankly, I've grown tired of this one."

"Get him out of my sight." Rynok turned his back on him. Moryn stood, almost turned to leave, but stopped.

"What of the boy? The Filfilled?" Rynok didn't respond. "I'll be locked away. What's the harm?"

He still didn't turn, but he answered. "Dead. Bled out in his father's arms."

"Did he say anything?"

"Yes, 'He's coming. They're all coming.'" With that, he turned and left. The guard didn't have to lay a hand on him again, he had accepted his fate willingly. The boy's last words rang in his ears. *'He'? Could it be Athan?* It didn't sound right, not from what he had told him the last time they met in the forest. *'They're all coming'? It had to be the children. If they aren't dead, then what?* The closer he got to the dungeon door, the less the questions plagued him. After so long fighting alone and so long stressed to the breaking point, he was tired. He was getting too old for this young man's world. All he wanted was some rest. If it had to be at the bottom of a dark damp hole, then so be it. But he would never see Rynok again. That thought alone brought a smile to his worn old face.

-O-

Paladin rose from the floor. He pulled the arrow out of his palm, but he felt no pain, just a need for vengeance. He snapped it in half, the metal tip in one hand and the razor feathered back in the other. They would have to do, his weapons were nowhere in sight. "Get away from her!"

Reaper laughed, but he swore there was a glimmer of fear in his eyes. "And here I was thinking I wouldn't get to kill you myself." He turned to his Berserker. "Keep him busy till I'm done with her."

"Yes boss." He charged Paladin. He was fast, far faster than his size would have led on. He caught him by the throat and slammed him right through the wooden floor.

Reaper's voice followed amidst the debris. "Let the fifth round begin!"

They crashed through three more floors before Paladin got the upper hand. He rode down another five stories on Berserker's back, stabbing him as they fell. The arrow shattered to pieces against his iron-hard scales. He kicked off and crashed hard into the next level below him. Berserker continued through, but Paladin only left a cracked dent. He took a moment to collect himself, but three cracked ribs made it tough to breath.

He rolled over to look in the Berserker-sized hole. Paladin must have been on the second floor now, because Berserker was lying in his own crater covered in dark soil. He jumped to his feet like the fall hadn't hurt one bit.

An arrow flew over his shoulder and hit Berserker square in the chest, but it turned to dust and splinters on impact. "I'm coming!" It was Archer. He was jumping down floors at a time, firing from midair.

"No! Go back! Protect the Princess!" The ground shook beneath him. He looked down to find Berserker smashing through the supports for his level. Archer landed right next to him and fired another barrage. They were just as ineffective.

The ground was about to give way. There was only one support beam left, and Berserker had his malicious eyes zeroed in on it. Paladin grabbed Archer and threw him up to the third level. He jumped to follow, but his timing was off by a millisecond. The floor fell and his jump was too short, but he still managed to catch a hand on a jagged floorboard.

"Get down here!" Berserker cried in protest. He climbed the piles of debris and headed for the support columns further out.

Paladin's handhold snapped and he started to fall, but then a hand reached over the edge and caught him. "I got you." Archer said, strain in his voice. "Climb up."

Archer started pulling him up. He had the strength, but the floor beneath him didn't. The wood was creaking and cracking underneath where he was lying. "Stop. It won't hold. Just go. Get back up there. Get back to her."

"I'm not letting you go. Not with that thing down there."

He looked down. Berserker reached another column and took it out with a crushing blow. The whole building sank on that side. "He's going to bring this whole place down. I have to stop him. And you have to save her."

Archer's eyes darted back and forth between him and the ground floor. Tears welled in his eyes. "I can't."

"Yes you can. Just let go."

"No, not that. I can't protect her." Tears fell past him. "I'm not strong. I'm not like you." Paladin was confused. He had fought by Archer's side, he knew how strong he was. He had survived against Reaper's forces longer than anyone else. He infiltrated the arena single-handedly. Archer sniffed and continued. "You saved my life. Those Hunters should have killed me. I was weak. I am weak. I don't deserve to still be alive."

And there it was. It hit him like a knife in the heart. The last time he heard those words they were coming out of his mouth. He had spent so much time dwelling on the past, he never bothered to look at the present. Archer was right about one thing: Paladin was strong now. He may have been weak at one point but not anymore, and if he could do it so could

Archer. "Look at me. You were weak before, so what? So was I once. But look at what you've done. You marched straight into an enemy's home not once, but twice. You've saved me more times now than I have you. You are one of the strongest and bravest people I've ever known." The building shook again, and the floor crumbled even more. The building couldn't take much more abuse. He had to get down there. Archer had to believe what he was saying.

Archer looked in his eyes for a long moment. Paladin couldn't tell what he was thinking. He didn't know if it worked, if he believed. Archer finally spoke, soft and still. "Kick his ass."

"You too." They released and Paladin plummeted. As he fell, he watched Archer jump up until he was out of view. He landed on his feet surrounded by piles of smashed wood and iron. Berserker was thirty feet ahead, ready to smash another support. "That's enough!" He stopped. When he turned around, a scaly grin was on his dark green face.

He moved towards Paladin slowly. "You really disappointed me back in Crater Field. As soon as I saw you fight, I knew you would be the one. The one to finally make it to me." The heaps of rubble gave way under his feet as he walked. He cracked his knuckles, the sound of scales grinding together drowning out the pops. "But your tiny friend had to come and ruin it for me." He stopped five feet in front of him.

"Well, now's your chance. What were the rules again? Unarmed?"

"Not that it matters. I'm no Djinn. I don't have a weak spot. I'm faster, stronger, smarter. What do you have?"

Paladin looked up the hole leading all the way back up to the top floor. The floor where Princess was facing Reaper. *I'll be there soon.* He glared at Berserker. "Something worth fighting for." He lunged. No weapons. No armor. Just his bare hands and pure strength of will.

-O-

Princess watched helplessly as Berserker plunged Paladin into the floor and disappeared into it. "Let the fifth round begin!" Reaper shouted down after him. He turned to her, an evil smirk on his face. "Looks like it's just you and me."

She looked around. Archer was gone. Only the lifeless victims of the Shade remained. She really was alone with him. She tried to control her fear the way Paladin had taught her, the way the Xyrith said to, but she couldn't. She faked confidence. "Good. No one to get in the way."

"Stop your lies. I can see into your mind. You're riddled with fear. All the training in the world can't compete with my strength. It's a gift from Gylum Himself. Face it, you're out matched. It's not too late. Join me and you can be a queen."

She loosened her grip on her shield, just enough to get a glimpse of her Birthright. It hid behind an old dirty bandage, but the light permeated through. She held it up to him. "I already am." This time her confidence was real, and he knew it.

She swung first. He dodged and attacked back, but she was ready with her shield. The dance lasted for a while, going back and forth and around the hole in the floor. For the first time, she didn't see a single hint of surprise in an opponent's eyes. Usually, they underestimated her skill, and it would provide enough for her to gain the upper hand. Not from Reaper though. He knew her, he had been in her mind. He was still in her mind, even as they fought. It felt like she was fighting Paladin.

His attacks seemed slow and paced. It was like he was just toying with her. She was growing tired, and the longer they battled the less he was holding back. Soon she wasn't able to get in any blows. She was too focused on defense and staying alive. He laughed as he battered away. She started seeing shavings off her shield rain down around her feet. "Give up little girl. You don't have to die this night."

"But you do!" She blasted him with her shield and knocked him back. She followed quickly with a frenzy of sword swings. He blocked most of them with his claw, but one sliced down his right arm. Blood dripped down her blade. He looked at it, and rage burned in his eyes.

"So be it. You had your chance." He swung his claw wide. She blocked it, but felt a sharp pain in her arm. He had dug his fingers into the face of her shield. Four of his razor-tipped fingers protruded though, the fifth imbedded into her forearm. He yanked hard, and the leather strap snapped off her arm. He tossed the shield aside and down the hole.

She grabbed her left arm, a deep puncture wound right between the bones. Reaper showed her the blood on his claw. "How good are you without something to hide behind? No white knight to save you. Your Archer has abandoned you. Even your last line of defense, your little shield, all gone."

"You're wrong. My friends don't abandon me." She nodded her head over his shoulder. His smile faded and an arrow shot out the front of his chest, just left of his heart. Archer landed on the far side of the hole in the floor, already placing his next arrow in the drawstring.

"Hope I didn't keep you waiting too long." He muttered with a wink. He shot again, but Reaper turned and caught it out of the air. Archer's face turned cold.

Reaper threw the arrow like a knife, hitting Archer in the shoulder. "No!" she yelled. She swung at him again, but he sidestepped and kicked her in the gut. All the wind rushed out of her lungs. She fell in a heap coughing for air.

Reaper turned and jumped over to Archer. He pulled the arrow out of his chest from the front, the whole thing passing through him yet he didn't even tremble. "Always fighting from a safe distance. Never getting your hands dirty." Archer was crawling backwards on his back. He looked terrified. She wanted to go and help him up, but she still couldn't stand. Reaper stabbed his arrow into Archer's other shoulder. He cried in pain. Reaper picked him up by grabbing both arrows and lifted him up. Archer's toes were swaying nearly three feet off the ground. "I get my hands dirty." He released him and drove his claw into Archer's stomach.

"No!" She cried again. She rose to her feet, but stumbled back down. She crawled with one hand down, the other clenching her stomach. Her sword fell from her weak grip, and bounced down to the next level. She continued towards Archer without it.

Reaper tossed his body aside. He was still alive, gasping for air through choked sobs. She reached him and fell beside him. She held his head in her lap. Blood was everywhere; it pooled in his gut, ran down his chest piece from both shoulders, and dripped from his mouth. "I-I'm sorry," he muttered softly.

"Just stay with me. Please." She tried desperately to wipe the blood and tears from his face, but there was too much.

"I thought… I thought I was strong enough." Reaper circled the two of them. He could have easily finished them both off right then and there, but he was just watching. He was enjoying it. She looked back to Archer. "Just promise you'll get out of here. Survive." His eyes closed with his final word.

"No! No! Stay with me! Please wake up!" She shook him, slapped his cheek, whatever she could, but he didn't wake up. She pulled him in and cried over him.

"How touching." Reaper smirked.

"You monster!" She felt around for her sword, but remembered she didn't have it.

"It doesn't matter. Even if you had your weapon, you can't defeat me. No one can." Reaper raised his arms. "I am a god among men! The Immortal Forest is mine to command! And with it, I am immortal!"

He flexed his claw, preparing for a single slice to end her life once and for all. She didn't want to leave Archer, and she probably wouldn't have been able to out run him anyway. She was as prepared as she could be for death. She closed her eyes and thought about all the regrets she would have: breaking her promise to Archer's dying wish, the sacrifice Paladin had made by dedicating his life to keeping her alive all being for nothing, and never getting the chance to avenge her mother's death.

She heard the sound of a blade ripping flesh and expected it to be her own, but felt nothing. She opened her eyes and saw the tip of her sword. It was coated in blood, sticking out right in front of her through Reaper's heart. He fell to his knees with a look of pure surprise. The man standing behind him was almost unrecognizable. He was completely covered in blood, dirt, and dust. It was the eyes that she recognized, Paladin's eyes. He was breathing heavy like he had just gone to hell and back.

"You want the forest so bad?" He picked Reaper up with the blade and turned hum to face the hole he had just climbed out of. "You can have it!" He kicked Reaper off the sword and his limp body fell all the way to the soil below. The bending and cracking of Grim Wood roots echoed up all the way to her ears. Paladin fell to his knees and loosened his grip on Princess's sword. It clattered to the ground. "Are you okay?"

"Are you? Dear Gylum, you look like death." Before he could say anything the building shifted further down the way it had been sagging.

"We have to get out of here." Paladin rose to his feet slowly. "This whole place is coming down."

She clutched Archer tighter. "What about him? We can't leave him."

Paladin scooped him up, being careful of his wounds. "Now come on. We need to find a way out." The building crumbled more and more. Princess found it difficult to stay standing. They crossed over to a window on the lower side of the room. Mage's cart had rolled down there, and a strange whimpering sound combined with the clattering of glass came from its direction. She approached it cautiously and lifted the cloth that draped over its edge.

Hiding and quivering beneath it was Mage, the box of Birthrights shaking in his tight grip. "Please don't kill me!" he squeaked.

"I'm not going to hurt you." She assured him. Somehow he survived the Shade's attack. The light from the Birthrights probably saved his life. She held out her hand. "It's not safe here. We have to go."

He reluctantly took her hand and crawled out. They joined Paladin at the window. When he saw Mage, he drew out her sword and pointed it at him. "What is he doing here?"

Princess put her hand on his, lowering the blade. "It's okay. He's not like the others."

Mage trembled and hid behind her. "Yes, she's right. I never hurt anyone. I help people." He looked at Archer in Paladin's arms. "I know how to save your friend. Just take me with you."

Paladin put the sword down. Princess looked around. She didn't see a way out. "How do we get down from here?"

Paladin looked over the edge. "The old fashioned way. We jump."

"What? It's too far. We can't survive that. I can't…"

He shifted Archer into one arm and grabbed her with the other. "But I can." He jumped. Mage whined and complained, but followed.

It was fifty feet before they hit the treetops. Branches whipped past them smacking against their legs, arms, and armor. She had her face buried in Paladin's chest, and her arms wrapped so tightly around him she was worried she would crack his ribs more than they already were. Paladin was slowing down their descent with the branches to the point that when his feet touched down they were all still alive.

He set Archer down, released Princess, and collapsed to the ground. She stood there alone. The massive structure finally succumbed and fell under its own weight. A wave of wind and dust rushed past her as it was reduced to a pile of wooden splinters and twisted metal.

Reaper's troops began filing into the forest and surrounded them. She looked down at Archer, he still wasn't moving. He was alive, just barely, but not for much longer. Paladin was getting up again, even slower than the last few times. It seemed impossible that he could be standing in his condition, but she couldn't do it without him.

All of the men around them unsheathed their weapons. She was having trouble finding hope in this situation. On a good day they wouldn't have stood a chance but with only one sword between them, Archer down, and Paladin hardly able to keep on his feet, they were done for. After everything they went through with Reaper, it would all mean nothing.

"Wait!" Mage hopped out of the nearest tree and stood between Reaper's men and them. "He's dead! They killed him!"

What's he doing? That wasn't exactly the smartest thing to say to an enemy army, that they just killed their leader. She thought Mage was supposed to be helping them.

"Is that true?" One of the larger men asked. "Did you really kill him?"

Paladin forced himself to stand tall. "Yes. Yes I did."

The large man dropped his axe and one by one, the others around him followed suit. After a moment, they were all unarmed.

Princess was in shock of it. *What just happened? Are they afraid of us? Surely they know they could easily kill us right now?* She was so confused she almost forgot about Archer. She ran over and pulled Mage by his arm. "You said you could help him. Please do something."

"We must hurry, bring him to the infirmary." The group of men around them parted, leaving a pathway back into the camp. Mage ran through and Princess followed, Archer in her arms. Mage turned to the crowd. "And bring the other one."

Paladin remained behind. He couldn't stand any longer. He hit the ground, losing consciousness even before his knees reached the dirt. She turned back just before leaving the tree line. Two of the men picked him up and started following after her. Whatever their reason was for surrendering to them, it was genuine. They were going to be okay.

Princess put Archer down on one of the beds when she reached the infirmary. Mage had already prepared a combination of Integro root and a few other herbs she didn't recognize. "Will that work? The wound is too deep. You said you could save him." She was starting to worry again. Integro root was good for healing small wounds like the stab on her arm, but not something as severe as what happened to him.

"Not alone it won't, but with these." Mage pulled out a handful of Birthrights. "Stand back." He dropped them into the mixing bowl and crushed them. He stirred it until it was a smooth paste, and then poured it into Archer's stomach. "Alright Doc, wrap him up." A man she hadn't noticed standing in the corner came over and wrapped up Archer's stomach. "It shouldn't take long now."

By the time the two men came in with Paladin, Archer opened his eyes. He looked around the room. He saw Paladin badly beaten and battered but alive, and then he looked to her. "We're alive?"

Tears of joy filled her eyes. "We're alive."

CHAPTER 21: THERE'S A NEW SHERIFF IN TOWN

"Change is an inevitable part of life. Whether the bad becomes better, or the good gets worse, nothing is ever the same as the moment preceding it. All one can hope for is Gylum to bless the good to grow better, and prevent the bad from getting worse."

                                                    – The Xyrith: 84: 69-71

Athan had been walking for five long months. Five thousand miles of Djinn, Dao Wings, Zed Wolves, Knixx Vipers, and Shades; however, the thing that worried him most was that aside from that first child, he hadn't seen any more since. It was a large moon and there would only be around a thousand children out there at any given time, but he still should have crossed paths with someone.

The Altar came into view. He was alleviated beyond words. As he got closer to the clearing, he heard strained cries coming from the Altar. There was a woman giving birth, her husband and servant were with her. She was young, it was probably her first child. The husband was much older, but Athan didn't recognize him. He wasn't surprised, between the dungeon and the forest he wouldn't know anyone who Fulfilled any time in the past eighteen years.

Athan held back and remained hidden. As desperate as he was for any human contact, he had no idea where their allegiances may lie. The husband could be a member of the royal guard for all he knew, he could have orders to kill him on site. On the other hand, he could be part of some resistance Moryn, or anyone, had formed in his absence. It was entirely possible he had no clue who Athan was and couldn't care less about it.

He crept out further, closer to the clearing. He was trying to find their carriage; they must have taken one to get this far outside the village. He saw nothing, just the three of them on and around the Altar. Suddenly he remembered his vision, the one of ancient soldiers marching through the bridge. He had lost sight of them when they marched through and into the other realm. *Maybe that's where their carriage is. Maybe it's just on the other side where I can't see it.*

He kept an eye on the husband as he moved closer.

The women were easily too preoccupied to be paying any attention outside the pillars, but the husband was another story. He would walk out a ways and stare off into the forest periodically. He waited until the husband turned his back and he made a run for it. It was only forty feet from the tree line to the nearest pillar. He covered it in no time at all. He hid behind it for a moment before poking his head around to see if it was still clear.

He saw the front bumper of an old style carriage. The rest of the vehicle passed behind one of the two pillars opposite the road leading back to the village. The majority of it should have been visible, the pillar wasn't that thick. Now there was no doubt what the ancient Warlock told him was true. The pillars truly were a bridge between realms.

He looked over to the three at the Altar. The husband had his full attention on his wife now. She must've been close. Now was his chance. He sprinted for the carriage, making sure to pass through the pillars to enter the side he needed to. He half expected to feel something as he passed, some kind of wave or field but there was nothing. If he didn't already know, he never would have guessed anything was there.

He made it to the carriage and hopped into the driver's seat. He checked the mirror to see if he had been spotted. He was clear, but he noticed a finely crafted sword in the back seat. He pulled it up into the front with him and examined it. *This will come in handy.* He heard the faint sound of a baby crying, and looked back in the mirror. The father took his newborn daughter from his servant. In their culture, firstborn daughters were a sign of weakness in a father unable to conceive a son. If he was right and that was their firstborn, then he should have looked incredibly upset, but that wasn't the case. The father smiled and hugged his daughter with affection.

Athan felt terrible stealing their only means of transportation, but it was a necessary evil. With the child being a girl, that left one man alone in the forest with three helpless women. He would send someone to get them as soon as he could, but he really hoped they would survive until then. He started up the engine and peeled down the road. He watched in the rear view mirror as he left. The man handed the child off and started chasing after him, but it was useless. The carriage was much faster and long gone before he even reached the edge of the clearing.

It would be a while before he reached Tuckkar, and he still wasn't sure what he would do when he got there. He'd had years to plot his revenge; first, when he was locked away, then all of the time in the forest, and yet he still had nothing. A big part of that was he had no idea what he would be walking into. It had been forever since he made contact with Moryn, any number of things could have changed in that time.

The highest point of the castle came into view over the horizon, he was close. Despite everything, he knew one thing for certain. He had known it for eighteen years. He was going to kill Rynok. Not just for what he had done to him, but for what he had done to everyone. He killed Ivary, Nimm, and countless others. He drove Tuckkar into the ground, if it was still standing he would be surprised.

For the first time in a long time, he entered through the main gate into the village. A nervousness crept up his spine. Memories of Rynok standing over him like a titan flooded his mind. He had to remind himself that was years ago. He was ten times stronger now; the forest had transformed his former weak frame into one of chiseled stone. His memories were deceptive. He remembered his brother as a giant, but the reality was, his mind exaggerated over time. He knew that he was now far bigger and stronger than his brother had been, but the image in his mind still scared him to a degree.

The streets were empty, every business closed. There must have been a town meeting going on. That was perfect. He would know exactly where to find Rynok, and the whole village could witness their liberation from the tyrant. The only downside: normally he'd only have two or so guards with him, but at the meeting every single one would be there. It would be a virtually unstoppable wall of the finest trained men Tuckkar had to offer between Rynok and him. All he had was a stolen sword.

He pulled right up to the front door. The guards hadn't stopped him yet, they must have recognized the carriage and believed it was the three from the Altar returning. As soon as he exited the driver's seat, the two guards at the door knew something was wrong. "Halt!" one of them demanded. "Who are you? Where is Jodin?" They closed in on him. Their blood red armor glistened in the light emanating from the open door behind them. Whatever it took, he would get through that door.

Athan pulled down the hood of his long cloak. "My quarrel is not with you. Stand down and I won't hurt you." He placed his hand on the hilt of his sword.

"Wait, that hair. Could it be?" the same one asked with confusion in his voice.

"It is!" The second one extended out his twin claws. "Kill him!"

"As you wish." Athan drew his sword with lightning speed. He drove the base of the hilt into one of the guard's helmet, denting it inward significantly. He blocked the second one's strike in the same movement. His blade had caught between the guard's massive claws, so he twisted it over in a full three-sixty, snapping the bones in his arm in several places. He freed his sword and plunged it into the man's shoulder, pinning him to the wall but not killing him. He checked on the first guard, who was motionless at his feet. Dead or just knocked out, he didn't know. The one with the sword in his chest fought to free himself, but it was futile. "I told you, my fight is not with you."

Athan ripped off his helmet. "Well my fight is with you! You betrayed our king, killed the queen, and his heir!" There was a pure hatred in his eyes. He was definitely old enough to have known the queen personally, by the looks of it.

"You have been lied to. I swear to you, everything will become clear soon. I'm sorry for this." Athan bashed the man in the temple with his own helmet, and set it down beside him. He decided to leave his sword as it was, so he removed the man's clawed gauntlet and put it on. He tested the blades to make sure they weren't damaged. They retracted and extended smoothly, he was ready to go.

A handful of the villagers in the back of the room had heard the commotion and were peeking outside. He strolled inside and they parted fearfully out of his way. He heard whisperings over the sound of the village preacher reading lines from the Xyrith. His name was buzzing through the crowd. He was catching wind of some of the rumors that must have been spreading about him, many of them very farfetched. He reached the middle of the room still unnoticed by the cabinet members or guards in the front. He saw Rynok sitting on the throne, listening to the scripture intently.

"Brother!" Athan roared at the top of his lungs. Every single eye fell on him and every mouth fell silent. His word echoed through the throne room several times over, eventually fading to dead silence. Rynok's jaw dropped when he realized who he was. Whether it was the shock of seeing him alive, or the fact that he was triple the size he had been the last time he saw him, he wasn't sure.

As soon as the shock wore off, he jumped out of his seat. "Guards! Kill him! Kill him now!" The line of guards fanned out and encircled Athan. All of them extended their blades in unison.

"Afraid to face me yourself?" Athan called out over the heads of the crowd. "Hiding behind your guards like a coward?" He knew that would drive him crazy.

"Wait!" The men stopped advancing on his word. Rynok stepped down from his raised platform and joined the circle of guards. He tilted his head to one of them, but never broke eye contact with Athan. "Bring me my broadsword." The crowd gasped, whispered, cheered, and mumbled about themselves as the guard rushed off to Rynok's personal armory. "Tonight!" He faced his people. "Tonight, our queen shall be avenged!"

The crowd broke into thunderous applause. Athan glared at Rynok until he got his attention and the cheers died down enough for him to be heard. "Only we know how true that statement really is." He drew his claws not to attack, but to illustrate a point; he would willingly wait for Rynok to be armed. The queen would be avenged because he was going to kill Rynok, and restore order to his home.

The man returned quickly with Rynok's broadsword. It was massive, almost twice as long as he was tall, and just as broad as he was wide. The guard could hardly hold it, but when he handed it over Rynok wielded it with ease. The blade was forged of the finest steel in all of Tuckkar. Light reflected off its mirror-like surface. Athan could see himself clearly in it when Rynok brought it up. "Ready brother?"

Athan raised his arm to the ready. He couldn't help but compare the weapons. His stolen gauntlet was excellently crafted. It was far better than any makeshift weapon he had used in the forest, or even the blade he had used moments before. The metal would hold up against Rynok's sword, although he would have to compensate for the weight behind it. They only extended three feet beyond his hand making his reach far less, but if he got in close he would have the advantage. The grip was much more secure than a sword, but it limited his options as far as strikes. He would have to make it work. "You should have killed me when you had the chance."

"Duly noted." Rynok swung the sword up and around his head. The point extended out over the heads of the on-looking villagers. The guards extended their perimeter accordingly.

Athan saw it coming, but it was much faster than he thought possible given its size. If he blocked a strike like that, it would pulverize the bones in his forearm to dust. Instead, he dove forward and rolled beneath it. The sound of it slicing through the air rang in his ears. He popped back up onto his feet immediately, but Rynok had already started his next attack. The blade was vertical, coming down on top of him at the speed of sound.

There was no time to dive out of the way, and he couldn't block a force that strong. He raised his claws and forced Rynok's blow to glance off just enough. The top third of the sword dug into the solid stone floor. Athan's whole arm was reverberating from the deflection, filling his arm with pins and needles. Rynok pulled on the sword with both hands, but it was no use. The sword was buried so deeply into the stone floor that it would take an army to pull it free. Now was his chance. Athan exploded forward, bringing his claws out to bear with everything he had.

His forward momentum stopped abruptly. He looked down his arm expecting to find blood, but the only thing on his claws was a single callused hand. Rynok had caught them mid-strike. His hand cupped the top of the blades, keeping the razor sharp edge down and away from cutting himself. He squeezed and bent the metal until they touched, then swept up and took Athan by the throat with his free hand.

Athan was bewildered. He had underestimated his brother far too much, and he was now suffering for it. The back of his skull cracked against the rough stone floor and his windpipe crushed under the grip of his brother's hand. His vision began filling with blood, and his lungs ached as they begged for air. He felt like he was dying and if he didn't do something in the next few seconds, he would be.

Rynok whispered through gritted teeth as he pressed down on his throat even more, trying to snap Athan's neck under his weight. "You are pathetic. Even with seven years to prepare, you are still nothing." With the mountain of pain coursing through his nervous system from his head and neck, he barely noticed a lump pressing into his lower back. "It was never enough for you, was it? Always trying to tell me how to run my kingdom. Always thinking you knew what was best. Always pressuring me!" His voice was getting progressively louder, and the crowd was quieting their cheers to listen in. Athan slowly moved his hand behind his back to see what was prodding him. "It was your fault! It was! You may not have given the order or held the sword, but you drove me to it! Every day with your endless cabinet meetings and statistics and your Gylum damned science!"

The crowd was dead silent now and they had no problem hearing Rynok, who was yelling at that point but seemed to neither notice nor care. "You drove me to it! You drove me to the brink and I snapped! You had everyone against me! You had them think me weak! That you should have been king, not me!" Athan's hand found what was underneath his back, and he gripped it tight. He was only moment's from losing consciousness, he had to act now. "So yes! I did it! When Gylum shamed me with a daughter, I snapped!" The crowd gasped, but Rynok was still too upset to notice his audience. Athan forced himself to stay awake, he had to hear what Rynok was confessing. "I killed them." His voice was soft again, tears filling his eyes. "I killed them all." He pulled out a large dagger from his boot and held it high over Athan's head. "Because of you!"

Now! Athan pulled his hand out from beneath his back and plunged the old, worn, dull knife Garm had given him right into Rynok's exposed carotid artery. *Thank you Garm. That was for you.* He remained conscious just long enough to watch Rynok fall down beside him in a pool of his own bright red blood. He twitched for a few seconds, and then croaked out a bubbly final breath. He had won. Not only was Rynok dead, but he had also confessed to killing the queen, framing him for it, and even that his firstborn had been a daughter. And he confessed before the entire village. The last sight he had before slipping away was that of the guards hovering over him, not to kill him, but to help him.

-O-

Paladin climbed the stairs of the newly erected tower, the replacement for the one they had destroyed thirteen months ago. Princess was waiting for him at the top. Today was her eighteenth birthday, and in a few minutes she would Fulfill her Birthright and return to her home awaiting her in Tuckkar.

With every passing step, the nervousness in his gut grew. He wished that they had more time. For the past few months, he was spending every possible second with her, trying to squeeze a lifetime in before he'd lose her, possibly forever. But for the entirety of that day, their very last day, she had made a strange request. She asked to be left alone.

He didn't understand what she needed to be alone for, especially on this day of all days. It had driven him crazy, and now that she finally called for him he would barely get the goodbye he had always wished for. If he was to be honest with himself though, he didn't want to say goodbye at all.

The first person he saw waiting at the top of the stairs was a bit of a surprise. It was Archer, who after a significant growth spurt, stood only a head shorter than him. He was glad to see his old friend, but a part of him wanted to be alone with her. She was special to him and he was to her, more so than anyone, even Archer. He smiled when he spotted him coming up. "Oh, you're early. Good."

Early? You mean she wanted even less time with me before leaving? He shrugged away the negative thoughts. He wanted to be happy for her. It would be the last time he could be happy. "Ya, big day you know." He reached the top and looked around. Princess was nowhere to be seen. "Where's the birthday girl?"

Archer glanced over to the balcony. "Waiting for you."

Paladin walked over to the drapes separating the room from the uncovered walkway beyond. He turned, Archer wasn't coming with him. *Good, she does want to be alone.* As soon as he stepped outside, he saw her standing at the railing. The dim red light of Gylum high on the horizon silhouetted her beautiful figure. She wore a long tight dress with her hair done up. It reminded him of the way Reaper presented her at the arena, only none of the unpleasant memories broke through to the surface. It was going to be a good day, whether he liked it or not. "You look beautiful."

She smiled her shy smile. "Thanks."

"They're going to love you." It took him a moment to register, something was missing. Someone wasn't there. "Where's Mage? We don't have much time. If we miss it I swear I'll…"

She pressed her finger gently to his lips. He silenced and calmed when she did. "He's coming. He's just running a little errand for me."

What errand? Doesn't she realize how important this is? If Mage wasn't there when it happened, then he couldn't prepare the trace spell he needed to track her through her Fulfillment. Without that, he would never find Tuckkar. Without that, he would never find her again. If she only knew how hard it had been to get his hands on enough Birthrights. Reaper had burned through all but a handful in his quest to master the process. Under their leadership he would only take them from volunteers, and it was not easy to find people willing to give up their futures willingly. "I hope it was important."

"The most important thing in my life." She replied. She was way too calm. He felt like she didn't even care, like their relationship meant nothing to her.

"It's all my fault." He said as calmly as he could. He was fighting off tears.

"What?" She was genuinely confused.

"It never should have happened this way. I should have prepared better. I should be in Tuckkar waiting for you right now, not stuck here watching you go."

"No, stop, you don't have to…" She tried to calm him down again, but it didn't work. He wanted his last words to her to be sweet and loving, but he had to get everything off his chest because his broken heart wouldn't be able to carry it.

"I caused the Reaper to become what he was. I allowed us to get captured. I should've fought harder, I should have killed him sooner. My whole life all I thought about was protecting you until this day, and maybe it's selfish of me but what does that mean if it means losing you?"

She only had seconds left, and he had said everything he had wanted to except three words. If she knew him as well as he hoped she did, then she knew what those words were. Like reading his mind, she answered back perfectly. "I love you too." This was it. Her Birthright would begin taking her away, and without Mage's potion he would be losing her forever, but it didn't matter in that moment. He could be as angry as he wished later, but for that wonderful second everything was perfect. He grabbed her and kissed her with every inch of his heart, and he felt the same in return. He would kiss her until Gylum Himself reached down and plucked her away from him.

A minute passed, and she should have been gone, but she wasn't. He opened his eyes and noticed there was no light surrounding her, it was dark. He grabbed her left hand and found her palm stitched up and empty. "Wait. Where is it? What did you do?"

Just then, Mage tore through the drapes behind him wheezing from exhaustion. "Sorry I'm late milady." He held out a necklace eerily similar to Reaper's; the one he wore when he captured her Birthright. It even had a bright blue rounded stone in the middle.

"What is that?" He asked as he snatched it from him. He spun it around and gasped when he saw it. It was Reaper's necklace, and it was her Birthright in the center. The small glowing crown at the heart of it could be nothing else. "But…" He couldn't form any other words. He looked to her for answers.

"I wanted him to make sure it would be safe if I just removed it."

Mage had caught his breath. "Yes, it's not the Birthright that does the work, it's the person. As long as it wasn't physically in her hand at the time, then it'll remain as it is. Well, unless someone else Fulfills it, but, well, you know."

Paladin turned back to Princess. He didn't want answers to the magic or the science behind it. He wanted to know why she passed her one and only shot at her future. "But why? Now you can never go back. You can never return home."

"I don't owe anything to Tuckkar. I don't have any memories or knowledge of it like the rest of you. It's not my home, this is." She smiled at him and took his hand. She was right. They had built a life there. For over a year they had picked up the crumbled and broken system that had fallen apart without Reaper's manipulation, and had formed a functioning community. They had become the new leaders, not because they wanted it but because they were wanted. It wasn't perfect; there were fights, complaints, and people impatient to find Tuckkar. The difference now was they didn't want to go to war with it, but to return in peace.

"And you're sure this is what you want? You're not just doing it for me?"

"I've never been more sure of anything." She kissed him again. "You know, there is one matter that we've neglected to talk about."

"And what's that?"

"You Fulfilled, well, sort of, but that was over a year ago."

He wasn't sure where she was going, but he humored her. "Your point being?"

"You taught me that upon Fulfillment, you receive three things."

"Right. A career, a name and a wife."

"Yes. Well, you have a career, sort of, but you still don't have a name."

He laughed. "Right, well, I've gone nineteen years without one, I'm sure I'll be fine." She looked like she wanted to say something. "Unless you have any ideas."

"Ya, but I don't know if you'll like it."

"Tell me, I'm sure I'll love it."

"Well, you remember that story you used to tell me, the one about the brave white knight that saved Princess from monsters?"

"Of course. My father made that up to tell to my sister when she was a baby. You always loved that one."

"Well, I just thought, given everything we've been through. I think it fits quite well."

He thought about the name. He had always liked that story, and she was right, it did fit quite well. "Okay, I like it. That just leaves one more. A wife."

She laughed and smiled. "I don't think you have very many options around here."

"I only need one." He pulled her in close. "Just like the end of our story. He sweeps her off her feet, and they live happily ever after." He leaned over and kissed her passionately. It was a nice thought, but even though they were in the trawls of bliss then and there it wouldn't last. Ghor was too violent and dark for any happiness to exist for long. Their future had too many unknowns, and too much room for pain and misery. But in that perfect moment, he wanted her to believe. He wanted them both to believe that happy endings could exist outside of a fairytale made for a child. The real world of Ghor wasn't like his father's story; the one he aptly named: the Princess and the Paladin.

EPILOGUE:

Tinus started up the carriage and the headlights illuminated the road ahead. A trio of large blood red carriages roared down the road towards them. They slammed to a halt and surrounded him.

"Honey, what's going on?" Murel asked nervously.

"I don't know. Stay here." He got out of the vehicle and was confronted by two members of the royal guard. The rest, a mixture of royal and wall guards, poured out of the three carriages and sprinted off towards the Altar. "What is the meaning of this?" he demanded.

"Where is your child?" The first one asked.

The second didn't wait for an answer, he tore open the back seat and searched to see if a daughter was with them. "Not in here." He turned to shout after the other guards. "Find the boy!"

"What? You leave my son alone!" He took a swing at the second man, and the other's swarmed him and held him down. "What are you doing? Stop this!" He was not a small man; he fought them off for a while until they had enough to bring him down.

His head was halfway in the mud, but he saw a pair of boots walk up to him much different than the others. "Please, there is no need to fight. It's not what you think, we don't want to hurt you. Or your family." The voice sounded oddly familiar.

Tinus calmed down and stopped fighting. He would listen to what the man had to say. If he didn't like it, he would find a way to break free and kill him with his bare hands. They lifted him up to his feet, but didn't loosen their grip just yet. Now that he saw the man's face; more importantly, the shimmering gold of his hair, he recognized him. "Lord Athan? You're awake?"

"Yes, it wasn't as serious as the rumors floating around made it seem." There hadn't been any rumors. The whole village, himself included, had been there. It was only two days later, and he couldn't believe Athan was on his feet so soon. Tinus had been there, in the throne room. He had a front row spot during the fight between him and the former king. He saw what happened to him, all of the blood and broken bones.

"But, I still don't…" He looked around to try and figure everything out. The men were taking up positions around the Altar. Half of them were inside the circle of stone pillars looking outward, but the other half did something even stranger. The others were outside looking in as if they weren't trying to keep anything out, but keep it in. "What's going on?"

"I'm sorry, but it's much too complicated to explain right now but please, just trust me. The forest isn't safe for your son right now."

How can this man just waltz back into our village and think he knows what's best for me and my family? At first, he wanted to protest, but then he remembered. He remembered all the hard times over the years. He remembered the whisperings about Athan, how he was building strength in the forest, and how he was the true blood-born king of Tuckkar. Then there were the Fulfillments. The lack of Fulfillments to be precise. If it hadn't been for the mystical pull of the Altar, he and his wife never would have driven out there to begin with, but honor and tradition drove him to do so.

"We've got him!" A guard shouted in the distance. Tinus turned to face the voice, and found a man gripping his wet naked son upside down by an ankle. His son fought and squirmed, but it was useless. He was simply too small. It pained him to see his son like that, so helpless.

"What do you intend to do with him?" He said to Lord Athan. The guards must not have liked his tone because their grips tightened.

"As I said, don't worry. He will still be allowed to live free, just not out here. He'll have to stay close to the village where it's safe." Of course it wasn't safe. It was the Immortal Forest. It was the most dangerous place there was, but it was still the proving ground of their people.

They held the baby down in the back of one of the carriages. One of the men pulled out a knife. "What's he doing to my son?"

"Just an insurance policy. He'll be fine." The man used the knife and cut the Birthright out of his left hand.

"You monster! Stop this! You were supposed to change things!" he raged. Rynok may have been bad, he may have put restrictions on births, he may have enacted Rukor's

Law, but he never went after their children this early. All they had done was trade one evil for another. The guard threw Tinus's son into the back of the carriage and went inside. The door closed and the carriage took off back the way it came.

Athan looked at him, a look of real sincerity in his eyes. "I'm sorry. This pains me as much as it does you. I will explain my actions to you and the rest of the village in due time." He nodded to his men to release him. They returned to their vehicles. Other than the guards around the Altar, only he remained. "All you need to know for now is that there are forces out there beyond your comprehension. Someone or something out there is killing and kidnapping our children, and until I find them, the Pilgrimage is over. Whoever's out there, whoever's in charge, they have lost their chance. I will find them, and I will kill them. No negotiating, no discussions, nothing but their heads on my table."

TO BE CONTINUED...

CONTINUE THE ADVENTURE IN:

COMING SOON